THE LOVE PARADE

The Love Parade

Sergio Pitol

Translated from the Spanish by G. B. Henson

Deep Vellum Publishing
Dallas, Texas

Deep Vellum Publishing
3000 Commerce St., Dallas, Texas 75226
deepvellum.org · @deepvellum

Deep Vellum is a 501c3 nonprofit literary arts organization
founded in 2013 with the mission to bring
the world into conversation through literature.

ISBNs: 978-1-64605-113-7 (paperback) | 978-1-64605-114-4 (ebook)

LIBRARY OF CONGRESS CONTROL NUMBER: 2021948209

Front Cover Design by Kit Schluter
Interior Layout and Typesetting by KGT

Printed in the United States of America

For Lya and Luis Cardoza y Aragón,
Luz del Amo, Margo Glantz,
Carlos Monsiváis, and Luis Prieto.

CONTENTS

CHARACTERS

(in order of appearance)

THE MINERVA BUILDING – the name Pitol gives to the iconic Rio de Janeiro Building, located in Mexico City's Colonia Roma, known to many as the House of Witches

MIGUEL DEL SOLAR – the novel's protagonist, a historian who lived at the Minerva in 1942 at the time of a shooting, the mystery around which he is attempting to uncover

DIONISIO ZEPEDA and EDUVIGES BRIONES DE DÍAZ ZEPEDA – Del Solar's aunt and uncle, residents at the Minerva; Dionisio is Del Solar's mother's brother

AMPARO – Dionisio and Eduviges's daughter and Del Solar's cousin

ANTONIO – Dionisio and Eduviges's son; although sickly as a child, he'd go on to hold a government position and be implicated in a corruption scandal

ARNULFO BRIONES – Eduviges's brother, shady figure and businessman, husband of Adele Waltzer Briones

ADELE WALTZER BRIONES – Arnulfo's German wife and mother of Erich Maria Pistauer

ERICH MARIA PISTAUER – son of Adele Waltzer and Hanno Pistauer, stepson of Arnulfo Briones; killed following a party given at the home of Delfina Uribe at the Minerva

MARTÍNEZ – the so-called "consultant" to Arnulfo Briones; in fact, his fixer

DELFINA URIBE – a gallery owner and former tenant in the Minerva Building

RICARDO RUBIO – Delfina Uribe's son, who was injured during the shooting

CRISTÓBAL RUBIO – Delfina Uribe's former husband

JULIO ESCOBEDO – an established Mexican artist, client and friend of Delfina Uribe

RUTH ESCOBEDO – Julio's wife

CECILIA – Del Solar's wife, now deceased

LUIS URIBE – father of Delfina Uribe, once a prominent politician, known as the Licenciado, a univeristy title that can denote an attorney or a courtesy title extended to men of high political rank

PEDRO BALMORÁN – an eccentric tenant at the Minerva with ties to Mexico's ultraconservative Catholic movement, and who claims to have in his possession the account of a nineteenth-century Mexican castrato

IDA WERFEL – a German-Jewish Hispanist who resided at the Minerva at the time of the shooting

EMMA WERFEL – daughter and personal secretary of Ida Werfel

MALÚ – Delfina Uribe's sister-in-law

DERNY GOENAGA – Miguel del Solar's cousin; Arnulfo Briones's nephew; a successful advertising executive

CRUZ-GARCÍA – the publisher of Miguel del Solar's historical books

THE BOMBÓN SISTERS – two entertainers who attended the party at the Minerva

THE CASTRATO – a nineteenth-century indigenous singer

CHAPTER 1

Minerva

A MAN STOPPED IN FRONT OF the gate of a redbrick building in the heart of Colonia Roma one afternoon in mid-January 1973. Four unwonted turrets, also brick, sit atop the building's corners. For decades, the building has epitomized an architectural extravagance in a neighborhood of tranquil residences of another style. Truth be told, in the last few years everything has become discordant, as the entire neighborhood has lost its harmony. The hulking mass of the new buildings crushes the graceful homes of two, at most three, floors, built according to the Belle Époque style in Bordeaux, Biarritz, and Auteil. There is something sad and dirty in the district that until recently still maintained certain displays of elegance, of a once powerful class, wronged but not defeated. The opening of the subway station, the ragtag hordes that it regularly vomits, the countless stalls of fried foods, tacos, quesadillas, and elotes, of newspapers and secondhand books, the hawkers that sell dogs, cheap toys, and miracle drugs, have heralded the true demise of that part of the city, the beginning of a different era.

Dusk fell. The man pushed open the metal door, walked toward the interior courtyard, looked up, and surveyed the squalid spectacle of an edifice on the brink of ruin. Just as the building didn't conform to the neighborhood, and, on second thought, to the city, its internal structure was inconsistent with its faux Gothic façade, with its mansards, porthole windows, and four turrets. The man surveyed the corridors that encircled each of the building's floors, irregular oases created by clusters of flowerpots and tin pails of different shapes and sizes where palms, lilies, rosebushes, and bougainvillea were growing. The arrangement of the flowers breaks the monotony of the cement, creates an asymmetrical and ultimately harmonious ensemble, and evokes the interior of the city's humble tenements.

"Palms with slender stems used to grow in the jardinières," he tells himself. He wonders if his memory might be laying a trap. His stay here emerges, fades, and reappears in his memories as if drawn in a palatial setting. At that moment, as he examines the interior with care, the spaces, despite their size, seem much smaller than how he's stored them in his memory. A torrent of words spoken thirty years before rushes over him, echoes of conversations suggest elegance, the building's social prestige, its art deco interior designed by one of the most renowned architects of the time in 1914, precisely the year in which his book is set, a style superimposed on the original bricks, unfinished just as they appear on the exterior. What he sees at that moment are walls about to implode, crumble before his eyes.

The man must be about forty years old. He's wearing thick, dark brown flannel trousers and a slightly marbled tweed jacket of the same color. His tie is made of woven wool, ochre. In that corner, and especially in that portico, his attire, as well as his particular way of standing, of bringing his hand to his chin, are absolutely natural, in tune with the tall, dirty reddish brick walls, like those of many London walls and porticos. Under his arm, he's carrying the newly corrected proofs of his latest book and a treatise on the language of Machiavelli, which he just bought at an Italian bookstore nearby.

Frankly, he could characterize as disappointing the last

two days, which he spent revising the proofs of the book he'd worked on over the last few years: a chronicle of the events that took place in Mexico City from Victoriano Huerta's departure to Carranza's arrival. He found the style crude and presumptuous. At some times, it seemed incoherent and pedantic; at others, overly affected. But what was worse, the spirit of the book had begun to slip away from him. Did it really make sense to have spent so much time buried in archives and libraries, breathing stale air, coating his hair and lungs with dust, to achieve such mediocre results? It seemed as though during each of his past vacations in Mexico, he'd done nothing but search for, classify, and decipher papers. Suddenly, as he pored with fatigue over those pages, now free of typos, awaiting his final approval, he felt that his work could have been done by any scribe who possessed a modicum of instruction in the technique of evaluating and selecting the information scattered in letters, public and private documents, and the press of a given era. His book was called *The Year 1914*, although the action also took place during a large part of the following year. He had used 1914 in the title because it was the year of the Convention of Aguascalientes, which was critical to the basis of his work. The story of a city without a government: the capital that, though in the hands of the different factions, is controlled by none of them. During such disarray, in the heart of chaos, anything can happen: Vasconcelos improvises a ministry of public instruction; outside his door, from time to time, soldiers shoot their rifles into the air, obeying who knows what reflexes; etc.

It was necessary to leave that now distant Mexico to find peace. If there was anything that kept him going for the moment, it was a deep interest in studying a series of materials that aspired to be a new book. A few months before, while still in Bristol, he'd discovered the correspondence between the administrator of an

English oil company in Mexico's Huasteca region and its head-quarters in London during the oil conflicts that led to the expropriation of the companies and the subsequent break in relations between England and Mexico. He extended his curiosity to the continuation of these difficult relations, the resumption of which was made possible by the war, to the visits paid to General Cedillo by prominent British intellectuals and journalists (Waugh, no less!), who insisted on seeing him as the noble savage in whom the seed of catechism had indeed taken root. The man necessary to defeat chaos. The world press expressed itself without the least sentimentality: if Cedillo refused to lead the rebellion, or if he was defeated, the only way forward was armed intervention. To quell the disorder. He took some notes at the time; he'd reviewed and expanded on them in Mexico. And just two or three weeks earlier, just before the end of the year, he met a fellow student, Mercedes Ríos, with whom he discussed his readings at the time and some still-vague research projects. Mercedes lent him some photocopies of a bundle of papers dealing with the more or less clandestine activities of certain German agents active in Mexico during that same period. These documents had belonged to an uncle of hers, a high-ranking official of the Secretariat of Home Affairs during the war, and she imagined he might find them interesting, since they were in some way linked to his topic. He had thought about doing more focused research—the actions taken by oil companies against Mexico, the outbreak of the Second World War, the country's participation in the Allied cause, de facto solutions to the problems created by expropriation, etc.—but reading those documents made him aware of a thousand other possibilities. He decided to broaden his scope, to study Mexico's situation in relation to the international one, and not just in regard to the countries to which the expropriated companies belonged. An extremely stimulating period. Elsewhere he began to find materials that renewed his interest in that critical period, which, despite its proximity in time, seemed as remote as that in which José María Luis Mora attempted to plant the ideas of the Enlightenment in the country and to bring Mexico closer to the Age of Reason. Mercedes had been right about the interest that such documents would arouse in him. He plunged into them one weekend. A bitter perfume of mystery emanated from those scant biographical notes. In a way, they recreated the atmosphere of certain films, certain novels that one is accustomed to finding in Istanbul, Lisbon, Athens, or Shanghai but never in Mexico. There were just over fifty pages. He read them on a Saturday night and was so excited that he couldn't sleep. On Sunday he studied them again, took notes, and reflected on the information they contained. It was thanks to them that he was there, in the courtyard of that bizarre redbrick building, and he looked indecisively at a corner of the second floor where he supposed, without being entirely sure, that his bedroom had been thirty-one years before, during the months he lived with his Uncle Dionisio and Aunt Eduviges. Dionisio Zepeda and Eduviges Briones de Díaz Zepeda, as she liked to point out.

The bundle of papers that had excited him consisted almost exclusively of this: a dry collection of biographical notes, almost completely without glosses in the margin. The majority of these synoptic biographies were devoid of apparent interest, at least for the time being. As a historian, the only thing he's learned for certain is that there is no point in time that doesn't lend itself to the juiciest revelations. There was the possibility that once the names included on that list and the information that accompanied it, for the moment neutral, began to be linked to others, to the corresponding persons and institutions, they would expand, branch out, and lead the researcher to broader areas, some truly significant.

Its mere existence constituted a store of priceless information:

Johannes Holtz, for example, landed in Veracruz in February 1938; he worked as a chemical engineer for a company that manufactured essences and perfumes. He was twenty-seven years old at the time of his arrival. He established residence at the Anatole France, 68B, Colonia Polanco. During the first months of his stay in the country, he established contacts with Rainer Schwartz and Bodo Wünger, both owners of fertilizer concerns. Holtz often traveled, sometimes alone, sometimes in the company of some of the aforementioned German nationals, to Cuernavaca, where he attended meetings that were suspected of providing political instruction, though they may well have been for recreation. He had a relationship, whose intimate nature was taken for granted, with the widow Eliza Franger, the daughter of a German father and a Colombian mother, in whose apartment, located at Luis Moya 95-9, he regularly spent the night every Friday. On April 10, 1943, he embarked at Tampico bound for Brazil. As far as anyone knew, he hadn't reentered Mexico, at least not under the name of Johannes Holtz.

Some of those listed were Germans born in Guatemala, educated in Germany, perfectly bilingual, engaged in carrying out not-so-dangerous work: establishing contacts with Germans residing in Mexico and sponsoring proselytizing activities. At an establishment located on Avenida Juárez, near the corner of Dolores, two or three of those who were trained professionally in complex and delicate work—which they constantly perfected—employed highly sophisticated methods, according to the Home Affairs document, for sending messages to a central receiver in Germany. All this was contained in the brief account, the comings and goings of a handful of gray individuals, linked only tangentially on the edge of what we consider the true story. In fact, it was little more than a cursory police dossier. Notes,

notes, and more notes on individuals with Teutonic names, which repeated with monotony their date of entry into Mexico, their domiciles, associations, and trips throughout the country. There was no mention, which would have made them truly interesting, of their contacts with the centers of national Nazism, with those deranged and exalted apostles of the Mexican radical right. Perhaps that was described in another dossier, in some confidential file. The dreaded fifth column! In short, there must have been other important files, and it was possible that they were now available for consultation. He had to try. Perhaps pay a visit to the National Archives. It's important to note that in the interim he hadn't been inactive and that during the moments when he wasn't correcting the proofs of the book he preferred not to think about, he'd visited the newspaper archives and read the newspapers for the month of November 1942. He needed to corroborate certain information from 1914 about which he wasn't very sure, although in fact he should confess that he made that visit for a more intimate reason.

His friend's anodyne files had fascinated him for two reasons, one minor and another rather amusing: discovering that the father of a law school classmate, whom at one point he'd begun to detest, was linked to this network of clandestine activities and had transported some German agents in a small plane belonging to him, once to Tampico and several times to San Luis Potosí. He'd met him. Yes, a hazy figure whom on two or three occasions he saw crossing the garden of his detestable classmate's home with an uncertain look and the air of having fallen into a labyrinth with no exit. At the end of the note, a comment disabused any notion that he was a dangerous agent; to the contrary, it celebrated his many indiscretions (thanks to which it had been possible to learn about some of the suspicious movements of others). Alcohol, it was said, produced an uncontainable logorrhea in him. He found it queer that the man in the dossier and the maniacally silent old man he'd met were the same; nevertheless, there was no doubt whatsoever about his identity. His name and address were listed there, the same home he'd visited on so many occasions during his adolescence and to which he swore each time not to return. He imagined his friend's father during that time: a young braggart, newly arrived in the country, whom two glasses of brandy transformed into a parrot disposed to talk a blue streak. The authorities had taken full advantage of his trumpeting his exploits. Perhaps his subsequent silence had been penitential. Every project in which he'd participated failed because of him.

The other surprise, which indeed gave him a start, an indescribable excitement, was contained in the final two lines of the dossier. They indicated that the murders in the Minerva Building, the very one in whose courtyard he found himself at that moment, were possibly linked to a dramatic settling of scores between German agents and their local henchmen. He'd lived in this house at the time of these events! He would have been ten years old at the time. An age at which it's possible to remember everything, or almost everything . . . And, of course, he remembered many things . . . But in what an absurd, muddled, and incoherent way! It's possible that the facts he had in mind weren't those mentioned in the dossier. Where had the shooting taken place, for example? In the courtyard facing him? On the stairs? Where had the shots actually been fired? Once, when recalling his childhood, he'd felt a flutter, the echo of lost memories, which linked him to the shooting that had disturbed the family's life. What he felt was a vague echo, despite the impact it had that night on his life, so profound, in fact, that he wasn't able to finish the school year and had to leave Mexico City.

A thousand times, as he passed the building during

university, when his classmates commented with a mixture of enthusiasm and mocking on the eccentricity of its architecture, the spectral air that gradually enveloped it, the look of a Dickens's novel illustration that its balconies, walls, and towers radiated, he took pride in revealing to them that part of his childhood had been spent in that very building. And he repeated sentences from his archive of familial nostalgia: no one could imagine, when passing in front of that ruin, the elegance of its interiors, the exquisite wood of its parquets and doors, the spaciousness of its rooms, the height of its ceilings. The building, he explained, had been built, just as its twin located on the streets of Marseille, for the purpose of offering quality accommodation to the staff from foreign embassies and legations, less costly and easier to care for than private residences. Small and dark, the ground-floor apartments were less appealing. Those on the second floor, where he lived with his relatives, on the other hand, were palatial. The entire floor was occupied by only two apartments, each with grand living rooms, a large dining room, and long hallways that connected an endless number of bedrooms, studies, sewing rooms, etc. On the upper floors, the apartments were less spacious but no less impressive: they were simply made for smaller families. The system of corridors surrounding a large interior courtyard, unusual at the time of its construction in the late nineteenth century, when in Mexico real estate speculation had exploded, distinguished it from any other building in the city, contemporary or thereafter.

From the interior windows the tenants were able to see the kind of visitors the neighbors received. This ability, in a Mexico like that of the 1940s, still full of provincial vices, must have been very attractive. He'd watch the foreign tenants greet each other unhurriedly, exchanging a few words in unintelligible languages; say goodbye with the same ceremoniousness; then go on their way. He imagines that they visited each other only on prior arrangement. No one would meddle in other people's affairs, although he couldn't know for certain, since, as far as his Aunt Eduviges was concerned, she'd done nothing but meddle in other people's affairs. Her brother, Arnulfo Briones, an old codger whom he'd always disliked, with a shrill voice, dirty, yellow-stained teeth and moustache, and inexpressive eyes that looked to be made of glass, subjected him on several occasions to veritable interrogations, dry, inhospitable, and lacking in affection, about the children with whom he used to play in the courtyard and their families—interrogations to which he later also subjected his Aunt Eduviges, Amparo, and even the servants. Yes, it was a matter of rummaging in his memory. He was already ten when the German was killed.

At that age one remembers everything, he'd said, but it turned out that in his case it wasn't true. On two or three occasions he'd been in Delfina Uribe's gallery, had exchanged a few words with her, and yet he didn't realize that she was linked to the tragedy until much later, when he visited the newspaper archives and consulted a number of old newspapers. He knew Julio Escobedo better, although that also meant little. At one time he'd dealt with him relatively often. At their wedding, some of his wife Cecilia's cousins had given them one of his oils, which ultimately became his favorite painting: a gray cat playing with a spinning top. In the background, a vase of blue and purple flowers. Never, of this he is sure, did he imagine that the party that had ended so badly might have been offered in the painter's honor. What's certain is that he knew, and at the same time he knew nothing, about what had happened there. Nor did a ten-year-old boy have any reason to know that a party was being held in the apartment next door for a painter who over time would become famous. He hadn't gone to the newspaper archives to find out the details of the case (in the Home Affairs dossier, the word "murders" was used, in the plural, which intrigued him, as if Arnulfo Briones's stepson hadn't been the only victim) but to verify some information about which he'd suddenly felt unsure after reading the latest proofs of *The Year 1914*. Finding no errors, he was satisfied. The information about which he'd at one point been in doubt was correct, but since he was there, he told himself, he'd take the opportunity to scan the press from 1942. It wasn't difficult to pinpoint the date. He was in his fourth year of primary school, so it must have been 1942. The period of the blackouts: air-raid drills over Mexico City. The city would grow completely dark under the roar of the planes flying overhead. The shooting, he thought, must have taken place toward the end of the year. It took him no more than half an hour to find the newspapers he was looking for. The party, he was able to confirm, took place on the night of November 14, 1942. On the front page of one of the newspapers, a headline, in large print, read CRIME COMMITTED IN THE HOUSE OF LUIS URIBE'S DAUGHTER, and the reader was referred to two inner sections—the society page and the nota roja. He read the society article first. The week before, Delfina Uribe celebrated the opening of her gallery and the inaugural Escobedo exhibition. Read thirty years later, the list of guests was a revealing document of the time. Almost everyone had been present that night. Painters, writers, politicians, filmmakers, theater people. Legendary figures, most of whom are gone. He was impressed by the compactness of the setting. A small city where, for that very reason, their personalities stood out more clearly. Delfina's family relationships and her personal talent allowed her to bring together the whole of Mexico City with little effort. The reporter described in words akin to ecstasy the elegance of that "extraordinary apartment that, because of its modern decor, would have been the pride of cities like Los Angeles or New York," which she concluded by describing as "a Hollywood dream!" She quoted remarks by some of the guests about aluminum columns, a pair of pre-Hispanic masks, and the portrait of the hostess, painted years before by the young Escobedo. She spoke of the dinner's French and Mexican dishes; she described at length the eveningwear of some of the most prominent social figures of the day: the contrast, for example, between Frida's opulently embroidered Oaxacan dress and the Greek-style draped tunic worn by Dolores del Río. She commented on the cosmopolitan atmosphere that suddenly flourished in some of the city's salons, where "because of its refined spirit, a gathering like Delfina Uribe's constituted *un vrai événement*, an entrée to a privileged space where all languages could be heard and spoken." The article was a hymn to harmony. Had she been a political reporter, the author would have mentioned the national unity slogan that was the order of the day. Politicians and artists comingled in perfect peace at the gathering; ladies and gentlemen, descendants of the old families, mixed and interacted without suspicion with those who only very recently—yesterday, as it were!—had moved up the social ladder. Like the dishes served that night, local and foreign guests seemed to coexist in the most convivial way. The society reporter left the gathering in a state of ecstasy, only to fall into a new delirium before the celestial spectacle. The night, still cold for that time of year, exposed a clearer sky than usual. Each of the stars that made up the Orion constellation sang praises in honor of Delfina and her new gallery and foretold happiness for the other guests. Is it possible that the commentator left the party before the shots were fired? It seemed evident to him that she had, and yet he sensed in her gilded tone an exaggeration intended to conceal something terrible. In the same newspaper, on the blood-spattered nota roja, the same gathering was reported in very different terms. It was described as sinister. A devious plot devised by a highly criminal mind. The toll: one German murdered and two Mexicans who lay dying in the hospital. The deceased, this he knew well, was the stepson of Arnulfo Briones, the brother of his Aunt Eduviges, a boy who'd recently arrived in Mexico. The two wounded: Delfina's own son and a certain Pedro Balmorán, whose name, although vaguely familiar, he was unable to place. He checked the newspapers from that day and the following days. Unfortunately, he was unable to find in the newspaper archives any of the scandal rags of the time, which would surely be more explicit. In any case, the pages dedicated to the nota roja were virulent and sensationalist. Delfina declared that she didn't know the deceased, whose name was Erich Maria Pistauer, nor had she invited him to her home. During the ten days that followed, all the newspapers alluded to the passionate and political motives of the crime. The articles hinted, in one way or another, at Delfina's connection to the murder. One newspaper portrayed her as an example of revolutionary corruption: easy money, scandalous luxury, passing affairs, frivolity galore. It was said that the fight had begun in her apartment, that the Uribe brothers had run off the troublemakers, and that the shots only rang out after they reached the streets. Another journalist commented on circulating rumors: an effort to achieve from the top, by decree, a contrived national unity had ended in failure. From the beginning, certain fissures had been exposed that would eventually become deep cracks. The crime was portrayed to the public as the fruit of a new schism in the revolutionary family. Gun in hand, General Torner had threatened the painter Julio Escobedo. The unifying project turned out to be a fiction. The military, it was clear, caused the civilians to feel the full weight of its force. Had the caciques resumed the struggle for power? What at the end of the day was the Machiavellian

Licenciado Uribe's ultimate goal? Let him speak! Let him lay his cards honorably on the table! A bush-league journalist with a reputation for pedantry commented in a far right-wing newspaper that it was not an anomaly that the tragedy had taken place there. The Minerva Building had become a perilous new Babel, invaded by foreigners of the worst sort. Semites who had emerged from Lithuania's murkiest sewers and the Black Sea had transformed it into their theater of operations. But the police were keeping a close eye on their activities. He emphasized the fact that the Hebrew Ida Werfel had started the battle by attempting to send a coded message, using as a cover—oh, the gall!—phrases by the immortal Spanish religious author of passion plays, Tirso de Molina. The Werfel woman and her henchmen should be careful! The authorities were neither blind nor deaf; in a few days they'd reveal shocking news. No obituary was published. The name Arnulfo Briones was mentioned with relative discretion on two or three occasions. Fifteen days later the news disappeared, except for one or two fleeting references, which were slipped into the unruliest newspapers, in reference to the fight between General Torner and the painter Escobedo. Always with the same tenor of unreality. It was obvious that Delfina's father or brothers had intervened to silence the scandal. Perhaps the standing of many of those attending the party, two cabinet members among them, also contributed to this silence.

Consternation reigned in his aunt and uncle's home. He would be lying if he said he'd heard the shots that night. His room had no windows facing the street. The next morning, Amparo awoke at first light to tell him that Erich, the son of his Uncle Arnulfo's wife, had been killed. He dressed quickly and joined the family in the dining room, where they were already having breakfast. His aunt seemed to have gone mad. Neither she nor his Uncle Dionisio had been to bed all night. At one point, she rose and, with an imposing gesture, made him and Amparo swear that they wouldn't leave the apartment all day. Then she fell into a chair and, with a voice and expressions of defeat, asked them not to go into Antonio's room so as not to worry him with the news, as any shock could be fatal for a child with a liver ailment. They were to speak to no one about what had happened. Not the neighbors and not the servants. "Don't say anything! Keep your mouths shut! Not a single word to strangers!" Dionisio shouted. She, on the other hand, did nothing but send the servants to find out what they could and then relay the information she received by phone to who knows how many places. When his uncle returned, he found her feeling faint but able to be revived at any moment to hear any rumor provided by the doorwoman, the neighbors, Delfina's servants, and those of the Colombian and Uruguayan diplomats living on an upper floor. She locked herself away for a while with her husband, then emerged distressed, telling him that he was wrong, that her family knew nothing about any bloody incidents, that the person responsible for what had happened, as she'd been insisting since the previous night and had predicted long before, was one of the injured, whom Del Solar was able to identify in the newspapers as Pedro Balmorán. The fact that he'd been seriously wounded seemed to confirm her suspicions. Throughout the day she tried to locate Delfina, but she hadn't returned from the clinic where they operated on her son. She knew that several police inspectors had gone to her apartment and that the Uribes had been responsible for receiving them and then seeing them off. Amparo and he lingered at a bureau next to a window to watch the photographers take photographs. Later, the inspectors arrived at their apartment, and his Aunt Eduviges shouted that she knew nothing, that she was terrified, that she was a poor, desolate mother with a child who suffered from infantile hepatitis, whose life hung by a thread, which was the result of living in such a sinister building, that the only thing she could state was that Pedro Balmorán, who claimed to be a writer and journalist and lived on the top floor, was the worst sort of scoundrel, surely mixed up in the murder of Pistauer.

As the days passed, calm seemed to return to the building, but it no longer reigned in his aunt and uncle's house. Arnulfo stopped visiting them. Del Solar knew nothing about Erich's funeral. He only remembers having seen his mother, a German, once, when his aunt forced him to accompany her on a visit from which she returned very annoyed. They hadn't been able to understand each other because the German woman, a tall blonde who didn't smile even once, didn't speak Spanish or French, and his aunt didn't understand a word of German. The visit, which was very brief given the enmity with which they were received, consisted of little more than an inspection of the kitchen, especially the refrigerator, accompanied by numerous frantic gestures that meant that the butter wasn't as good as that which she bought at the San Juan Market, that she should be careful with the fish, and that she should only buy it when she knew the fishmonger very well, that the best fillet of beef could be bought at a butcher's shop in Colonia Juárez, although in Colonia San Juan they also knew how to cut it as it should be, and she indulged in bitter remarks after arriving home, directed just at him, since Amparo had stayed to keep Antonio company, regarding her brother Arnulfo's foolishness, the most recent consisting of involving himself with a woman so unpleasant that she would end up getting him into trouble. Which eventually happened. The police detained the two girls who worked in the home for interrogation, and his uncle had to go to the police station to look for them, but they refused to work for them any longer; they returned, frightened to death, only to pick up their belongings. His aunt remained silent, or almost, for several days, teary-eyed. Amparo learned that they'd have to move, that her Uncle Arnulfo had disappeared along with his wife and would no longer pay the rent; that they'd been offered a more modest rental house in the same neighborhood, a few blocks from the building. The doctor was very concerned about the deterioration of Antonio's condition; he said the anxiety in the house had penetrated his bedroom and poisoned his organism, that they might admit him to the clinic for a few days so that the move wouldn't affect him. Del Solar didn't experience the move, since, although there were still several months remaining in the school year, his parents decided he should join them in Córdoba, where he lived during the ensuing years and continued his studies until the time came to return to Mexico City and enter university.

As he examined the building again, he felt that the games in the courtyard, the blackouts, his aunt's frenzied confessions, all had been part of an idyllic existence that forgetfulness had barely managed to conceal. More than the children's games, he missed the endless mysteries he'd divined from his aunt's conversations with her husband, with her brother Arnulfo, with unknown interlocutors with whom she communicated by telephone. His aunt's uncontainable exuberance, which as an adult he always considered loathsome, was perhaps the element he missed most. Strange but true! He never noticed that Eduviges was a monster and that over time she'd become worse. That she'd spoken to him and Amparo as she would to a pair of adults, that she'd shared with them, as if with accomplices, the thousand and one vicissitudes of her daily life, despite the fact that they could only understand a fraction of her verbal torrent, had given Miguel del Solar a pleasure that he'd never again find in his dealings with people. And Antonio, of course, barely registered in his memory, invisible as he was in his sickroom.

Perhaps having been nurtured in a fountain that always confused familial tribulations with the country's disasters defined his later vocation, his determination to continue despite family opinion, which considered the study of history to be of little import, too imprecise. Yes, he abandoned the study of law a year after starting in order to devote himself fully to history.

That building with its gangrenous walls, the Minerva, wasn't even a shadow of what he once knew. It needed painting, lacked dignity; its eccentricity was mixed with misfortune, categories that never work well together. Parts of it reminded him more of a tenement than residences built originally for elegant tenants. Even so, he couldn't deny its charm. His aunt and uncle's apartment consisted of two wings, which formed a triangle. Nonetheless, he was unable to pinpoint the location of his own room.

At the back of the courtyard, around a small fountain, people were working, apparently without success, to repair a water pump. A young woman, humble, with a fresh smile, approached him to ask if he was looking for someone, if he would like anything, adding:

"I'm the doorwoman."

He felt as if he'd been caught in a harmless act. He said, hurriedly, that as he was passing by he wondered if there was an apartment available.

"I don't think so," replied the young woman. "But who knows if one will be vacant soon? The building superintendent could tell you, but he's not here now. Would you like to come back later?"

He said goodbye. No, he certainly didn't intend to live there. He surveyed the interior of the building again. A house of witches. A ruin, with a lot of character, yes, but surely unlivable. If his sabbatical weren't about to end, perhaps he'd consider it.

A few minutes later he set out for Calle de Tabasco, where he was to turn in the corrected proofs of his book.

He's a historian, that much is clear. His name is Miguel del Solar, recently widowed. For the last seven years, he's lived in England, where he's a professor of Latin American history at the University of Bristol. The visit he just paid has moved him. He feels an almost physical need to know the circumstances and details of the crime related to the Minerva Building. He believes it touches him personally.

CHAPTER 2

The Vanquished Party

LOCATING HIS AUNT HAD BEEN A test of patience. When he called her, a woman's voice asked who he was. He said his name. What did he wish to say to the señora? they wanted to know. He insisted: he was her nephew; he just wanted to say hello. A silence and then another question. Which nephew? What did he say his name was? He should wait a moment; they would see if by chance Sra. Briones de Díaz Zepeda was still at home. A few minutes later a man's voice was heard on the receiver. A rather gravelly tone. He wanted to know who was calling. Del Solar explained, on the verge of losing his patience, who he was, and that he merely wanted to say hello to his aunt. Again: he should wait a moment; it seemed that the señora had gone out . . . Two or three minutes passed, and another voice answered again. In falsetto. It was difficult to know if it belonged to a child or an old woman. An unpleasant voice, extremely contrived. It all seemed like a joke. They asked him the same questions again. He was beyond impatient but decided not to hang up.

"Del Solar! Miguel del Solar!" he shouted.

"For goodness' sake! Why didn't you say so?" the voice responded. "Why so much mystery?" The voice was shrill, disagreeable, but somehow more normal. "Are you in Mexico? This is Amparo. Mamá can't come to the phone. She can't move at the moment. They gave her a sedative injection. She has to stay in bed for at least an hour after the injection. They were harassing her on the phone all last night."

He made clear that there was no mystery on his part; he'd said who he was from the beginning and that he merely wanted to say hello. He asked his cousin when he could pay them a visit.

"Let me discuss it with Mamá. Would you prefer to come for lunch or dinner?" And then without transition she asked him if he was still living abroad or had decided to stay in Mexico. If he was getting along in England, such a humid place. Del Solar felt that his cousin was trying to buy some time, to divert the conversation, to turn the appointment into something imprecise, to say goodbye without committing to anything. That's why he insisted. He preferred not to bother his aunt by demanding a lunch or dinner, he told her; he merely wanted to drop by to say hello and have a cup of coffee with them; that was all.

"I'd love to see the two of you," he repeated again.

"It's odd that you would say that, after having not so much as called us all this time, don't you think?"

He decided to ignore the impertinent remark, and he continued to speak as if the trust they shared in childhood still existed. He was likely to stay in Bristol for another year, perhaps he'd return next year and settle permanently in Mexico. Nowhere, he was convinced, could he work better than in his own country; he'd grown weary of teaching students who would never manage to understand anything. Besides, his children needed to come back. Keeping them in England without their mother was in fact impossible. And without giving her time to dither or beg off, he told her that he'd drop by to see her—he cleverly used the singular—the next afternoon. Would six be a good time? Amparo answered yes, said goodbye sounding a bit confused, and hung up.

Del Solar commented to his mother how strange that call

was; the different voices he'd heard at first, Amparo's reticent tone. He asked her if the relationship between her and Eduviges had worsened.

"I wouldn't say it's bad," she said, and after a pause added: "but not good either; rather nonexistent, which I suppose is the same as saying it's bad, isn't it? It never crossed my mind. Since she became a widow we hardly see each other. Antonio's career has her in a daze. Every now and then we bump into each other at someone's home. Once I went to visit her in Coyoacán. She's become even more impertinent and high-handed than before, if that's possible. When Dionisio died, I was the first to show up at her house. They didn't live nearly as comfortably as they do now, you'll see. When I saw their house, I thought she'd become common. Do you think that's possible at her age? Losing one's taste, I mean . . ." She remained silent for a moment, then continued: "Antonio seemed very affected that day. That's when I realized how much like his father he was. I always thought he'd never amount to much, but just look at him, he's a very bright boy. Sometimes I think Eduviges considered Dionisio's death a victory, to be able to have her son all to herself. Anyone else would have lost their spirit, like what happened to Dionisio after he married her, but it wasn't like that with Antonio. On the contrary, the boy's full of ambition. I don't think he gets along with this government very well. I don't know if you've seen how the newspapers treat him. He must have done something wrong because they're making things very hard for him. I haven't seen him since the funeral. He asked me about you, about your work. Even Eduviges seemed to be proud to be related to you when your book appeared; but only at the beginning, then she changed. She's always been selfish. She wants any success to be her son's."

The next day, at six o'clock, as he and his cousin had

agreed, Del Solar entered a home in Coyoacán from the middle of the eighteenth century. He passed through a large garden surrounded by arches. He walked behind the maid who'd come out to open the gate. They walked through a dimly lit room. He tried to focus his attention on two paintings before going up the stairs. Two beautiful French landscapes, perhaps also from the eighteenth century. The maid turned on the light. The rest was jumbled, incoherent, trivial. An excess of expensive objects in disarray; brass, porcelain, crystal. Good silver, but too much of it. The maid paused, as if the meeting were to take place in that room. Del Solar felt that this was a mandatory layover so visitors could appreciate the furniture and objects. Then they went up a staircase of wide red tiles, before walking down another hallway to the small room where his aunt was waiting for him. A much more pleasant room, unlike the mass confusion on the ground floor.

It was difficult to take in his aunt's entirety at first glance. He'd last seen her a good dozen years before. By then her body had already begun the process of expanding and, given her height, had taken on a truly monumental shape. His mother had mentioned it, but the effect was much greater than expected. A mountain in perpetual motion wrapped in wool. She maintained her anachronistic and wholly particular way of dressing, which he liked. The same clothes he'd seen her wear as a child. A kind of evening dress that went down to her ankles, made of a thick gray flannel, actually more suitable for a man's overcoat, with antique black velvet trim on the breast and cuffs and jet-black vertical threads sewn on both sides. The kind of garment advertised in the magazines and newspapers of 1914 that he'd just researched. As if his aunt had been captivated in her childhood by her elders' clothing and decided to remain faithful to that fashion. Her glasses, just as thirty years ago, were tied around her neck with a thick black velvet ribbon. Her decidedly unkempt appearance surprised him, her lack of personal cleanliness: makeup poorly applied, neglected nails, disheveled hair, as seemingly dirty as the sable she wore around her neck. It seemed as though she'd slept several nights in the same dress, without repairing either to a commode or a bathroom.

When she saw her nephew she leapt from her chair with remarkable lightness. She ran to him, hugged him, and then pushed him unceremoniously into another chair, as if she'd suddenly grown tired of him or had come to the decision that she didn't need to be so affectionate. She brought her hands to her head and tousled her hair even more. She held out her hands in a dramatic expression and let them rest, open, atop a chest of drawers. Her fingernails were trimmed almost to the quick, neglected, and somewhat dirty. She walked toward the couch where she'd been reclining when he arrived, and nearly collapsed on it before changing her mind at the last moment and, on the verge of falling, performed a pirouette that reminded him of dolphins at sea. She returned to where he was, took him by the hand, forced him to stand, and led him to the back of the room, where she finally allowed him to sit on a high-backed settee, and she plopped down with all her weight beside him, against the backrest. Del Solar hadn't uttered even the most elementary words of greeting when she got up again, bumping into her nephew's knees, a basket full of newspapers and magazines, and a table on which she placed her hands and where she was able at last to regain her balance. There she rang an electric bell.

"I'll have them bring us something. I don't know what you'd like; I'm going to have a mint tea because coffee makes me very nervous. I'm seeing Dr. Murillo. He doesn't let me drink more than two cups a day, one at breakfast and one after lunch. Perhaps you'd prefer a whiskey." She waited at the door for the maid, and when she arrived, contrary to all that she'd said, she ordered a pot of coffee and two cups. "Later I'll offer you something else. Coffee must have its drawbacks; Murillo knows that better than anyone else, but the truth is that there's no better drink in this cold."

Del Solar employed with his aunt, in an attempt to soothe her, a method that almost always had good results: he began by telling her that she looked very well, that time seemed to have stood still, that he hadn't seen her so fit since the time they lived in the Minerva Building.

"Do you think?" she asked with a certain misgiving. "I think I've put on a bit of weight. I've been a bit negligent over the years. Don't you find me fatter?"

"It must be the dress. You're wearing very thick wool today."

"No, no, no," she repeated categorically. "I've put on a few pounds recently. And I've not been in good health at all. You've caught me a sight, my gallbladder is bad, my blood pressure and cholesterol are very high. Especially my nerves. I've felt so bad! Did you hear that they've started to fabricate lies about Antonio? I won't be able to recover until this situation is cleared up. There are people who are determined to harm him; they want to make him fall into a trap. Licenciado Armendáriz recommended that he leave the country. To spend some time, a year perhaps, abroad. To go, for example, to Spain. In the event he has to leave, and hopefully it won't reach that extreme, I think I'll have no choice but to go with him, at least for a while. He likes Madrid, but in this case perhaps the best thing is to take refuge in a less visible place, Málaga, or—and why not?—Torremolinos. I can't tolerate the poisonous nature of his detractors, let alone his false friends. You don't know how they torment me on the phone. I'm hurt by the pompous behavior of all those people my son has showered with favors. If they happen upon me, they pretend not to see me, or they greet me with outright mockery. It's reached the point that I don't leave the house. You were right to leave, to escape the savagery. They'll finish us off, just you wait. They vowed to do so long ago and have gone about doing it. They have it in for us, just as I'm telling you, Miguel." His aunt delivered these lamentations with prodigious speed, and with an abundant assortment of gestures and movements. Her face had turned to playdough. She moved her lips with exaggeration, and at the end of each sentence the corners of her mouth dropped so much so that she looked like an old bulldog at times. Her massive cheeks contracted and expanded just like her nostrils. At times her eyes were little more than slits lost among her abundant flesh, at others they bulged like balloons. "In our family, you know better than anyone else, you are a historian after all, no one has ever sullied their hands with other people's money. No one! I'd stand in front of the National Palace and shout it at the top of my lungs! No one! That's the bad thing! A lesson in dignity for which they won't forgive us. It's the man at the bottom who steals, and the first thing he does is to blame the person above him. Six years later, you find yourself among savages disguised as gentlemen. We've always been respectable. Your family, no offense, not as much as the Brioneses, but honorable to a fault, no one should doubt it. My husband paid off the house in Colonia Valle just a year before he died." She paused, rang the bell again, waited for the coffee to arrive, and then continued: "They won't do to Antonio, I swear it, what they did to my brother. I won't let them touch him. I have much to say. If I decided to talk!" Suddenly she became the Phantom of Justice, a mighty goddess of punishment, the Queen of Swords, Turandot the Merciless. But the effect lasted only a moment; all at once she collapsed. She began to roll about on the sofa, a defenseless, gelatinous, frightened mass. "I'm so scared," she gasped in a weak voice. "I haven't been so scared in quite a while." She swallowed her coffee in two gulps and poured another, smeared a piece of toast with orange marmalade that she devoured as ferociously as she drank the coffee. She seemed to forget that there was another person in the room and began to leaf through some magazines. Del Solar cleared his throat. Finally she noticed her nephew again. She looked at him with bewildered eyes, her mouth half-open, and said, "Thank you for coming to keep me company at this time. Have you heard anything new? Have you come to tell me something?"

"No, I never imagined the situation was so serious." He told her that his mother thought that Antonio had made some enemies who were trying to oust him; he thought that the situation was merely a six-year rotation to get rid of some officials politically and to fill the open spaces with other people.

"Your mother, forgive me for saying so, doesn't have the faintest." And she returned to her lamentations. Her son salvaged some government ventures that he'd found on the brink of collapse, and on his way out he left them flourishing, no matter what they said. He made no concessions, that was all. His only crime was that he belonged to a family that for many years they'd been determined to discredit and eliminate

If he allowed her to continue to speak, she'd spend the afternoon repeating the same refrain, without reaching the point that interested him. It was time to intervene in the conversation. He asked her if, in her opinion, they were attacking her family more fiercely now or during the time they lived in the Minerva Building.

"What do you mean, then or now?" she shouted in astonishment, "Have I not told you always? I find it hard to believe that you're the one asking! You, the historian! They've persecuted us since the beginning of this century, perhaps even before, since Dr. Mora, whom you defend so ardently, organized Freemasonry in this country. I suffered personally, before and after my marriage, true hardships. And I've lived constantly in terror. My husband, like you, never managed to learn anything; he was never interested in doing so."

"But I am interested. Even as a child, when I lived with you in Colonia Roma, I realized that strange things happened around us. Do you remember the shooting that took place in the building? A German boy was killed, if I'm not mistaken."

Eduviges Briones narrowed her eyes; two slits fixed on him with absolute malevolence. She seemed unable to decide whether to talk. At last, she said with spite and ill humor:

"He was Austrian, not German. His name was Pistauer. Erich Maria Pistauer was his full name. Everyone always says the German boy and the Austrian woman, and it was just the opposite. Adele was German, and Erich and his father Austrian. They lived in Berlin. There, much to his misfortune, my brother met that detestable woman."

"It's as if I were reliving those days," said Del Solar, without paying much attention to the clarification about nationalities in which his aunt was still engaged. "Have you gone back to the Minerva?"

"Never!" she shouted, with such violence and such a profound expression of disgust that he considered these excesses to be wholly unrelated to his anodyne question. "Why would I set foot in there again? Why would you even ask? So someone can shoot me too? So a car can run me over? When Antonio had power, I was forever asking him to order a number of places to be cleaned out, that one in particular. To expel from the country, by whatever means necessary, the degenerate from the fourth floor who's responsible for all the evil that has happened to us. One of the culprits, because behind him there must have been powerful people. Someone protects him. No one will ever convince me otherwise. If I were a man, I would have finished Balmorán off long ago, I assure you. I would have ripped him to pieces. He's the author of our ruin. I told Arnulfo as much, but he didn't listen to me, and he got himself killed."

"The German boy? He was his stepson, wasn't he?" Del Solar asked, not understanding her.

"The Austrian boy!" she shouted, "Erich Maria Pistauer was Austrian! Yes, I mean him, but also Arnulfo, my brother. Are you going to tell me that you don't know about his death? They killed him. They refused to investigate further. My husband was out of work for quite some time. We got by with his translations. They were terrible years. I don't even know how I managed to provide for Antonio. And thirty years later, history is repeating itself. Even now, Balmorán's hand is at work."

"Balmorán? Who was also injured at the Minerva?"

"Let me tell you just one thing. One day last week I opened the newspaper. There was a vile article in which they slandered your cousin, yes, Antonio, and on the same page, next to that pack of lies, an interview in which Balmorán spoke of public corruption. He claimed that he was giving an interview to the press for the first time in many years. Do you believe that's a coincidence? Tell it to the . . . ! He's forgotten that I've been around. I know too much about him. I know what he's up to. He's been after me for a long time. Me and my family. Who's he working for? That's what I'd like to know. I have my suspicions, yes, many. He's not that smart; he's never been arrested. That's no small thing. He not only obeys orders; he carries them out in spades, to vilify and destroy us. Several years ago he came to visit me. We were still living at the Minerva. He wanted to know if it was true that I was related to Gonzalo de la Caña. And the truth is, yes. He was my great-uncle. He told me he was doing research and was interested in learning more about that cursed poet. Look, Miguel, I don't even know why I'm telling you this. I promised myself once not to tell anyone. I know you won't divulge what we talk about; please, I'm asking you, don't fail me... Gonzalo de la Caña was a rake who published stories and poems in magazines in Guadalajara and here. It seems that they never appeared in a book, but I'm not certain. Tablada admired his stories. But for the family he was always a cross to bear. He was my grandmother's younger brother. We were a cultivated family. You probably know that my father's library had no equal in Mexico. On several occasions I witnessed Gamboa consulting it; Nervo as well, and many others. People never bother to think of those things. Talent has always abounded in our people. I don't know if you've talked to Derny lately; he can tell you very interesting things." I had to bring her back to the subject, to Balmorán's visit. "Ah, yes. I was saying that one day a boy with a lantern-jawed face and shifty eyes came to see me. He had all the defects I abhor in a person, a shrill voice, sweaty hands, no taste in clothes. A veritable tramp! To give you an idea, he was wearing mustard-colored socks . . . I can forget everything but that. Utterly unremarkable! But you should have seen the airs he put on! He introduced himself as a journalist and a student of literature. From the first moment, something told me that this idiot would bring me nothing but misfortune; one can sense these things. I didn't want to invite him in. But he made his way into the living room and sat down. He told me that he was writing a thesis on unknown authors and that he had happened upon Gonzalo de la Caña. He'd discovered that he was a relative of mine. How? I still can't explain it! He said he thought it was a stroke of good luck to be able to talk to me. I felt my blood run cold. Since I was a child I had been forbidden to utter my uncle's name. He lived I don't know how many years, all his adult life, locked away in shed at the rear of my grandparents' home. There was a considerable age difference between him and his siblings. There were thirteen of them; Gonzalo was the youngest. I was able to see him a few times at the end of his life. He was a frightful sight. They had taken him to Europe as a boy; while in Paris, an illness made him an idiot. When he returned to Mexico he was only twenty-two. In those days such matters weren't discussed in front of an unmarried woman. Today, I can imagine what illness it was. We were forbidden to mention even his existence. He was the bête noire of the family. A veritable cross for everyone. The servants told us horrible tales. At times he would undress in front of them and show them his private parts, laughing hysterically. He was the devil. Suffice it to say that the gardener had to take him his food. In the end, fortunately, the violent outbursts passed. He lived his last few years like a tumor, without talking, without moving, growing bigger and bigger. I told Balmorán that I didn't know what he was talking about. That poet wasn't a relative of mine; I'd never heard his name. And that clown dared to tell me that surely my family had hidden the fact from me as it had from everyone else, and that they'd altered the dates of his death and burial. He said that they'd found letters from another poet, a friend of De la Caña, in which he accused my grandfather of having kidnapped the ailing writer. The poet wrote that he even feared for his life. Balmorán told me, in hopes of enticing me to speak, I believe, that perhaps he'd been punished for writing a very decadent, very perverse story, the last one he'd published, in which he wantonly described a human body, declaring that it belonged to one of his sisters. Can you imagine, Miguel, how much they suffered at home with that savage! I resolved to show neither nerves nor fear. I managed to restrain myself during the whole interview, and I even managed to say goodbye to him casually. I believed I convinced him that I didn't know anything because there was nothing to know, that he was following a dead end. At the door he told me that we would see each other often because he also lived in the Minerva apartments. Can you imagine? How could he afford it? I wasn't able to find out. At the time I thought that he must be living on the roof, that someone had rented him a servant's room, a practice that your Uncle Dionisio and I were opposed to. We'd protested to the owners, as we sensed that riffraff was beginning to invade our world. We thought that dangerous elements could sneak in, criminals. We could never have imagined that the enemy had already infiltrated, that he was living among us. I learned from the servants that Balmorán lived better than I'd imagined; he'd settled in an apartment on the top floor, a studio, only two rooms, yes, but with a kitchen and a bathroom. After that I never let him out of my sight. One day I asked Delfina Uribe, the revolutionary's daughter, if she knew Balmorán. There's no reason for you to remember her; she lived next door to us while they were finishing her house in San Ángel. She told me that, yes, she knew him well, that they were friends, and that he was writing a very entertaining book about a castrato. I never asked, nor did anyone ever tell me about the illness my uncle suffered; I only knew that he'd gone mad, and it suddenly occurred to me that this man intended to incriminate my family, to reveal a secret that's been kept hidden with the greatest care, and perhaps to even accuse my grandfather of having castrated the madman so he'd stop going around showing his organs to the maids. From what my cousins and the servants told me, when they took him into the house and locked him away there was nothing castrated about him, on the contrary, they couldn't so much as go near him. I thought it was bad form that Delfina would entertain these conversations, much less repeat them.

I told her as much, and our friendship suffered forever. I realized that a plot was being contrived to harm my brother. I didn't know how, or what it entailed, only that there were people who detested him, Delfina and her relatives among them."

She seemed so exhausted at that point that she couldn't utter another word. She leaned her magnum body forward, reclined her head, breathed in through her mouth, and then threw herself suddenly backward until landing on the back of the settee; she whickered two or three times, brought her hands to her head, and tousled her hair even more.

"Why did they hate him?"

"I'll explain another day. Arnulfo's personality wasn't easy. On more than one occasion I gathered my courage and dared to speak to him. He was too intransigent a man. Even at that time it was no longer common for men to behave that way, but he was very old-fashioned, more so than my parents, for example, and even my grandparents. Which is why I was so surprised that he married that German woman. I gathered my courage. What do you want? At home we'd been taught that certain subjects were never to be discussed, least of all between siblings. But I dared to do it, knowing it was for his own good. If only he'd listened to me then! If he'd protected himself in time, perhaps he'd be here now, talking to us. I told him that a fellow who lived in the building had paid me a very suspicious visit, because he wanted to know certain intimate details about our family. I recounted his version of Gonzalo de la Caña, our uncle, and that it had given me goose bumps. I exaggerated the tone a bit to force him to act, but still I didn't succeed completely. I told him that Balmorán, which was the man's name, had begun to make inquiries among the neighbors to find out everything he could about us. I knew what would rankle him most, so I added that Delfina, Licenciado Uribe's daughter, had told me that Balmorán was aware that a relative of ours wasn't quite normal, that he wasn't all there, and that he boasted that he had the papers to prove it. The truth is I was more innocent, I swear to you, than anyone could conceive, and I didn't understand entirely what he was talking about. After mentioning Delfina Uribe, I realized that he was listening with greater interest, even if he did try to hide it. Finally he stopped reading the newspaper and asked who was visiting Delfina, and for some information about her friendship with Balmorán. A few days later a man he trusted, whom I couldn't stand the sight of, showed up at the apartment at a time when Arnulfo wasn't usually there, which seemed very strange to me. What's more, it was the first time this had happened since Arnulfo had arrived from Germany. I showed the character, Martínez was his name, to Arnulfo's office, and I'd barely done so when I remembered my brother's orders not to let anyone in, no one at all, not even his wife if she asked. I went in and told him that it would be better if he came to the living room to have a cup of coffee with me. It seemed that was what he wanted. He had a very engaging gift of gab. He commented on how much people had changed in Mexico in recent years. I said yes, that unfortunately everything was different. He had a way of pressuring you that caused you to begin to talk without realizing it, although I'm sure I didn't say anything that would compromise anyone. It was no secret that I disliked the environment in which I was living. All I did was tell him what I thought, that is, that I felt bad in this atmosphere. I described each and every one of the tenants until arriving at Balmorán. There, I indulged myself, of course. I repeated the same thing to him that I'd told my brother. I told him what I knew about my uncle, the poet. He was very interested, excessively. But I thought that since my brother was nervous about talking to me about certain subjects, he'd sent the aforementioned Martínez so that I'd open up, as if it would be less difficult for me to talk about these matters with a stranger than with him. And he wasn't wrong about that. Arnulfo was a sick man, a weakling. Which is why I don't understand his relationship with his wives even now. Well, to continue. I thought that later the two of them would discuss the matter alone without my having to touch on any salacious details in front of my brother. But when Arnulfo arrived I told him that his gunman had been there, since I had a hard time calling him his adviser, and it would be impossible for me to think of him as his associate, as Martínez himself sometimes suggested. He couldn't be his associate. My brother wouldn't allow such a mediocre person to be involved in business with him. Martínez was an oaf who had come up in the world. Now that I think of some of Arnulfo's quirks, I wouldn't be surprised. Anyway, I saw that my brother was so annoyed that I didn't dare repeat my conversation with him. He'd already spent his life accusing me of indiscretion. He didn't need anything else. Men don't understand anything. He accused me of being indiscreet, but here I am, ill but alive, and he, on the other hand, where's he? Six feet under! They've filled my son's head with the same old song, my indiscretion, my impertinence, my tactlessness, need I say more? If he'd only listened to me, if he'd put certain people in their place, he wouldn't be in the predicament he's in today. I'm a sincere woman who's different, who's known, what's more, how to see beyond what they've been able to see. I don't want to talk about it anymore. Don't you think it's unusual that Amparo hasn't come back?" she asked suddenly, apparently willing to change the subject. "She had to meet Gilda, my daughter-in-law, at Armendáriz's office. She knows my life is hanging by a thread, and she enjoys making me wait. She's always been that way, since she was a child, you must remember. She does it on purpose to upset me. All the satisfaction Antonio has given me in life, she returns to me as grief. She was excited by the idea of seeing you today. She went to the beauty salon this morning, as if it would do her any good! Sometimes I think her defect has become more noticeable over the years. If she wanted to see you so badly, she would've hurried, don't you think? She was ecstatic. But after lunch my daughter-in-law sent for her. She should have been back more than two hours ago. She could at least have phoned to say she was going to be late, in my opinion. Good God, I'm dying to know if they were able to sign those papers!"

Del Solar looked at the time on his watch. He needed to leave! He'd been invited to a dinner. He started to say goodbye, but she didn't seem willing to let him go. She began again to swear vows of honor. Hers was an honorable family. Her family couldn't take her to Europe because they were always short on money. The house seemed ostentatious, but it wasn't. Antonio had bought it for a song. He'd earned a very good salary and had been able to invest his money well. What's more, she'd taken care to marry him off well. Gilda was the daughter of a man of considerable wealth; a scatterbrain, poor thing, but that was another story. Not as much as a penny had gone to her son. That was obvious, unless some wanted to make a mountain out of a molehill. All that was left was for Gilda to agree that some properties would pass into Amparo's hands—nominally, it was understood. It would be a temporary measure to protect herself. To protect Antonio! The girl was descended from a family of imbeciles. She might have thought, under the present circumstances, that they wanted to keep properties that, in the end, in some way belonged to them. Antonio's interests would be better taken care of in their hands than in those of a certain Gildita.

He'd already put on his coat while she was drowning in her fits, and he asked her without any hint of emotion:

"Why did they kill the German boy in Delfina Uribe's house?"

"Erich? Erich Maria Pistauer?" she answered in bewilderment. "How should I know that?" And then she added angrily, perhaps because she'd been distracted from her primary concern: "I told you he wasn't German, but Austrian. The German was his mother, Adele. Besides, he wasn't killed at Delfina's house, but at the entrance to the building."

The phone rang. Eduviges shouted something to the maid from the door; she picked up the receiver and began to listen closely without uttering a word. She hung up in a fit. Del Solar had sat down again. He didn't allow her to explain who'd called.

"I've read several newspaper articles from the time," he said. "They said it happened at a party given by Delfina Uribe."

Eduviges paused to collect her thoughts. She didn't sit down, instead taking a few steps that made her immenseness even more absurd, her improbable clothes, the marten stole around her neck, her jewels. At last she opened her mouth, breathed deeply, and said:

"Yes, Erich was at the party. Delfina attempted to incriminate me, declaring with absolute certainty that I was the one who brought him to her house. Can you imagine anything more absurd? What interest could I have in taking my brother's stepson into that den of wolves? It's as clear as day: Delfina had set out to seduce him. She had a passion for young boys. She'd had a lover younger than her own son; she told me so herself. Erich was killed as he left the building. Delfina attempted to absolve herself of responsibility. She said she didn't understand what the boy was doing there. Of course no one believed a word she said. The only purpose of that was to mortify your uncle. It was a wake-up call. He was being cornered. The currents in which we moved were very murky, but one thing was clear: Delfina was in league with many people, with Balmorán, with General Torner. I'm telling you, she was the one who first told me about the story of the castrato. They were in league. Delfina's father, let's not forget, was one of the most powerful men in Mexico. Together they'd woven a very tight web to trap my brother. And he, poor fool, thinking he was so experienced, fell into it. First they killed his stepson. He couldn't have been more than twenty years old. He was struck down. They covered everything up with a smoke screen. The culprit was never caught. When I run into Delfina, I barely say hello to her. I wouldn't be surprised if she's behind Balmorán now too. What a coincidence, I'll say it again, that an article against your cousin appears in a newspaper next to an interview with that swine, talking about corrupt officials. The only thing that was missing was a photo of Delfina to complete the portrait. General Torner died recently. That night at Delfina's house he gave a very strange performance. He wanted to kill the painter Escobedo."

"Is she still alive?"

"Who, Delfina? Of course she's alive. She's become a witch, but also a millionaire. Of course no one goes after her or investigates her. That's how justice works in this wretched country!"

The phone rang. Eduviges acted the same again: listening while, downstairs, the maid or the driver answered. Suddenly her face lit up, she shouted yes, of course it was her, could she please have two minutes to say goodbye to her nephew. And then she called the maid, hugged him effusively, and sent him off in a hurry. When he was almost at the bottom of the stairs, he heard her voice again. She'd resumed her phone call with great enthusiasm.

CHAPTER 3

Perfect Hostess

VISITING DELFINA URIBE'S GALLERY IS SOMETHING that every Mexican like Miguel del Solar has done regularly over the years. It's the equivalent of attending a concert at Bellas Artes, for example, the retrospective exhibitions at the Museum of Modern Art, the annual film festival; in other words, it's part of the circuit through which that sector of the population interested in the arts, or what surrounds them, necessarily flows. He performed this ritual regularly in the years before his trip to England with Cecilia. He knows Delfina, has exchanged greetings with her occasionally in her realm and exchanged the occasional casual phrase about the merits of some exhibition, the virtues or shortcomings of this or that painter. If he thought about it, however, he'd have to confess that he's never, in fact, had a conversation with her.

For various reasons, Delfina has been a public figure since her youth. Her gallery became a necessary point of reference for tracing the recent history of national painting. She enjoyed a reputation for being intelligent, cultivated, generous. She also had the requisite number of detractors, who, unwittingly, helped to ensure her prestige. Painters who felt they'd been treated unfairly, whose work, due to their own negligence, failed to be recognized or elevated to the proper status. Some were bothered by her social whims, her qualities as a hostess, even her position, which events never fully bore out, as a patroness.

When Del Solar visited her home, he wasn't surprised by the arrangement of the spaces or their contents. Somehow he'd imagined it that way. Both gallery and home complemented each other and reflected a personal style, that is, Delfina's ascetic and rigorous physical nature. Perhaps he expected to find more paintings hanging, a greater mix of color on the walls. This was the only minor inconsistency between what he'd imagined and what was visible.

"The señora will be with you in a moment," a servant informed him, offering coffee at the same time.

While he waited for Delfina to appear, Del Solar occupied himself by examining the ground floor of the house: two large, luminous spaces, the first a living room, and the other a dining room, which opened onto other less spacious rooms. A strict, severe order, but not altogether cold. The most serious objection concerning the house that could be made, he thought, arose from its slightly scenographic quality, like that of almost any space that is seldom lived in. Some of the ceilings were painted in a very pale solferino, two of the walls in Siena red. Everything else was a radiant Moorish white. There was a pair of glass walls, one in the dining room, another in a small sitting room, both of which looked out onto an almost tropical garden. The furniture, displaying a clean, simple line, possessed a comfort undetectable to the naked eye. Delfina later explained that the design was by Alvar Aalto; she told him that a factory had been created in Mexico in the 1940s that produced the work of the most innovative designers of the time. She'd invested some money, but the business wasn't successful. The furniture was very expensive but lacked the air of opulence that the clientele demanded at the time. Del Solar strolled back and forth for a long moment in front of the paintings. On the wall hung a large Tamayo: a human figure made of superimposed discs of flashing red, peering out of a wide-frame window of an almost ontological gray. On the other walls, far apart, he could see the other paintings: a self-portrait of a young Frida Kahlo; a still life by Lazo; a Julio Escobedo signed in 1937: Japanese plum branches carried by two baroque angels who seemed to be entangled with them. In one of the small sitting rooms, a tremulous drawing by Matisse, opposite a wax-colored skull by Soriano. Everything in the house—the architecture, the furniture and its arrangement, the paintings—represented the embodiment of excellence dating to the end of the thirties and beginning of the forties. Delfina's home became frozen in time when she opened her gallery, when Miguel, at the age of ten, saw her hurry by, swathed in white organza with blue polka dots, putting on gloves that were surely blue and getting into a white car that she herself sometimes drove. At the end of the grand hall, on a narrow black table with slender legs, an immense wooden head with metallic nails, magnificent and ferocious, roared at the world; despite its size and aggressiveness it could only dominate a small part of the surrounding space. On the opposite wall, above a wide beam, six or seven Totonac figurines laughed mockingly at the African head. Delfina had promised to tell him on that day everything she remembered about the tragedy that ended her party in the Minerva Building.

They'd warned him that she would be difficult to talk to. Or rather, that it was difficult to get her to talk about anything other than painting. And for her, his informants had whispered, painting was limited to a dissertation on the painting business—the latest prices, the high and low prices of Tamayo, Gerzso, the muralists—and to recounting anecdotes about dealing with the painters in her gallery. But everything had happened differently, one might say surprisingly. After an initial and brusque conversation, it was almost impossible to imagine that he'd wait for her not long thereafter in her own home to have lunch and hear from her lips the true details unrevealed in the newspaper articles about Erich Maria Pistauer's murder. Nevertheless, it was true.

He'd ruled out using any of the renowned personalities that revolved around her and her gallery to arrange a first meeting; he assumed that, if he did, the conversation would be stiff from the beginning, that it would become impossible to speak naturally about the documents where the crimes at the Minerva were mentioned (or rather, crimes that he assumed had occurred at the Minerva). Instead, he turned to Delfina's niece, María Elena Uribe, whom he'd met casually at university. He asked her to accompany him on the visit, and over the course of two weeks he'd spoken to her twice, and by the third, the invitation to have lunch, she'd agreed, to his surprise, to assist him in his inquiries.

The first time she arranged to meet him at the gallery at midmorning. Del Solar brought a copy of his book on Dr. Mora, annoyed that it was taking so long for the new one to appear, the one dealing with 1914, in which on numerous occasions he commented on the ideas and policy management of Luis Uribe, Delfina's father.

She'd scarcely changed during the years that Del Solar lived outside of Mexico. He found her a little thinner; that was all. Smaller, more focused on herself, he ultimately concluded. Her same style of dress, on the edge of fashion, provided a momentary temptation to compare her with his Aunt Eduviges, although he thought better of it immediately, since Delfina's style lacked any hint of eccentricity and willful anachronism. Delfina didn't imitate styles. His aunt's dresses, on the other hand, were intended to express the fullness of the physical possibilities of her mother, her aunts, the Brioneses, the Calcaños, the Landas de Calcado, the Landas y Zerón, which the impoverished little girl, fearful of venturing into unknown territory and whose lack of resources might lead her to commit grave faux pas, adopted with total naturalness and for the rest of her life. Del Solar rummaged through his childhood memories. Delfina seemed the same then as during the numerous visits he'd made to her gallery over the years. She exuded a sense of coldness, confidence, excellence. When he was a child, he saw her as a figure more suited to the screen than to being contemplated in real life. Everything about her always seemed concentrated, light, and at the same time, inexplicably, ostentatious. Her movements during the interview in the gallery reminded him of those of a cat. She smoked, just as she did those distant times when he glimpsed her walking through the corridors or the foyer of the Minerva Building, through black or honey-colored cigarette holders. Except that in childhood, those holders had seemed massive to him, and perhaps they were.

It was evident that Delfina and María Elena had talked about him, because when he appeared in the gallery he was treated as an equal and was made to feel, with tact, gentleness, and humor, that Delfina knew and appreciated his professional activities. Something in her, discreetly assimilated but nonetheless present at all times, conveyed her status as a winner, that she'd imposed her rules on the world and won the game. Her personality was made up of antagonistic elements; it formed a multiple oxymoron: conviviality and reserve, talkativeness and discretion, intelligence and frivolity. He could list many other contradictions. It was difficult to know if her behavior was the result of her longtime dealings with painters, with her writer friends, with a group of sophisticated and powerful clients. Or if, on the contrary, a series of innate virtues had managed to turn every relationship into a success. He understood that the only possible way of dealing with her was to tell her the truth. It would have been absurd to insinuate an interest in buying paintings in order to make her reveal the secrets of that November 1942 once he'd gained her trust. That course would only lead him to make a fool of himself and to descend into grotesque scenes. He spoke, then, of his chronicle on 1914 that was about to appear and how his interest in this type of research had led him to plan another book, this time on the year 1942. A study that would focus on the pressures exerted on Mexico on the eve of the world war, the subsequent break with the Axis countries, the almost immediate declaration of war, and its international consequences.

"We were the ones who witnessed," exclaimed Delfina, suddenly interested, "how our country's place in the world had changed overnight; the adjectivization, of course, changed radically. Where 'chaotic' was written, 'exemplary' was read; the 'unacceptable practices of Mexican politics' was transformed into 'a shining example of democratic action for the continent.'"

"I wanted to address this topic," added Del Solar, "and make an initial foray into microhistory."

He said he envied novelists. He proposed to study the consequences of that conflict on the behavior of various social groups, if possible of a few representative personalities and others who were uncelebrated, without name or prestige. He was not yet clear about this. Delfina listened to him carefully. Del Solar then recounted how the project had been born; he told her about the correspondence he'd discovered between the manager of an oil company in Tamaulipas and its headquarters in London, about the pressure exerted on the government that emerged from those papers, about the English support for Cedillo, also about the documents that a friend had lent him recently about subversive activities in Mexico during the war period and the reference to a bloody event that had taken place just after a party in her apartment, that is, the murder of Pistauer, an Austrian citizen. As she listened to that connection, Delfina's expression became visibly transformed. Something in her face grew tense. The expression was, most of all, one of surprise.

"What!" she shouted, her voice shaken. "Those documents mention my party?"

"Not at all! What they record is that the activities of some German citizens, or those close to the Germans, were connected to the murders in the Minerva Building. I was surprised by the use of the plural, as if there had been several murders—strange, isn't it? I was looking for information in the newspapers of the time and read articles about your party. I must confess that my curiosity about this matter is completely different from what I felt when I wrote the book about 1914, not to mention when I worked on the one about Dr. Mora and the Mexican liberals. In this case it's a personal and concrete curiosity, since at the time Pistauer died I also lived in the Minerva Building. Yes, I was a neighbor of his, Delfina. Pistauer was the stepson of an aunt's brother; my aunt's husband was my mother's cousin . . . ," he finished, confused, pierced by Delfina's icy gaze.

"You mean you're Arnulfo Briones's nephew?"

Apparently, nothing had changed, but the sympathy in her demeanor was gone. The tension was palpable when she uttered the name Briones.

"No, not his. His sister, Eduviges Briones, was related by marriage to my mother. The families had little to do with each other. I suspect that my aunt and uncle were going through difficult times. My parents transferred a pension to them that must have been of some help." He felt he was becoming more and more muddled. He was sure he'd taken a wrong turn. Delfina remained silent. Del Solar continued, "I remember you very well; I saw you many times in the building. Perhaps what I liked best was to watch you drive off in a white convertible."

There was silence again. As if suddenly aware of her duties

in the gallery, Delfina shuffled some cards and put each one in a rectangular wooden box after having read it. It was likely a customer directory. She then spoke in a stern tone into the receiver, asked for some information about a gallery in San Francisco, and then, as if seeming to notice Del Solar again, said in a dry and affirmative manner:

"You must have been six or seven years old at the time." And she looked at him from head to toe with a displeasure that she made no effort to conceal.

"Ten."

"Did you talk to Eduviges about that crime? If anyone knows what happened, I imagine she does. The German was her brother's stepson. What's more, she always pretended to know everything. Everything about everything. Of course it's not true, but in this specific case I'm sure she knows more than what she said at the time. The murder was committed at the end of a party held at my home, but that was a mere coincidence. I didn't know Erich . . . What did you say his name was?"

"Pistauer. Erich Maria Pistauer. He was Austrian."

"I didn't know him. I'd never seen him except that night, and only in passing because there were so many people. I'd even forgotten his last name. If I ever knew it, it was because I'd read it in the newspapers in the days following his death. What was he doing in my house? Nobody invited him. Ask Eduviges why she brought him there. And why she denied it afterward."

"You know her well. You know how difficult it is to make sense of anything she says. A few days ago I went to see her and ended up not understanding anything. Her story was too confusing. According to her, she barely knew Pistauer; that may be true. There'd been no time for a friendship to develop between her and her brother's family. To begin with, her sister-in-law wanted nothing to do with her, which I can personally attest to.

The only thing she seems convinced of is that a journalist who lived in the same building, and who was dedicated to writing a story of an outcast poet, was somehow implicated in the crime."

Delfina seemed to relax, though not entirely, on hearing that fact. She burst out laughing furiously. Then she replied:

"The immarcescible Balmorán? Is Eduviges still insisting on that? It's hard to believe, unless she wants us to believe that she's gone completely mad. You have to be careful with her. She's smart, even if she doesn't seem to be; she has animal cunning. I've always thought her greatest skill was clinging to that absurdity so as not to say anything." She paused. She took another card, read it, wrote a few words in the margin. She picked up the receiver, but before she spoke she seemed to change her mind and hung up. "It's interesting what you say about those documents. My brothers thought it was a political crime. Perhaps they were right. We were at war, and during those days many great economic interests were suffering." She picked up the receiver again, this time using it. She called a secretary, who appeared immediately. She asked with visible impatience for some letters. The secretary left and a moment later returned with them. Delfina signed them. She asked for a file on the Phoenix Museum, and instructed her to prepare a letter for the director that morning. It was clear that she was ending her interview with Del Solar. To emphasize her intention, she stood; she then asked her niece, who during the interview had done nothing but leaf through a monograph on Zurbarán, about the health of her brothers and sisters and asked her to convey her greetings to them. Then she turned to him with her hand outstretched, and asked:

"So you've seen Eduviges recently? I'm told she's not well, is it true?"

"Extremely nervous. I hadn't seen her for years. I found

her more frantic than usual." He refused to add anything more about his aunt's recent vicissitudes, considering it inelegant.

"After my son's death, I decided to break off contact with her. Even before, we barely said hello to each other. The truth is we never cared for each other very much. I maintained a relationship without feeling the slightest affection for her," she concluded, as she directed the secretary to sit in the chair that Del Solar had just vacated.

"I won't say that I'd be sorry if they put her son in prison, because it's not true. The country is full of crooks. I wish they could punish them all!"

Days later, María Elena called him to convey an invitation from Delfina to have a drink at the gallery. He found that move intriguing indeed, given the dryness with which she'd ended their previous visit. He decided not to go. A while later the phone rang again. It was Delfina herself. As if she'd divined his mood, she was calling to reiterate the invitation. She was launching a book about painters in her gallery and thought he might be interested in attending. She decided to host only a few friends. She wanted it to be an intimate affair. No pomp or circumstance. Before hanging up, she added:

"I've thought about what you said about my party. I'd be interested in talking to you more."

And of course he was at the gallery on the exact day and time. But the few friends whom Delfina had alluded to on the phone turned out to be a crowd. Del Solar waved to the hostess and wasn't able to speak to her again until almost the moment of saying goodbye, when Delfina pulled him to her side as she held out her hand or offered her cheek to the stream of departing guests. In the end, he seemed to realize that it would be impossible to start the conversation he was interested in:

"I'm exhausted," she said. "They weren't able to regulate

the heat, and look, it's become an oven. I'm going straight home in a few minutes. I've tried to gather the materials you're interested in; please bear with me." She waved to a group, then turning back to him said, "What are you doing next Saturday? Could I trouble you to have lunch at my home? I live in San Ángel. I'm free on Saturdays. We'll eat light and, in the meantime, talk about whatever you'd like." Then, in a conspiratorial tone, she added, "Look, speak of the devil, just look who's here. Emma Werfel! Have you spoken to her? She was also at the party, and it would be worth talking to her. She's the daughter of Ida Werfel, the writer. Surely you've met her, no?" Del Solar replied that he'd heard some of her lectures years ago and had read several of her books, but she wasn't listening to him. "Try to remember; they lived in the Minerva Building too. You don't remember? Of course, you were a child. Come, I'll introduce you. This Saturday," she insisted, "we can talk in complete confidence. Come, or she'll get away! Her mother was one of the victims at that party."

But she never introduced them. The moment they started to walk, two obese young women, gaudily dressed, vulgarly bejeweled, cut her off, embraced her, and led her into a corner, shrieking and cackling. Delfina, apparently happy to run into them, allowed herself to be abducted.

Saturday came; he arrived, but apparently Delfina wasn't free that day either. She wasn't even home. They wouldn't be eating alone. After bringing him coffee, the maid began to set the table in front of him: five plates. It occurred to Miguel del Solar that perhaps Delfina had invited Emma Werfel, whom she hadn't been able to introduce the time before and who, as she herself had said, was a valuable witness to the night of Pistauer's murder. Who knows who the other guests would be!

Delfina arrived shortly afterward accompanied by a very

frail elderly woman, her sister-in-law, Malú, who, once introduced, walked toward the stairs and disappeared.

"Forgive my delay. I had to pick up Malú. The poor thing
doesn't drive, and on weekends she's left without a driver. When
my brother Bernardo, the archaeologist, is in Tehuacán, which is
almost always, the poor thing is absolutely lost. We've brought
some beautiful rosebushes. It's not the season for planting them,
but we'll see what the gardener can do. He has a delightfully
green thumb. The maid's brought you coffee, I see. Would you
like something less innocent?"

"I could use a scotch."

Delfina ordered two scotches to be served; she disappeared
up the stairs and came back down with a folder in her hand.

"I have the pictures from the party here. The press clip-
pings aren't even worth looking at. Based on what you said,
you've already seen them. I didn't fully remember how scandalous they were, how malicious, until I read them again. I'm
angrier now than I was then. Those vipers, by insulting me, were
expressing their malice toward my father. My niece Rosario is
going to join us; I don't think you know her, she's my right hand.
In fact, she runs the gallery; she just returned from Monterrey
yesterday. The Vélez family will also join us. We have enough
time. Luckily on Saturdays people are in no hurry."

"Will Emma Werfel be coming?"

"Emma? No, I don't think so, how dreadful! Why should
she come?" she said with a certain bewilderment. "We don't see
each other very often. Did she tell you she planned to come?"

He said no. It had occurred to him to ask because of something she'd said at her gallery about how useful it would be to
meet her. And suddenly he was in a bad mood. He understood
why so many people found Delfina exasperating. She never relin-
quished her role as an ideal hostess, a perfect society doyenne. He

would never be able to talk to her. She'd invited him to talk alone, about something that she was supposedly interested in, and she'd gone somewhere else, arriving late, talking about rosebushes, and instead of the personal conversation he expected, he was forced to attend a family lunch. Delfina herself had advised him to talk to Emma Werfel, and she'd all but alluded to arranging a meeting with her. It would have been interesting to know her version of that party where her mother had been insulted, two people were seriously injured, and Erich Maria Pistauer had lost his life.

Delfina seemed to guess his thoughts:

"Emma has led a regrettable life. The most prudent thing would be for you to talk to her alone," she recommended with a smile of reconciliation. "You never interacted with Ida, so that will allow the poor girl to place herself within the subject you're interested in. With me she does nothing but talk about her mother. For years she didn't dare say anything; she was a mere shadow of Ida, who always treated her like a misprint created by some diabolical printer just to ruin her most beautiful page. But when her mother died, she seemed to want to make up for her fifty years of silence. There's no way to keep her quiet. She makes me dizzy. She tells me stories I know better than she does, but she tells them in her own way. It turns out that Ida wouldn't take a step in life without consulting her first. It's too much! It'll be different with you, I can assure you." She adopted a serious expression and a confidential tone of voice. "As you might suspect, Miguel, the conversation we had in the gallery left me very troubled. That day, the one that interests you so much, defines my life, who I've been, who I am now. Lately I've begun to resent loneliness; I live in this house in the midst of things that I love dearly, but I'm alone. For years I've done nothing but work myself to the point of exhaustion. And for what? For whom? You must understand that discussing what happened in 1942, which

I haven't done in a very long time, isn't easy for me, even now. Remember that because of the shooting that took place outside the building, not only did the German die . . ."

"The Austrian!"

"What are you saying . . . ?"

"The Austrian. Pistauer."

"He wasn't the only one to die; my son did as well. Ricardo also lost his life."

"I read in the papers that he was injured."

"Yes, and he never recovered. They performed several operations on him; I never lost hope that he'd recover. It wasn't to be; he lived only three more years, as an invalid. It only took a simple cold for him to die. I've never been able to recover from that night, those gunshots. You were saying that my party was mentioned in some official file?"

"No, not exactly," he repeated again. "The file referred to the Minerva murders and connected them with the activities of a group of people in the service of Germany. You told me the other day that your brothers thought more or less the same thing, isn't that right?" She paused, but Delfina didn't respond. Del Solar continued, "I was surprised that the file mentioned murders or crimes. I don't remember which word was used, but it was in the plural. Perhaps they were referring not only to Pistauer's death, but to your son and perhaps the other wounded man; although the latter, I'm told, is still alive."

"Balmorán! You're just like your aunt! That report didn't refer to my son or Balmorán. It doesn't make any sense. In any case, it would more likely refer to Eduviges's brother."

"Arnulfo Briones?"

"Of course!" Del Solar sensed the same sullen tone in her voice that he'd heard in the first interview. "What does Eduviges think of her brother's death? Ask her."

"I visited her. I told you. But all I understood was that she insists on Pedro Balmorán's participation in the murder. I only spoke to her once. I found her on the verge of delirium, as if in a fever. The attacks on my cousin cause her to jumble everything up. As a boy, I enjoyed her extravagance, her excesses, but not anymore. My book, which I gave her, about the first Mexican liberals, irritated her as much as it did my cousin. Deep down, they've not been able to accept independence, much less the reform. She was also very rude about . . . Well, there's no point in talking about my aunt. What's strange is that you could have been friends, had she not tried to torment you for being the daughter of a man she surely detested."

"We were never that close, Miguel." She grew silent and began to arrange some flowers. "I don't know if it's just me, but it seems that in the last few years the roses are getting smaller and smaller, at least the ones in my garden . . . It's rather difficult to explain. Eduviges and I saw each other every day; however, we weren't friends. In the days before the party, I couldn't stand to so much as look at her. To be perfectly frank, I only invited her because I wanted to expose her publicly, to make her ignorance obvious to others, her lack of culture, her grotesque pretensions of moving in a world that wasn't hers. To ridicule her for daring to presume to lecture me. I was sick of her. For some reason that I was never able to figure out and that I still don't understand, she felt very cultivated. The true Minerva! Perhaps because she went to a French school as a child. Well, none of this matters. Only the facts matter. I don't know if the reference to a possible internal struggle between the Germans and their henchmen is true. It's possible that those who wrote the document you read jumped to conclusions: the dead boy was German . . . Yes, I know, please don't correct me again, Austrian. But the mother was German. Austria itself was German at that time, was it not?

They came from Berlin. It's possible that they entered Mexico with German passports. The easiest course was to avoid a criminal investigation by connecting them with the clandestine activities of their fellow countrymen. Now, if that was true, which today would be almost impossible to prove, then Pistauer's murder would be linked to that of Arnulfo Briones, his stepfather."

"But he wasn't at the party! He wasn't killed!" shouted Del Solar, who hadn't entirely followed Delfina's reasoning.

"Do you really think I could ever invite Arnulfo Briones to my house? Look, it's not possible to speak about his death with such certainty. He died shortly after the shooting at the Minerva. No one believed it was an accident. He spent his entire life involved in unpleasant activities. I never even said hello to him."

Voices could be heard. Delfina got up. She looked out of one of the glass walls overlooking the garden.

"Look, Rosario has arrived with the Vélezes. Today, when we were expecting them to arrive late, they decided to arrive early." She called for the maid and told her to inform her sister-in-law that the guests had arrived.

There were new introductions, another glass of scotch, and a short walk in the garden with the whole entourage, to decide where they would plant the rosebushes next Monday. Then, at the table, Del Solar sensed that Delfina's conversation, though general, was directed mainly at him.

She began by saying that the gallery was the backbone of her life or something like that. Everything she saw, for the last thirty years, everything she did and said, had been for the benefit of her gallery. Her activities were the flesh that over time was added to the skeleton to create a body. Del Solar found the metaphor dark and even repulsive. Vélez, the owner of a successful advertising agency, and Marina—he never knew if she was his wife or sister—not to mention the sister-in-law and niece, must have been accustomed to the verbal flow that meandered its natural course, which she mastered to perfection. Delfina spoke of her painters. She recounted amusing anecdotes, others with a certain dramatic flair. She knew, it must be said, how to wield her resources very well: the pauses were perfect; the accents fell exactly where they should. There was much self-congratulation in the hymn to her tenacity, to her stoicism in having supported Mexican art in difficult times, to her many abilities. She was too self-centered. The voice, the tone, the gestures, all contributed to her mastery of the story, accentuated her narcissism, and, in a complex way (given that the façade of perpetual and masterful hostess would make one think otherwise), revealed her will to exclude, her capacity to become lost in thought, far from the rest of the world; she seemed capable of satisfying her spiritual needs and those of any other kind with her own resources. She had to endure times of incomprehension, she said. But she never gave up; she never made concessions that, at times, would have seemed inevitable; no gallery like hers had existed in Mexico for many years. She'd opened it to entertain herself, and thirty years had passed since then. She planned to run it for four or five years more; then, if Rosario wanted to keep it, hand it over to her in the best possible condition. She would devote her time to traveling. When she opened the business she knew little about painting. She perhaps had a good eye and intuition. She'd been accustomed to seeing paintings since childhood, although her first true passion had been literature. She'd taken advantage of her father's periods of exile in Spain, the United States, and other countries to perfect her literary studies. She'd written a thesis, which for its time hadn't turned out altogether bad, on the dual personality in the Victorian novel: Jekyll and Hyde, Dorian Gray, Dickens's Edwin Drood, Kurtz from *Heart of*

Darkness, the protagonists of Wilkie Collins, etc. The university press had produced a beautiful edition, which had been sold out for many years. She had only one copy. She didn't dare reprint it; she'd have to reexamine the subject, update her knowledge, and such a task was impossible now, but in her youth that book had given her great satisfaction. She fell into painting by chance. Yes, the visits to the museums she'd talked about had played a role, but there was something else. One day she went to visit Titina Morales, the daughter of General Morales, who received her next to a beautiful portrait that Julio Escobedo—at the time a young unknown painter who was beginning to emerge—had just completed.

"It's sad to say, but at that time he painted his best portraits, when he was just a kid," she explained, adding that she'd felt such admiration and envy for the painting, that when her mother whispered to her later that "the Licenciado," as she was used to calling her husband, was planning to give her a car for her birthday, Delfina went to see him and told him she didn't want it, that all she wanted was a portrait painted by Julio Escobedo, the artist who'd just painted Titina Morales. "My papá was very enthusiastic about the idea of a portrait; he wanted Diego to paint me, but I dug in my heels and demanded that Escobedo do it. For my birthday I had the portrait and a car. My first car! It was beautiful! A Buick, pearl-colored! We've been friends ever since. At first, he made me a little tired. During the sessions he talked incessantly, about his family, his friends, about Ruth, whom he'd just married, his teachers, his enthusiasm for Zurbarán, for the pointillists, and above all, for Matisse, who even then drove him mad. I bought that drawing, which I like more and more every day," she vaguely gestured to the room where the Matisse was hanging, "as something of an homage to him, during a trip the three of us made to New York. I've been in love with Julio ever since, a kind of sexless eros, of course. Rather, one could say that I've been in love with the couple, whom I've never been able to separate. Even today I can't live without them. And you wouldn't believe how they try to ruin my life! It's not to be believed, and yet it's true: Julio didn't attend the book launch. One of these days you must call him, Rosario, and tell him for me that he's crossed the line this time. When they made the grotesque mistake of divorcing, I couldn't talk to them; it was as if they were incomplete, boring, miserable?" She paused; then in a professional voice, added, "Yes, Rosario, do it the day after tomorrow, a good slap on the wrist. Tell him that there are things that one simply cannot do."

They took their coffee in the living room. Delfina opened the folder and took out an envelope with several photographs. The ones from the party. She'd asked the society photographer to make her a full set. She kept a detailed record of all the openings and social events related to her gallery and her painters.

Her sister-in-law, Malú, who, like the others, had remained silent, seized the floor. The time had come for her to play her part:

"The grand party," she said in a didactic tone, "the opening of the gallery, had taken place two weeks before. These photos are from an intimate gathering; its purpose was different. There were people, even among the attendees themselves, who believed that Delfina was giving a party for Julio, when in fact she was celebrating her son, Ricardo, who'd spent several years studying in California." She showed a photo of a lanky youth with a boyish face, who looked very much like his mother, with his hair almost shaven, military style. She also showed one of Pistauer, the young Austrian, talking to two attractive women. Del Solar, on the other hand, found a picture of his Aunt Eduviges, very thin, with a hat that looked like a feather duster tied to her forehead, listening to an enormous woman, whom he recognized immediately: it was Ida Werfel. Next to her was her daughter, Emma, whom he'd just seen at the gallery. Those present went about identifying people from different backgrounds: politicians, writers, painters, doctors, bankers.

Miguel del Solar showed the photo he'd set apart and made a witty comment about his aunt's hat. Delfina said that hers, on the other hand, was a jewel, and she rummaged almost desperately among the photos to show it. She didn't find it, because, as Malú explained almost immediately, her sister-in-law was mixing up the gatherings.

"Delfina wouldn't receive guests at her home at night wearing a hat. The one she's looking for she wore to inaugurate the gallery. She'd bought it in New York. A beautiful design by Hattie Carnegie."

Del Solar asked the reason for Ida Werfel's eye patch, but no one could give him an answer.

"Let me see that picture," said Malú Uribe, and once she had it in her hands she added, "She looks as if she's about to fly away. This one next to her looks like a Colombian poet. Delfina, wasn't it a Colombian poet who fought with everyone?"

Delfina took the photo, looked at it for a few moments, then said in a neutral voice, very slowly, as if she wanted to emphasize every word.

"No, he was Mexican: the most sinister character I've ever met. Connected, by the way," she said, addressing Del Solar, "to your family. He wasn't invited either. He sneaked in, taking advantage of his ties to Eduviges. I shouldn't have had that party; my son couldn't have been less interested in dealing with that constellation of snobs. It was a pure act of vanity. I invited some people only because famous men drove Eduviges mad, and I wanted, as I said, to expose her boundless stupidity in front of everyone. Ridicule her. To show her, moreover, that I could bring these people together with absolute ease, which for her would have been impossible, even if she had their names on her lips all day long. People whom she didn't even know by sight!"

Del Solar looked again at the photo that interested him.

"I read in the press," he said, "that the fight started when Ida Werfel began to talk about Tirso de Molina."

"That's an opinion, and it must be taken as such," replied Malú. "Although, who knows, there may have been something of that. Do you remember, Delfina?"

But Delfina didn't answer. She gathered the photos, all but snatching them from her guests' hands, and returned them to a yellowed envelope. She scolded Malú for an inaccuracy in her reminiscence about an English conductor who'd given a concert the night before the party at Bellas Artes. And then, without transition, almost rudely, she began to speak to the Vélezes about the price of some parcel of land near the Ajusco. She seemed to forget completely about Miguel del Solar, who, soon after, aware that his turn had passed, hurried to say goodbye.

CHAPTER 4

Corridors and Surprises

MIGUEL DEL SOLAR DECIDED TO PAY a visit to the superintendent of the Minerva Building. But first, in his spare time, he
attended to two or three matters.

He repeated to himself that if he managed to solve the
mystery he'd be able to understand many of the pressures of
the moment: the decline of certain old regimes, the arrival of
new ones. He sensed the pungent aroma of the time. He often
complained that he'd not been fortunate enough to witness any
important events, one of those political and social cataclysms that
served the great chroniclers of antiquity as a thread to unravel
the skein of history. In that tumbledown redbrick building lay
the seed of a historical event (however minute its significance,
if any, may have been), the only one in his life he'd had a brush
with: the murder of a young Austrian, Erich Maria Pistauer, as
he left a party. This crime was alluded to in a confidential dossier of the Secretariat of Home Affairs. He didn't witness it in
person because he was sleeping at the time of the events, but
he was witness, more modestly, to the disturbances produced
during the ensuing days in the whole building and in his aunt and
uncle's apartment in particular. Detectives, police officers, photographers, journalists, flocks of curiosity seekers, detained servants, outbursts of hysteria, etc. It was impossible not to know
more precisely what had happened. It was worthwhile at least to

attempt to possess the information necessary to form an objective opinion of the facts, and then to deduce from those what should be deduced.

It might not be impossible, he told himself, to know what had happened. But after a few days he could see that neither would it be easy. His brother-in-law, who held a high government post, promised to help him. He called another functionary on the phone, informing him that, absent any objection, his brother-in-law, Miguel del Solar, the historian, would come by that same morning to personally ask for his help in researching a criminal act of interest to him that had occurred thirty years earlier. And he explained how necessary the criminal records of the case were for his research. Del Solar went to the attorney general's office immediately. The official in question welcomed him politely, wrote down on a card the information that Del Solar provided; he called a colleague whose face and gestures seemed to personify efficiency and who, with a stern and obstinate air, led him to a reading room; she gave instructions to an employee who appeared minutes later with the requested file: a file of reports from the last quarter of 1942, organized in chronological order. He located those from November 14 without difficulty. Reading the reports left him perplexed. In them it was stated that the Austrian citizen Erich Maria Pistauer Waltzer, son of Hanno Pistauer Kroetz, also Austrian by birth, and Adele Waltzer (her second surname wasn't mentioned), of German nationality, both residents of Mexico, had been killed by projectiles fired from a firearm. The report described the trajectory of the bullets (and their caliber) in the body of the deceased, who shortly before the shooting had left the building called Minerva, located at the corner of such and such streets in Colonia Roma. The victim had visited the Díaz Zepeda couple, relatives of his stepfather, tenants of the aforementioned building. As he was leaving, in an obvious state of intoxication, he attempted to get in a car parked in front of the building's gate, possibly confusing it for a taxi, and became violent when the driver prevented from entering his vehicle. In the face of the assailant's insistence, the driver, or someone else, fired from inside the car. Neither he nor his passengers could be identified. According to statements made by the Díaz Zepedas' servants, the deceased had consumed alcoholic drinks in excess and exhibited a difficult and easily excitable demeanor. A bystander, a Sr. Miguel Ángel Fierros, who at the time was walking his dog, Cobre, witnessed the fight and the subsequent shootings and stated that it was a normal-sized black car. He confessed to not knowing anything about car models or makes, as well as not knowing if more than one person was traveling inside the vehicle. The document that Miguel del Solar read didn't record Sr. Fierros's address.

The bewildered historian spoke to the employee and told her that the file must be incomplete, since it didn't match the information he had in his possession, nor that which the press had published in the days following the murder. The newspapers, he explained, had published the names of two additional wounded. There must have been some mistake. The victim had attended a party at the Minerva Building, he added. The employee, unfazed, spoke to someone on an internal telephone and, within minutes, the attendant returned; she handed him an index card on which she wrote a few lines. Shortly afterward, another file appeared. Del Solar opened it at the place marked by the card and read:

"Pistauer Waltzer, Erich Ma. Austrian nationality. Born in Linz, March 15, 1921. Son of Hanno Pistauer and Adele Waltzer. Domiciled in Mexico City since July 20, 1939." The technical description of the autopsy followed, and, at the end, a chronicle of the events from the night of his death, identical, word for word, to what he'd read minutes before.

He left the attorney general's office genuinely confused. Something had completely escaped his grasp. Both his Aunt Eduviges and Delfina Uribe had lied. What common interest could they share to distort the facts? Both had assured him of Pistauer's presence at the party. The newspapers stated that when he left, he was accompanied by two other people, one of them Ricardo Rubio, son of Delfina Uribe, who, according to her, had died shortly afterward as a result of his injuries. He returned to the office of his brother-in-law, who greeted him with a less affable smile and obvious signs of impatience. Del Solar presented the results of his research. The other man remained pensive for a moment, signing with a distracted air some documents brought by his secretary. When she left, he said:

"Look, Miguel, the Uribes, and you have to remember this at every moment, represented a very powerful clan. I don't know if the Licenciado was still alive at that time, I think he was. But even if he'd died, his sons, Delfina's brothers, were still alive. Andrés, the eldest, was a beast. It's possible that when the reports were filed they managed to redact Delfina's name to free her from any suspicion. Who wouldn't do the same for a sister? The Uribes were extremely tight-knit, you have no idea. A very simple explanation could be that the reports didn't lie, that everything was in order. The boy went to visit your aunt, perhaps to look for his stepfather; he didn't find him, and your aunt asked him to accompany her to the party for a moment. He could have stayed at Delfina's house for a while, left, tried to get into a car, thinking it was a taxi, and fallen victim to a driver who was scared as hell, who honestly thought he was being robbed. You see? There's no lie, only the omission of the young man's presence at the party, which could have been incidental, momentary.

It seems to me that you're brooding about something that may be less convoluted than you think."

It was a much-needed ice-water bath. He acknowledged having fallen prey to an abnormal state of excitement. He attributed the fever to a nervous current lurking inside him, a parasitic energy that took advantage of the slightest opportunity to manifest itself. He left the office quite calm. But on his way home he remembered that the records, read even with the most charitable eyes, contained unacceptable omissions. There had been two people wounded, two unimpeachable witnesses, not even mentioned in the document. Instead, a single complete stranger was recorded, whose address wasn't listed, although his dog's name was "Cobre." A minute later he recapped. The statements must have been taken when Balmorán and Delfina's son were in the hospital, without the opportunity to speak, and that's why their testimony was omitted. But why wasn't their presence and the violence to which they'd been subjected even mentioned?

When he returned home, he attempted to talk to his mother. He found her almost dozing, her mind slow, scattered. He thought with sadness about her life. She had friends, she visited them, they visited her; sometimes they went out to eat together, to the theater, to see exhibitions; they played bridge. She read one book or another. At present she took care of his children, Juan and Irma. She tried to be interested in his work, in his courses, in his publications, but, he assumed, with rather scant results. It would have been something else if instead of writing about José María Luis Mora, he'd written about Carlyle or Mirabeau. If instead of Mexico in 1914, it had been the same year, but in Berlin, Paris, or London. Everything would be different then; there would be something to boast about to her friends. Clemenceau, Bismarck, Francisco José, a trail of names much more attractive than those of Eulalio Gutiérrez, Roque González, or Genovevo de la O. He remembered again how much he loved her and how much she exasperated him at the same time. The same was probably true for his children; they surely loved and pitied her. But that day, her tone seemed more exhausting than usual. She was talking about Eduviges and Antonio. The midday newspapers announced his cousin's arrest warrant. His whereabouts were unknown. He'd undoubtedly left the country. She said she'd spoken on the phone with Eduviges. After much effort to locate her, she'd barely been able to talk to her. Eduviges had given vent to a fit of wailing and imprecations. Frankly, the situation was bad: Antonio wouldn't be able to return for a long time. And she must have been very well aware.

He then commented that on the day he'd visited his aunt, she'd done nothing but complain about the persecution to which her family had been subjected since almost the turn of the century.

"She's exaggerating, she's always been prone to exaggeration, but to some extent she's right. During the Revolution they confiscated their house, precisely in the year 1914 that you've been studying; they stole objects of great value, and destroyed what they couldn't take. I imagine that the family was running out of money and the Revolution merely struck the final blow. We had only a distant family relationship with Dionisio, but my parents treated him like another son. I was a child when he was already in college. He was a saint, I had heard it said since I was old enough to understand, and from personal experience I can attest to it. He didn't have eyes for any other woman. He was always shy, studious, well educated. As a young man he met, at university I imagine, Eduviges's brother, who most certainly introduced them. There were three Briones: Arnulfo, the eldest, and two girls. By the way, the other one, Gloria, died recently in Italy, and I didn't offer my condolences to Eduviges. She left Mexico with her husband a long time ago; a Peña, from Querétaro. Newly wedded, they preferred to settle in France. She wasn't pretty, although much prettier than Eduviges, of course. She was widowed in Europe and remarried an Italian count. Eduviges was fond of mentioning her brother-in-law and sister, the countess, at every opportunity. She's always been a bore of a woman, pretentious, conniving. If she'd not been so ugly, I believe she might have aged more gracefully. Her family was *the* family, the only one. She wrote to her sister almost daily, and the countess answered her with a postcard on Easter and Saint John's Eve. Arnulfo didn't find the marriage amusing. He was a detestable man. He manipulated Dionisio however he saw fit, and Dionisio let him. He even seemed happy not to have to make decisions. Anyway, he never shared his pigheadedness. Arnulfo forced him to marry Eduviges, whom everyone thought unmarriable; I imagine he was afraid he was going to have to provide for her. Single or married, Dionisio maintained his usual habits: his work, his books, his translations; that was his salvation. He taught at the university. At first Eduviges needed to make him feel at all times that she and her brother, not to mention the countess, belonged to a higher class. Dionisio listened to her with resignation, patience, even some humor. What could he do! If there was ever anything more than a disagreement between them, it was no doubt due to Arnulfo's meddling, his mania for interfering in the lives of others. Their friendship from their time at university gradually cooled. By the time Arnulfo began working with the Germans, they were barely speaking to each other. Except for saying hello, of course. That happened to Arnulfo with a lot of people. With my parents, for example. Not with me, because I had no use for him from the start. Your father despised him. What I can't forgive Dionisio for is not having warned us that, when you lived with them, Arnulfo had his office in the apartment. That's the only thing I have against him. We gave them a rather generous amount each month for your expenses, and then we learned that the person paying for the house was Arnulfo Briones. An unjustifiable lack of courtesy, in my opinion."

"What Germans do you mean?"

"Germans?" she asked distractedly.

"You said that after Arnulfo Briones started working for them he barely spoke to my Uncle Dionisio."

"Ah! He represented some commercial firms in Mexico. He exported goods. I've never liked to discuss things I don't know much about, but there was a time when he traveled frequently to Germany. He spent one or two long periods there, a year or so. From the last trip, he came back married. Then Dionisio suffered several hardships. His salary at the university was all but symbolic, and from the government, I imagine, he also earned very little; that's when you went to live with them; it seemed like a discreet way of helping him. He was paying for the land where years later they built a house in Colonia del Valle, and they were having a lot of trouble getting by. Your father, on the other hand, was doing very well at the sugar mill, and having you in Mexico City until you finished the school year was a solution. Of course, the help that really mattered to them was Arnulfo's, which must have been a hard pill for Dionisio to swallow, because, as I told you, the friendship between them was strained. Poor Dionisio! He was always afraid, even more after the death of Briones! I went to see him two or three times, and I couldn't understand what was going on. They wanted for everything; they had nothing. It was impossible to get a word out of Dionisio, and Eduviges did nothing but talk, willy-nilly. She'd say things and regret them immediately, she contradicted herself. She wanted to go and live with her sister Gloria, but of course you couldn't travel to Europe at the time, and she didn't have the money anyway. She feared for her life and her children's. She saw enemies everywhere. She lived without maids for fear of being spied on in the house. Can you believe it? Arnulfo's death kept her unbalanced for a long time."

"According to her," he said, "the family persecution continues, and the campaign against Antonio is an extension of the conspiracy against her brother. She went so far as to say that Arnulfo was murdered . . ."

"We always took it for granted, your father and I, I mean. Arnulfo was a man with many enemies. I repeat, in the end no one had anything to do with him, except Haroldo Goenaga, his cousin. What a pair, good gracious! What a ridiculous couple of buffoons! I saw them together at Sagrada Familia when one of the Roizes got married. That was a thousand years ago, but from time to time I still seem to see the old pair of sacristans with blank eyes, beating their chests, infuriated, as if they were competing with each other in devotion." Del Solar listened with surprise. He couldn't remember ever hearing such liberal outbursts from her. "Goenaga was even more reactionary than Arnulfo. His son, on the other hand, is something else, delightful, as if he'd been cut from a different cloth. Did you know that Arnulfo had to hide at one time on a Tamaulipas ranch? It was after the Cristero uprising. Do you remember Arnulfo?"

She didn't wait for the answer because she heard yelling from the children, who were fighting elsewhere in the house, probably in the dining room, and went to quiet them. Del Solar took a short nap, and shortly after, when he asked his mother on what basis she believed Arnulfo's death to be a murder, she set aside a magazine, stared at him blankly, and after a few moments of silence, replied:

"I don't remember; too much time has passed. What I'm

sure of, however, is that they must have told me; I didn't make it up. Eduviges spoke about a very strange story, blackmail. Someone demanded money from Arnulfo not to reveal a family matter, secrets concerning a relative, it seems, a degenerate or some such. A blackmailer had come into some documents. She was very upset; she was talking, I told you, a blue streak, but none of it made sense. Arnulfo was always a bore; he berated Dionisio for teaching at the university, for working in government. He humiliated him at every turn. My poor cousin only began to hold his head up after his brother-in-law died. Much later. But if Eduviges thinks the same thing is happening to Antonio as did to her brother, that proves that it's worse than I imagined. Antonio got rich in a scandalous way, that's the problem, and in view of everyone. They'd do well to arrest him and put him in jail," she concluded in a sudden fit of anger.

Neither that day nor during the following days was Del Solar able to talk to his mother about the subject again. Her mood turned foul; she'd shut down, say she didn't remember anything. She insisted that at that time she didn't live in Mexico City but in Córdoba; her husband was the manager of the most important sugar mill in the region. Was he going to write an account of the tribulations of Eduviges? Was that why he'd chosen a career in history? she asked bitterly.

On that occassion, when she told him about the bad aura that surrounded Arnulfo Briones during his final years, Del Solar noticed that everyone considered his death a crime, and it seemed natural that it was the case. That same afternoon he left his house, crossed the Paseo de la Reforma, walked through Colonia Juárez, and entered Roma. It was a very cold afternoon. He enjoyed walking in the winter cold. It rescued him from the bad mood in which the last part of the conversation with his mother had left him. He suddenly felt that leaving his children in her care had been a very risky decision. He should reconsider the situation. Perhaps it would be best to give up his job in England. Living with children in Bristol, as he'd done at the end of the last semester, was madness. Getting married on the spur of the moment so that someone else could deal with them, even worse. He needed to think things through more calmly. There were job opportunities in Mexico, and good ones. He would devote his time to rigorously studying Mexico's foreign relations during the first year of the war. He would write *The Year 1942*.

He suddenly finds himself in the middle of the courtyard. What a vague chronology of childhood memories, yet how precise certain details are! For his cousin it was a year of illness. He can see him lying in bed, with an album of stamps next to him. Amparo is always a sharp, well-defined figure. But without a doubt the image that stands out most is his Aunt Eduviges. He sees himself playing in the central courtyard with Spanish and South American children, until the European children approached timidly: one from Hungary, another from Holland, Germans. The situations may be blurry, but not his aunt's penchant for monologues. She talked to him and Amparo about topics his parents would never have broached in his presence. She didn't differentiate between children and adults, perhaps because a seed of infantilism always flourished in her. Del Solar remembers a smattering of anecdotes, grumblings, diatribes, but they lack a common thread, the bridge necessary to bring the fragments into a unitary whole. There was a warmth in his aunt's voice that faded until completely extinguished. People refer to his uncle's angelic virtues; he, on the other hand, recalls him as an insignificant little man dressed in dark suits, with a black briefcase under his arm, withered, distant.

The memory exercise also allowed the abhorrent figure of Arnulfo Briones to filter through. Several times he saw him sitting in the living room, reading the newspaper, drinking a cup of coffee, or merely dozing. He sees him leave, accompanied by some silent somebody whose job, it seems, was to just listen. On two or three occasions, Briones subjected him to nasty interrogations about the opinions of his playmates. Once, at the end of his stay at the apartment, shortly before Erich Maria Pistauer's murder, Eduviges demanded that her brother forbid his bodyguard from entering the building when he wasn't present, because he disturbed everyone, especially the maids. It was a raucous argument. His aunt, more defiant than usual, told her brother to be careful with Martínez "because it was difficult to conceive of a more false and disloyal man," who at the most opportune moment (and her intuition always considered that moment imminent) would stab him in the back, or, in the best of cases, end up selling him for thirty coins. Briones blew his top. He shouted that women were by nature incapable of understanding anything. His sister, without hearing, added that her husband thought the same. Briones let out an eerie laugh, like scratched glass, and replied that, for that matter, it didn't matter, since she'd taken it upon herself to destroy what little manhood he possessed, that it wasn't even clear if he was a man or an old woman. He spoke of the family's decline, its laxness, of the collapse of the home. Eduviges listened to him calmly. She dutifully began to apologize for her words; she promised to remain silent regardless of the dangers she saw lurking around him.

But—and here she abandoned the submissive tone and began the great performance—who was he to determine the rules of behavior? First, he'd introduced a guttersnipe into the bosom of the family, then a divorcée. The first among the Brioneses! She knew that his wife's husband was alive and had followed her to Mexico! She added that the henchman he'd taken into his confidence wasn't as trustworthy as he supposed;

she'd begun to make inquiries about Adele and her family with the Jewish women on the upper floor, who knew very well—she repeated the "very well" with a contemptuous tone and scowl—about the past of his German wife and her husband, the surgeon. Eduviges insisted that she felt cheated, deceived, hurt, and, because of her inability to pretend, had spoken to Adele's son, and the conversation left no room for error. The boy responded nonchalantly, because those people ended up believing everything was normal, that, yes, his father was in Mexico. Arnulfo, having lost his composure, pounded the table. He shouted for her to shut her trap unless she wanted all relations between them to be severed forever. He had vipers instead of sisters! Their marriage was legitimate. His wife's previous marriage hadn't been sanctioned by the church. His confessor had raised no objections. His rage disappeared; his voice became less violent, more uncertain, then almost pleading when he asked anxiously about Martínez's encounters with the Jewish women upstairs. It's possible that someone arrived at that moment, or that the brother and sister had locked themselves in the office, because he can't remember the end. He and Amparo had witnessed the scene from an adjoining room, lying on the floor, pretending to read their storybooks. The truth was, they didn't take their eyes off his aunt. A door panel kept them from seeing Briones. He couldn't see them either. Only Eduviges. Having an audience, albeit a couple of children, must have helped her maintain her marmoreal attitude and speak with the craftiness she would have on a stage. It had been thirty years since he'd remembered that episode, which had arisen suddenly and with a sharpness that frightened him. Of course it could be distorted. He'd told his parents about it when he met them in Córdoba. Perhaps at the moment he recounted it for the first time he'd added a theatrical tenor, and that was how his memory had preserved it.

•

Del Solar asked a couple of youths who were coming down the building stairs, loaded with books, where the superintendent's apartment was. One of them gestured with the corner of his eye and a movement of his head toward the door at the back of the ground floor.

The historian sat down in front of a portly man with long hair and thick side-whiskers that grew down greasy jowl-like cheeks, a cup of coffee in his hand. In a corner of the room, a tiny woman was cutting a maroon cloth on a tailor's table. The historian began by expressing to the superintendent his interest in finding an apartment. It had to be large and on the second floor, since he had two children, a ten-year-old boy and a seven-year-old girl, and he didn't want them to walk the corridors of the upper floors because he thought they were unsafe. He said that as a child he'd played in the central courtyard. He had friends in the building. That was a whopping thirty years ago. Time had certainly flown by! It was a different place then . . . They hadn't yet built that horrible concrete building next to it, whose size strangled the Minerva, with the risk of causing it to implode someday.

"Did you have friends in the building, señor?"

"Yes, the children of South Americans. I don't remember if they were Colombians or Uruguayans. Also some Spanish and German boys; as I said, it's been a long time."

The superintendent's wife, still cutting the fabric and comparing the size of each piece, narrowed her eyes and looked at him with surprise.

The superintendent said he'd lived there for at least twenty years. His mother-in-law was in charge of the lobby and had gotten him a job as an errand boy at the owner's house.

He gradually climbed the ladder; he wouldn't want to live anywhere else. His wife also came from the lower ranks, the daughter of a doorwoman, a position very different from superintendent, but she'd learned a more honorable trade, and she never wanted for work. She was a curtain-maker. The conversation flowed gaily. Del Solar commented that he knew of an architecture book where the building was mentioned, accompanied by photos and its history. He commented that he was a historian, and that was why he would like to live there. A building like that was very tempting. Just walking down the street, he had the urge to write about everything that had happened inside it.

"But an apartment like the one you need isn't really an option. Sometimes the ones on the top floor are available; unfortunately, they're the smaller ones. As a rule, young people live up there. They stay a year or two, then leave. Those who live in the large ones don't give them up." He spoke of some famous tenants whom a writer of history would have liked to meet: "Licenciado Villegas, for example. He had to be thrown out because of his scandals. Little Villegas! There was no way to stop him. What vices! Who would have guessed that a few years later he'd be appointed a representative of the Public Ministry in Tijuana! Lots of strange people have lived here: painters, journalists, a lady boxer, writers, quite a few foreigners. You'll have to tell me the name of the book."

Miguel del Solar explained that the book was about the building as a work of architecture. Unfortunately, there wasn't one that talked about the tenants. He recalled that when he used to play there, there was talk of a notorious crime committed not long before in front of the entryway.

The woman held the scissors in midair and stared at him again.

"There's been a bit of everything here," replied the superintendent, scratching his sideburns with a plump finger; "there's been no shortage of tragedies, things that could happen anywhere. Not long ago a maid died of a nervous breakdown. And, yes, many years ago an American woman threw herself from the roof. She began to scream, take her clothes off, attract the attention of the neighbors, and when they went out into the corridors, she threw herself into the courtyard. She was on drugs, they later said. Maybe that's the case you're talking about."

No, he explained, that wasn't the case. His, so to speak, had happened thirty years ago. A young Austrian or German man had been shot from a car, and two others had been wounded. The superintendent didn't remember anything. Del Solar added that the murdered young man had attended a party held in the building by one of the most famous women of the time, Delfina Uribe, the daughter of Licenciado Uribe.

"Now I follow you." And the superintendent commented that he hadn't yet arrived when that happened, but that his mother-in-law had told him about the incident. Of course he knew about it; it was a crime of passion. A general who was in love with an actress had the German killed out of jealousy. "Do you remember anything?" he said to his wife.

"No, nothing," she said in a muted voice.

"My wife was just a girl. At that time a better class of people lived here. The ones today, as you can see, are more modest; on the one hand, it's a pity, but it doesn't lead to crimes of passion, and that, I assure you, is a big advantage."

"Did all those people leave?"

"Who?"

"The tenants on the top floor."

"Yes, señor, that's over and done with. All the elegance is gone, and in their place came more humble people; truth be told, sometimes nothing but rabble. The building is a disaster, as you can see. They all left; of course, Sr. Balmorán is still here. He's also a writer, by the way. An article recently came out in the newspaper with his picture. Yes, the only ones left are Balmorán and a German woman."

"Emma Werfel?"

"Do you know her? Emmita and her mother lived here until eight or ten years ago. They moved into a beautiful house, so they say. They deserved it. The doctor died recently, two years ago, I think. No, no, the German woman was already here when I got here. I'm sure you don't know her; there's no way anyone knows her. For us, she's a problem. You pass in front of her door, and it stinks to high heaven. The neighbors give me no peace. Not a day passes without a complaint. She only speaks to her family members; they bring her food. She's not been able to go up or down the stairs for a long time. She can barely move. An old bat! The neighbors in the apartment downstairs complained one day that water was leaking. It was a real fight just so the plumbers could get in to check the place. The old woman's son and I had to be present, on behalf of the owner. Enough to make a person sick to his stomach, I promise you. The floor is sinking under the weight of all the clutter. Every so often her son shows up, a man who's rather old himself, and reeks so bad of alcohol that it'd make you pass out just walking past him. He comes with a large cardboard box. Food, I guess. Sometimes the grandson comes. They don't talk to anyone either. They pay the rent on time, I can say that much. The owner says that as long as they pay the rent, there's no problem. But, Licenciado, let me tell you that's not the case; there are problems. We can't have better tenants, like the owner wants, and like we'd all like, as long as the floor stinks to high heaven. If you want to know stories about this building, talk to Sr. Balmorán, maybe you know him, and he'll tell them to you. Don't waste your time with the woman. And don't even think about talking to her because she won't open the door for you."

Shortly before leaving, Del Solar caught in the mirror the look of uneasiness, distrust, almost bitterness, with which the curtain-maker continued to watch him.

CHAPTER 5

Ida Werfel Speaks to Her Daughter

IT WASN'T DIFFICULT TO VISIT EMMA WERFEL. Miguel del Solar phoned her one morning, and the next afternoon he was already in her home. The insignificant figure whom he'd vaguely glimpsed at Delfina Uribe's gallery came out to open the door. A pair of round wide-rimmed glasses covered much of her face, giving her the appearance of a praying mantis. Her entire body, her gestures, her expressions and silences gave off an air of exaltation and martyrdom. She wore a dark brown robe like that worn by some women in fulfillment of religious vows. Except for her glasses, everything in her was stunted, sparse, diminished. However, at the most unpredictable times, a boundless fervor could erupt from those bones covered with yellowish, stained, and resentful skin. Her age was next to impossible to surmise. The tiny body, the furtive movements, a certain candor of voice made her seem almost like a little girl. The opaque skin, the washed-out face, the sunken, colorless eyes behind the lenses were those of an old woman.

The house was located on a narrow street in Colonia Condesa. The façade was as anodyne as the street. Not so inside. After crossing through the entrance hall, he entered a rather large room where the only thing visible was a bronze figure perched on a black marble Solomonic column: it was undoubtedly the bust of Ida Werfel. Six or seven rays of light from different points of the ceiling converged on that piece of sculpture: a chest and shoulders of more than generous dimensions and a tiny, chickpea-like head, with a forehead reminiscent of Cranach's bald women. A discreet silver laurel wreath pressed against the temples of the distinguished woman.

"You're standing before Ida Werfel!" said the diminutive woman in a victorious tone.

Del Solar thought about the genetic contradiction implicit in the fact that those exaggeratedly opulent shoulders and breasts, as well as the elegantly bovine neck he contemplated at that moment beneath the shower of light, corresponded to the progenitor of that tiny mouse who, in a heroic tone, had uttered the sentence of introduction.

He replied that the warning wasn't necessary. He had known her mother, although, to tell the truth, he'd never dealt with her personally. He attended several of her lectures years ago; he knew, of course, her essays. He even had the vague notion that as a child he'd seen both mother and daughter in the corridors of a unique building where his relatives lived at the time. He began, without delay, to explain the draft of his next book. A chronicle of 1942. The building to which he referred, the Minerva, could be the starting point, as it had housed refugees of different nationalities, political currents, and stripes. In addition to foreigners, in that building, in the 1940s, there lived relatives of Mexican revolutionaries alongside people linked to the most extreme factions.

"Many people, yes, who came as you say from the most distant corners, but, if I may point out, only one Ida Werfel."

"Indeed," he said, surprised by her new triumphant outburst. "She was the towering figure of that community, at least from an intellectual point of view. If I may be so bold, you could help me a great deal by explaining to me, for example, what atmosphere your mother found in Mexico on her arrival. Was it conducive to her work after that?"

"Yes and no. Such things can't be explained in that way, all at once. If you analyze German emigration, you will understand why. She had no political commitments. The only obligation that bound her was to the word; that is, to the highest expression of being. We are completing the remodeling of this research center so that new generations of scholars can benefit from her findings. I will help you in any way I can. Everything that is here is at your disposal: the library, the archive, her notes. Ida Werfel did in one day what takes other people entire weeks. She left an immense archive, which we have managed to organize. She would be turning eighty-five on March 15 of next year. For that reason, I intend to pay the greatest tribute that a daughter can render to her mother. The center for literary studies that will carry her name will be inaugurated here on her birthday. We will also announce"—she then narrowed her eyes, contracted the muscles of her face, and continued in a hushed but intense voice—"a commemorative edition that, I can assure you now, will be a joy and an absolute surprise to her readers."

"Unpublished work?"

"Yes, from beginning to end. Although this isn't the usual posthumous publication of incomplete and poorly crafted texts. The project is much, much more complex. It's been thrilling to bring it to fruition. But, come, you still haven't seen our institute."

The great hall contained only the illuminated bust of the celebrated Hispanist. The rest of the ground floor consisted of a considerable library, occupying several small rooms. The shelves ran from floor to ceiling, with worktables in each room.

Miguel del Solar went upstairs next, where he imagined Emma Werfel undertaking her relentless work, living in utmost modesty. He supposed that behind one of the doors would be a bedroom, a small dining room, certainly a minimal kitchen. The main room consisted of an ample study with a large window overlooking a terrace dotted with palms and azaleas.

"This is where she worked. Look," she said, pointing to a wall that was the perfect monument to vanity, "I've hung her diplomas, her degrees, her decorations, some commemorative photos. She actually couldn't care less about any of this. She needed no confirmation or recognition of the virtues of her work. The only importance she attributed to those documents and medals was to increase the dissemination of her ideas. It's the only meaning fame can have, don't you think?"

"Yes, perhaps," he replied, taken by surprise, without conviction.

Emma directed her guest to a seat. She sat in the chair behind the large worktable. For a moment she was the great Ida Werfel, the luminary. She sighed, embarrassed, unable to maintain the stature. There was something in her that pulled her down, diminished her, and condemned her irretrievably to being only and in perpetuity the selfless daughter of a great woman.

"Did you tell me," she continued in a dry, metallic voice, which nonetheless attempted to show some warmth, "that you are interested in some aspects of Ida Werfel's work?"

Del Solar replied that he was interested in several. Her studies on Spanish syncretism, for example, which the author later extended to New Spain.

"And even to present-day Mexico," the daughter added. "Almost all of her recent work focuses on some contemporary concern. I've been gathering her lectures, her final notes."

"For the commemorative edition?"

"No, for another one that will be published in a regular edition. She would have edited it with the same consistency with which she submitted her originals to the press every couple of years. Moreover, it's a book where some ideas are only outlined. A commemorative edition, if I may say, has other requirements."

"And she deserves an extraordinary one. Reading her, I understood the meaning, if not of history," he said in a high-pitched voice, suddenly infected by the dithyrambic tone of that impassioned old little girl, "which is almost impossible, then certainly that of working on history. The first thing I read by your mother, you should know, was an essay on Tirso de Molina, in a literary supplement."

The little woman said that he was likely referring to "Meditations on Tirso," the first work she completed after arriving in Mexico. She added that her mother was fascinated by Tirso, always returning to him, even though her views on the Mercedarian friar gave her many headaches, as her vision differed from traditional concepts.

"The article examined the misogyny of Tirso." Del Solar had searched the previous afternoon for that old issue of *Cuadernos Americanos*, a magazine with which he'd collaborated regularly at one time, in part to have points of reference during the conversation, but especially because he knew that a discussion about Tirso, initiated by Ida Werfel, had caused a scandal, the initial one, at Delfina Uribe's house on the night of the party. "What you say is very true; in that article your mother contradicted the opinion of many renowned commentators, Bergamín among others, who overidealized the femininity of Tirso's heroines. Your mother pointed out the mix of horror and fascination the author felt for his female characters. Woman transformed into a scourge and punishment for the man with whom she becomes infatuated. Tirso's world, she pointed out, makes up one of the most poisoned strongholds of sexuality. The female's function seems to have no other reason than that of castrating her suitor."

"You've read it very well," the woman interrupted him. "But you must have been a child when her 'Meditations' appeared."

"Indeed, but I read that chapter in a journal later."

Ida Werfel's daughter adopted a doctoral tone and in a neutral voice explained that, apparently, the book was viewed with suspicion by some traditional Hispanists. Her mother despised them, especially Vossler, for a number of complicated reasons that Del Solar didn't understand. Her mother wasn't interested in repeating hackneyed concepts, but rather in creating, thinking, on her own. She was interested in ideas. In the force of the classics, for example, to know where and why their language and their subjects continued being relevant. She maintained that every work was sustained by those few fragments in which language lived and radiated light on the linguistic canvas. Those passages were everything. Their sum constituted the literature of a nation. They were those passages that didn't require footnotes or margin notes for their enjoyment, even if some or many of the words were unknown to us. On the other hand, some parts of the works were decaying. This was the case for Tirso, Góngora, Cervantes. The most perfect works of the writers of the past, and even those by living writers, possessed those areas where the language becomes covered in mold and ossifies. A work was saved only when it contained a spark of truth, that very strange aura that nourishes or invigorates language. The work of the scholar should be to detect that spark and, in its light, to study the structures, the stylistic problems, the authors' obsessions.

"Do you follow me?" she asked at the end of the lengthy disquisition she'd recited without stopping, almost without taking a breath: "You're interested in her concepts of literary exegetics, are you not?"

"In part, yes, but not only that. The flow of writers, thinkers, scientists that came from different parts of Europe in 1939 and remained until the end of the war produced a kind of renaissance in various areas of Mexican life. You know this better than anyone, since you lived at that time and participated in the phenomenon. Of course, not all of those who arrived were, by any means, of the same stature as your mother. I don't think it can be said that we were languishing, that wasn't the case at all, but we were at a point where the influence of other ways of thinking and new methods of research produced an obvious euphoria."

"I wasn't just Ida Werfel's daughter," said the little woman, who apparently hadn't paid much attention to Del Solar's words. "I was also her secretary, her driver, her sister, her confidante, and, above all, her friend."

"That must be a source of great pride."

"Her curiosity knew no bounds, nor did she allow herself to be bridled. Her days must have had thirty-six hours. She was interested in everything: Spanish literature, Mexican literature, universal literature, history, painting, ethnography, music, philosophy, gastronomy, travel. In her final years, she saw much of the world. She gave classes in the United States and lectures in Spain, Brazil, Israel, Buenos Aires. She attended many international conferences. She was honorary president of various institutions. In her final years she reaped some of what she sowed. This house is the fruit and the reflection of her labor. Are you especially interested in her work on the Golden Age? Tirso, you said, yes. The Golden Age was her greatest passion. She introduced ideas that other critics have since adopted as their own. Her first book secured her reputation: *El pícaro y su cuerpo*, was its title in Spanish. I'm told that a Russian studied the same topic, only much later, and with reference to Rabelais. The picaro's body! The role of the viscera! A book too strong for its time!

The relationship between literature and the intestines simply horrified the traditionalists. The Leipzig edition is from 1916, the first Spanish one is from 1933. That a woman dared to examine such a subject was tantamount to streetwalking. Despite everything, the book now has had eight editions in Spanish and has been translated into several languages."

"That's what interests me. To know how, in the puritan Mexico of the time, theses as bold as hers forged their way; I'd like to know her influence on the thought of the time."

For a moment, the first of that encounter, the diminutive woman remained silent, apparently lost in her own reflections. Then, as if climbing out the pit of memory until arriving in full light, in a hesitant voice that transformed gradually into metal and victory, she said:

"You must know that when we arrived in Mexico she wasn't unknown. By no means! Several of her books had been published in Spain and Buenos Aires. She was an eminent figure in her field. She joined the university almost immediately. What's more, the Swiss ambassador, Mme. Desilly, who was born in Argentina and had met her in Europe, organized a group of diplomatic students who met once a week to listen to her at different legations. Other Mexican women, at the behest of a banker's wife, decided to emulate the ambassador and host lectures. They proposed a series titled "The Books That Shaped Humanity." Of course, the title was theirs. How laughable! Ida Werfel was obliged to explain the ABCs of literature and thought, *Don Quixote*, *The Critique of Pure Reason*, *The Kamasutra*!—just imagine!—before such an absurd constellation of presumptuous and ignorant women. I did the summaries at night and wrote the necessary reading notes, which I extracted from an encyclopedia. I couldn't allow her to waste time that she could—and did!—spend on weightier things. They came for her in a magnificent car; she read my notes and delivered them only in the grand salons of those voluptuous sirens. She was a born actress, a sorceress, a prodigious phenomenon of nature. They listened to her in astonishment, mesmerized, despite not understanding a hint of what she was telling them. Now and then I accompanied her to the lectures. Those elegant and frivolous she-asses looked like priestesses officiating in silence at the altar of their Goddess. It wasn't the money, that was well known, that motivated Ida Werfel, nor the influence that naturally emanated from that coterie of ladies who feigned thirst for enlightenment, but the illusion, the hope that some thought would penetrate their empty little heads. 'Imagine,' she told me, 'that some idea, some ambition, might penetrate their mosquito brains; that instead of spending the day scheming among themselves, thinking about cheating on their husbands and betraying their friends, it occurred to them to continue reading, to better themselves, to discover the inadequacy, the banality of their lives, to aspire to a higher goal.' To live in paideia was her ideal, which I unfortunately never shared. Those mosquito brains, as she affectionately called them, once the lesson was over, would tire themselves out with no thought other than acquiring a new outlandish hat, discovering new creams and perfumes, or going to a fashionable cabaret at night to dance."

"Was she well received in academic circles, among intellectuals?"

"The contact was immediate and ideal. How could it have been otherwise! A group of writers, almost all young, gathered around her. She gave them life, she passed on to them the miracle of her own different youth."

"That's precisely what I'm interested in delving into," Del Solar interrupted. "I recently read something that made me feel that, at that time, certain topics of an academic nature were completely alive and contemporary. A newspaper article referenced a verbal altercation in Bellas Artes on the day of a performance of *The Suspicious Truth*. I was also told that a quarrel your mother had with someone, to be honest I don't know whom, about Tirso de Molina, broke up a party given by Delfina Uribe. Nowadays, it would be inconceivable that anyone would argue because someone had disparaged Ruiz de Alarcón or praised Tirso too effusively. There was, thanks in large part to immigration, a new and intense cultural climate."

"My mother's work isn't composed of written criticism alone," said Emma Werfel, with a harshness she hadn't expressed previously, and without Miguel del Solar being able to establish a relationship between the answer and the words he'd just uttered. "Her oral expression, her pedagogical work, was equally as important as her books. In the classroom she employed her great intuition: later she'd develop it calmly at home, here at this much beloved worktable."

"It was in November of 1942, if I remember correctly, when the quarrel about Tirso that I referenced occurred. Delfina Uribe gave a party to celebrate an exhibition by Julio Escobedo, which inaugurated her gallery. Why such passion? I imagine she must have argued with one of those newly arrived intransigent Spaniards."

"My mother didn't argue with anyone, nor did she attempt to provoke a fight. Nothing could be further from the truth. She was attacked out of the blue by a maniac, an enraged madman. I've never experienced anything like it in terms of violence. That bedlamite was completely out of his mind. Before the terrifying incident, I already referred to him, whenever I needed to speak of him, as 'that lunatic.' You can't imagine how dreadful it was! He attacked her with his fists, kicked her. Saying that he was going to be a writer! Nothing could be further from the truth! He was a veritable hooligan! A brute!"

"But why did he attack her for talking about Tirso? How did that affect him?"

"He attacked her because he was mad, I just told you. He was a psychopath. It was a night of absurd confusion. If I've ever felt demons on the loose and prowling around me, it was that night. Did you know that at the end of the party one person was killed and several others were injured?"

"Yes, Delfina told me that her son was injured."

"Her son? Oh, yes, of course! He was one of the injured. They killed a young acquaintance of ours. His father was a very fine man."

"Was the man who attacked your mother armed?"

Emma K. Werfel shuddered. She sighed agonizingly. At last she replied:

"It's possible; I don't know. He was a wicked individual. Delfina assured us that she hadn't invited him. The incident horrified her immensely. She couldn't apologize enough. You can't imagine the effect that night had on Ida Werfel. There were days when she trembled like a leaf at the mere mention of the attack. 'We fled barbarism, and we've fallen into it again,' she'd say. Other times she believed that the shots that night were intended for her."

"Had you just arrived?"

"In Mexico? Yes, but not entirely. We'd not just gotten off the boat. I want you to understand that. We arrived in 1938, four years before the dreadful incident. We'd left Germany in 1933. On the surface, an extremely complicated story, don't you agree? We left Berlin in 1933 and landed in Veracruz in 1938. Did we, then, float in the middle of the ocean for the next five years? What could have happened to us? Nothing in particular, don't be alarmed. My parents had moved to Amsterdam, and in 1938, sensing what was about to happen, we set out for Mexico. Thanks to their foresight, Ida Werfel was able to transport her books, her papers, some objects to which she was very attached. Those who came later arrived with barely the clothes on their back. This small lapis lazuli beetle, for example," she said, taking an object into her hands and placing it in the light of a table lamp, although not actually bothering to look at it, "had a very special meaning to her. According to Licenciado Reyes, at the university, this mix of rationalism and profound intuition, of magic, in other words, added a unique appeal to my mother's personality."

"What made her decide to come to Mexico? German emigration had a very obvious political nature; almost all German émigrés returned to Europe at the end of the war."

"Language was essential for her research. Libraries, new editions, the specialized and even the merely informative press, interacting with colleagues, grooming protégés; that only happens in a suitable linguistic environment. What would Ida Werfel do in Australia?"

"I'm not saying Australia, but at the time it seemed more logical to me that a person such as she would have been attracted to Buenos Aires or the Hispanic Studies department of an American university. We enjoyed a dismal reputation in Europe at the time. Oil interests had created the blackest legend imaginable around Mexico. I would have found it less strange," Del Solar asserted emphatically, annoyed at not being able to lead the conversation along the correct course and not knowing how to get out of the mess, "had Lukács or Heinrich Mann come, for example. There was an important Communist group here and an antifascist newspaper published in German. As far as I know, Sra. Werfel wasn't interested in political activity."

"Ida Werfel," she said in a lecturing tone, which seemed to indicate that this was the correct way to refer to the Hispanist, "had, of course, her convictions. As a Jew, she couldn't simply watch what was happening in other parts of the world. I remember accompanying her to several public events where she took the floor."

"I still don't understand," Del Solar said with a tone of boredom that was in itself a provocation, as if he'd suddenly become uninterested in the subject and was about to succumb to the temptation to suspend the conversation, to leave the premises, without taking notes, without specifying his interest in anything. "Why did you choose Mexico? It was quite difficult to enter the country at the time. Did your parents have friends here?"

"Well," the other replied, with an air of dealing with a mere procedural matter, "she was interested in Mexico in a real sense. She'd corresponded with some writers. In this file there are two or three letters from Alfonso Reyes. In one article, Reyes treated with a certain irony, in a cursory manner, and with a humor that I'd dare to call somewhat vulgar, the connections established by Ida Werfel between the picaresque and the gastrointestinal functions. Once in Mexico, any difference that might have arisen between the two completely disappeared. My mother celebrated, in an article written on the ship itself and published when she arrived in the New World, the virtues of the earlier transcription into modern Spanish of the *Cantar del Mío Cid* by Reyes. She declined, as it didn't seem tasteful to her to arrive in the country with her sword drawn, to point out certain errors, which were colossal, in her opinion. It will soon be known what she really thought of Reyes, Américo Castro, Amado, Dámaso Alonso, Brennan, and Solalinde. Her unvarnished opinion about people, books, countries. The world will discover a portrait of Karl Vossler never before known: you'll find yourself amid a band of true scorpions, of whitewashed tombs. The work that will be published on the occasion of her birthday will include everything, as I've already told you, books, friends, everyday life." As she mentioned the commemorative edition, Emma Werfel's gaze became lost in a seraphic vision. "For the first time," she concluded, "her thoughts laid bare on subjects, except for one in particular, that preoccupied her throughout her life, will be exposed."

"You've yet to tell me what caused her to decide to settle in Mexico. Did she receive an invitation from the university?"

"I just can't understand why you're so interested in that detail. The surname Werfel, which we both bear with great pride, is her maiden name, the K, which I place before mine—surely you saw the plate on the door!—belongs to my father. Emma K. Werfel, that's me! The surname Kalisz reduced to its minimum expression, to an initial." She finally placed on the table the lapis lazuli beetle that she'd been holding all that time; she began to rummage in a malachite box, took out a few clips, looked at them, returned them, shook the corner of the table-cloth with one hand, as if she wanted to gain time, as if her words were as banal and insignificant as her gestures, and she then continued contemptuously, "Dr. Kalisz, my father, was an allergy specialist. He studied the nervous character of those ailments. He'd come to Mexico on one occasion for I don't know what conference. A Hungarian who owned some laboratories here became interested in his theories and invited him to collaborate with him. He liked something here. I never concerned myself with knowing what it was. When he returned to Amsterdam, he spoke only of Mexico, of the climate and its benefits, of the people and the markets of the cordillera, and of the volcano he said he could see from his hotel window. Ida Werfel, who was very forward-thinking, encouraged him to accept the invitation. She didn't need to insist, since the allergist Kalisz, as I've already told you, was crazy about Mexico. The decision proved to be most prudent, as a few months later the war broke out. We came with all our belongings, determined to stay here for a long time. There are those for whom instability has something deceptive and comical about it: Kalisz, Mexico's frenzied lover, Kalisz, the volcanoes' beau, fled a few months after arriving. We, the silent ones, sparing in words, remained. It goes without saying, as everything in this house is a testament to that."

"Did he return to Europe?"

"My father? No, not at all. He left for the United States, for some impossible place in a Dakota. He wanted her to accompany him, which would have meant uprooting her from her cultural environment, burying her. Of course she refused; she explained why in the most reasonable way, since until that day she'd been convinced that she had a husband who, although not brilliant, was at least proper. It was one of her few mistakes. He was hired by an institute to develop I don't know what allergy vaccine. He signed a one-year contract. However, he didn't return. During that first year he wrote regularly, sent money at the end of each month. Afterward, he began to drag his feet on the matter of returning; his letters became more and more infrequent. One day, it must have been around 1946, because the war was over, my mother received a legal notice. She was divorced without ever giving her consent. What am I saying? Without even knowing about the process."

"It must have affected her a great deal," he said to fill the silence.

"No, not too much. What surprised her, and significantly, was the erratic behavior of the allergist Kalisz, my father, having disappeared without a word. Whatever news we had about him was always secondhand."

"Did you ever see him again?"

"We never saw him again. But history, as a wise man once

said, knows no waste. Kalisz died a few weeks after Ida Werfel's death. Does it not seem significant to you that he wasn't able to survive her? He had become rich, thanks to some psychiatric treatments—what did he know about that, good gracious!—to cure skin ailments. My mother commented, when we got the news, that in the end his true personality had emerged, that of a false shaman, a charlatan. When he died, he left a considerable sum to Ida Werfel, which passed to me, as her sole heir. I've always found that detail queer. He must have known she was dead, and yet he didn't modify his will. Maybe he didn't have time. I'll never know. The American taxes were brutal, but even so the amount that I received was enough to create the trust that will allow this institution to go on. At first, I didn't want to accept the inheritance. Personally, I don't need money. I have what I need. Then I thought about it more. If I accepted the amount, I wouldn't need to sell the house in Cuernavaca, where we were both so happy, in order to pay for the tribute Ida Werfel deserves," her face suddenly lit up with joy, "the publication of her magnum opus. There, as I said, you'll find her complete body of work. What she thought of the affairs of this world, and even of the divine? Everything will be known."

"Her diaries?"

"You're on fire! On fire!" she shouted, applauding enthusiastically, and then added quickly, "In a way it can be said that it's a sort of diary, though with special characteristics. A diary, if you want to call it that, but not written by her, and for that reason more spontaneous, without the barriers that censorship necessarily raises. For years I made notes of her conversations, her reflections, and I recounted what could be called the meaningful aspects of her life. In the end, when she became aware of my work, because it was impossible to keep it a secret, she'd deliver monologues aloud in front of me. It was a remarkable effort; it gave meaning to my life. It all started the morning we boarded in Rotterdam. Perhaps she noticed my despair. I wasn't able to accept the fact of leaving Europe; I wasn't ready for the trip. I was afraid of the future, not so much for me but for her. I don't know why, but I couldn't imagine her on another continent. The truth is that she suggested that I record in a notebook, much like a log, the events of the voyage. But what importance could lie in knowing whether or not we had disembarked in the Canary Islands or in Curaçao? What could I say about what we saw in Havana, when I had the opportunity to record Ida Werfel's impressions? Living at her side was my true university. From 1938 until the day of her death I transcribed everything important that happened in her life . . . Thirty years! . . . Except, of course, during her travels abroad, or in certain periods, brief but terrible, during which she withdrew into herself. There were days when it was impossible for her to open up to the outside world. She had to store, reflect, digest, to be able to later express. Though difficult, I accepted that situation as normal; others who were unable to understand our relationship didn't. There are those who have even accused her of cruelty—poor people, they didn't understand anything! There were times, sometimes weeks, when she avoided me. She'd walk past me with an air of defiance and a scowl, answering me in monosyllables, or with a nod, until the moment her impenetrability showed cracks, began to open up little by little, and, like the cocoon when it releases the chrysalis, she opened herself to the word, to the relationship between man and the world, literary passion, the salvation of culture, the hidden meaning of life, everything appeared in those monologues that burst forth at my side, when I least expected it."

She stood up as if possessed, walked to an armoire, opened it, and pulled out several large files. He went to help her, certain that he'd find valuable keys, solutions. The material formed two tall columns on the worktable.

"You must have worked a ridiculous amount."

"Yes, day and night, since she died. But I'm used to it. During our first years in Mexico I did the same, worked at night, recording all the events of the day, trying to recover all of her words. I also did secretarial work, which wasn't light: typing her writings, proofreading, preparing reading notes, summaries for her classes, a thousand other things. On her death I typed everything. I revised. I corrected. Well, *correct* isn't the word. Who am I to correct Ida Werfel? What in the world! What I did was to withhold certain passages, which will form another small, intimate book, and will see the light of day only when I'm no longer on earth. At first when she discovered my activities, she seemed upset; she accused me of having spied on her for years. In time, she recognized the utility of my work. Sometimes she'd ask me to consult a conversation with a California professor who'd come years before to meet her, or to look for possible allusions she'd made over the years to a particular topic, which she was interested in developing in a new essay or lecture. My budget is considerable, but it doesn't matter. Everything is ready to send to the press. For a while, I considered entitling it *Ida Werfel Speaks to Emma, Her Daughter*; but I realized that it could be interpreted as a vain gesture on my part, a forced attempt to insert my name next to hers; I decided on a plainer title: *Ida Werfel Speaks to Her Daughter*. I omitted my name."

"Did you order the material chronologically or thematically?"

"I preferred chronological order. In that way, the reader will be able to know the fluctuations in her thinking, her discoveries, her advances, her refinements."

Miguel del Solar commented to Emma K. Werfel that the

work would be invaluable to his research. Amid that treasure trove lay information about the period he proposed to study. Would she allow him to see any passages? The one pertaining to the quarrel surrounding Tirso at Delfina Uribe's house that culminated in a shooting, for example.

"I may not have expressed myself clearly," she replied brusquely. "It wasn't a quarrel but an outright assault, carried out by a lunatic, the germ of which was possibly some kind of pent-up anti-Semitism."

"What, then, did Tirso have to do with it?"

"Nothing! It was a mere coincidence that at that moment they were discussing one of his works. It could just as easily have been Beethoven's quartets, or the baroque altar of Tepotzotlán, or the weather; it was already starting to get cold at that time."

"Why don't we look at the volume? Do me that immense favor, I beg you! From a historian's point of view it was a remarkable event. This party was attended by many of the celebrities of the time: politicians, painters, writers. If you need the date, it was November 14, 1942."

The woman looked for the date with a certain reluctance. She read the allusive pages softly, then commented:

"At the time, I became too lost in the details. Over time, I became stricter, more succinct. Yes," she read her notes again, "Delfina Uribe had invited us to her party, and we were almost not going to attend. 'The night of the great imbroglio!': that's how I titled that entry in my notebook. My mother suffered from an acute case of conjunctivitis. Her left eye was so irritated that she could barely open it. At the last minute we improvised a kind of black velvet patch: 'We shall say this is our personal tribute to the Princess of Eboli,' she said with her characteristic humor. She insisted that I should also cover an eye. There was a certain dose of eccentricity in her, a playful quality that fortunately she

never lost. I don't possess it; many of her virtues weren't passed
on to me. I suggested that instead of the patch she wear a hat
with a thick veil to cover her eyes, and at first the idea seemed
to excite her. Then she dismissed it. She would have to lift her
veil to eat, and everyone would see the patch; so we attended as
one-eyed women, she, making witty jokes all the while, and I,
needless to say, mortified, half-dead from embarrassment. We
spent a good amount of time on the preparations; when we went
down to Delfina's apartment the party was already very lively.
Martínez—it had to be that monster!—came out to welcome us.
We'd told him that afternoon, when he was in our home, that
we wouldn't attend, because of my mother's conjunctivitis, and
he seemed very surprised to see us. But, in the end, happy to
be able to take refuge in that environment under the prestige of
my mother. He shooed some people from a sofa with a haughtiness that left us frozen and made us sit there, as if he were
our host; as if, moreover, people could be treated with such vulgarity. We'd just sat down when a boy appeared, obviously very
drunk, who began to talk to my mother as if he'd known her all
his life. 'Yes, Huehue,' he said to her. Look, I wrote 'Huehue'
here, but maybe it should be written 'Ueue' or 'Wewe,' with a
'W' so it'll sound like 'U,' just like in Wenceslaus, for example.
To be honest, I don't know what the correct spelling would be.
'Yes, Huehue, at that moment, I had to choose to be Mexican,
you understand?' The boy's voice was shrill; it seemed to modu-
late in the stomach like that of the ventriloquists. 'We were in the
second act of *Pelléas et Mélisande*, directed, just imagine, by no
less than Ansermet. Papá approached me and said to me in that
condescending little tone that really bugs me, you know which
one, that it'd already been decided: we'd go back to Mexico, and
I had to take Mexican citizenship. You know how he is, Huehue,
you know him, so his antics won't surprise you. He blurted it out

just like that, without the slightest tact, delighted by my bewilderment. Can you imagine, Huehue? Suddenly, in the shadow of Debussy, I knew he was serious about being Mexican, that it wasn't an affectionate nickname the way I took it sometimes. That's not possible, I told him, suddenly short of breath. I didn't understand anything, I was desperate, I would gladly have cried. "We're going to Mexico," the ogre of the lake repeated with delight. "*Comment?*" I cried out, in anguish. At that moment, it was too much. Of course, I knew that my grandparents, that my father had come from here. But these are things, Huehue, that one knows and doesn't really understand. Ansermet, Debussy, Pelléas, La Tournier, who was, I have to tell you, a marvelous Mélisande, everything was spinning around and becoming confused with frightful stone images. I didn't roll on the floor, because God was great. I sank into my seat, and I remained there without seeing or hearing or knowing anything, until Granny got me in the car and took me home. To have known you then, Huehue!' . . . Ida Werfel listened to that stranger with the greatest attention, and I can say even with sympathy. The young man, after a pause, added: 'The next day I woke up tormented by the same thing. You know, as a kid, at school they called me *le mexicain*. I'd been born there, spent my life there. There and in England, of course, at boarding school. And suddenly it turned out that I was Mexican, it wasn't just a nickname! That I had to go to the Mexican Consulate that day, to take Mexican citizenship! We were leaving Europe because of the war; it was necessary, yes, but it seems incomprehensible to me . . . And now, in contrast, you see . . .' A waiter passed by; without seeing him, as if obeying a reflex, he stretched out his arm and took a glass of whiskey. He emptied it in a few sips, got up, and left. We were sitting next to Martínez and a neighbor in the building. A scary woman, a schemer. The lunatic seemed to be interested in deciphering what the name Huehue meant. 'It must mean Werfel and he's mispronouncing it,' I said. 'No, child,' said my mother, 'it's obviously a result of confusion. Recently I've been working precisely on impersonation, concealment, and confusion of personalities.'

"'I found out from some friends who're taking your courses that a book of yours has just come out,' said the idiot of a neighbor. Ida Werfel condescended to answer her with a slight nod. But the lunatic was still interested in why that boy, the grandson of one of Díaz's ministers, had addressed my mother with such familiarity, calling her by such a queer name. That name, Martínez insinuated, was a nom de guerre; it hid a key."

"Why was this Martínez fellow so interested in that? Was he a good friend of yours?"

"Of ours?" she shouted angrily, her face suddenly flushed. "We knew him, that was all. It was impossible not to run into him in the corridors of the building. You say you knew the Minerva as a child, didn't you? It was beautiful then; it deteriorated very quickly. By the time we moved into this house it had already become a pigsty. It was beautiful in its day, I repeat, but unlivable. A nest of poisonous vipers, some foolish and others lecherous, but all poisonous. Martínez was always there, lurking. One day, that neighbor I was telling you about stopped us at the entrance of the building to introduce us. It seemed strange to us, because we scarcely knew that neighbor by sight. Under the pretext of that introduction, he showed up at our home when we least expected it. He asked me leading questions. He wanted to know everything, about us, about the rest of the tenants, even about my mother's students. He liked to insinuate that his profession was in some way diplomatic. Who knows what that means! He oozed vulgarity. We thought he was attempting to find out who the tenants of the building were. Many were foreigners; we were Germans; and we were, let's not forget, in a time of war. Delfina Uribe told me that she wouldn't be surprised if he was a police agent. I get goose bumps when I remember the attitude that handsome young man adopted when addressing Ida Werfel. I told her what Delfina had told me, but she didn't seem to care. In a way she found the brute entertaining. I imagined that his cocksure airs, his airs of a conqueror, of a caliph, must have seemed grotesque to her. That wasn't the case . . . When I turn to dust, the world will know aspects of her life as a woman that I don't dare to insinuate now . . ."

"Do you mean . . . ?"

"I don't mean anything; it's not the time. In fact, if I'm to be frank, Ida Werfel wouldn't have been opposed to even greater familiarity. On that occasion, I still didn't realize what was happening. She tried to calm me down. She told me that we didn't have to worry, that the best way to behave was to answer his questions naturally, casually. We had nothing to hide. We were respectable working people; the sooner I accepted it, the better. I found him utterly repugnant. He looked at my mother as if he had her at his feet. He could never stand still. When he spoke to me he avoided looking me in the eye, only to, at the most unexpected moments, let out a horrible laugh, like a horse's snort, as if he'd found me guilty of something and held me in his hands. Then, yes, he looked squarely into my eyes, with his own filthy pop eyes. I should tell you that at times he frightened me. And that night was one of them. He was unusually agitated; he'd certainly had a lot to drink. 'I didn't know she was on such intimate terms with these refined young men,' he said reprovingly. 'What would her husband say if he found out about her meeting with that boy? Oh, Huehue, Huehue! So that was the little name she traveled around Europe with?'"

"And why did they call your mother that? Who was Huehue?" Del Solar asked, feeling lost at that point in the story.

Emma K. Werfel read her notebooks with relish. She finally raised her head. She'd apparently not heard the question, as was almost always the case. She continued the narration, consulting the notebook from time to time:

"The neighbor interrupted Martínez. She wouldn't let him talk, which put him in an even fouler mood: he began to gesture, to snarl, to mumble words that no one understood. Yes, that woman, a veritable macaw, was momentarily a barrier for us against the lunatic's wrath. She's still alive. They just confirmed that her son was a thief. If she opened her mouth, the whole world had to remain silent. She began to talk about Mexican gastronomic excellence and all the dishes we were to eat that evening, as she'd already prowled around the kitchen. We would taste nogada, the delicate, the most exquisite chiles en nogada. One of the last opportunities of the year, because walnut season was about to end. We'd have to wait until next August to enjoy them again. She asked my mother if we'd grown accustomed to piquant flavors. As you know, having read her, Ida Werfel was a superior spirit. By temperament, by culture, she didn't accept taboos. How else could she have written a book about the picaro's body? And the body of the picaro was, first and foremost, the stomach, several meters of intestines, and, you must forgive me, an ass from which to defecate. She had sufficient stature to be able to say it all. Her sense of humor, her indescribable *charme* became apparent when she blurted out the greatest absurdities. She tried to clear the field of the banality imposed by that mediocre woman. She replied that yes, she liked chiles, but in moderate amounts, that when she ate one for the first time it was as if she'd ingested liquid fire, lava. 'The characteristic of that fire is that it burns twice,' she said at the top of her lungs, winking at Martínez, as if trying to ingratiate herself with him for not responding to his twaddle. 'It burns on entering, not to mention on exiting, does it not?' There was silence around us. A bit of dismay perhaps. She loved those effects. 'Polish, you piece-of-shit shoeshine woman!' shouted the lunatic, his face contorted with anger. We didn't know what he meant; we weren't familiar with his regional argot. Ida Werfel—how innocent!—thought he was thanking her and celebrating her comment, and she laughed, very pleased, which ended up infuriating the monster. She got up and was about to withdraw when the young aristocrat returned with another glass of whiskey filled to the top. He was walking upright, but swaying back and forth, like a sailor when the sea is rough. With the same flutelike voice that sprang from the pit of his stomach, he called out 'Huehue!'

"'At your service!' my mother replied jovially.

"'Excuse me!' said the boy. The velvet patch over Ida Werfel's eye seemed to baffle him. 'Excuse me!' he repeated. 'Have you seen Huencho? You know him, don't you? I left him here a moment ago.'

"'Do you see? It's a case of mistaken identity,' she said. 'I've been working on the subject for the last few days. What sustains the intrigue of the comedies of the Spanish Golden Age is the confusion of characters. But in Tirso de Molina the confusion reaches delirium. Take any of his works, *The Garden of Juan Fernández*, for example. Nobody knows who they're talking to. The characters appear with false names and fictitious biographies before other characters with the same characteristics, that is, who are not who they claim to be. A carnivalesque game of disguises ensues. They pretend to third parties to be other characters who don't correspond to either their personality or to the pretense under which we just met them.' My mother was truly seductive when she talked about what interested her deeply. Several people had come closer to hear her. She spoke with ease and mastery. Upon seeing the crazy little man sitting in front of her, contorted by fury, prey to his tics and his incoherent gestures, she spoke to him again, as if to include him in the dialogue and calm him down. 'Sometimes, I've come to think, my dear Martínez, that the whole world has become the garden of Juan Fernández, that we all traipse through life without knowing who is who, at times not even who we are, or what higher design we serve.'

" 'Without knowing whether or not we're Huehues? There are people who just need to know that they have to obey certain Protocols of certain Learned Elders, of a certain Zion,' the lout barked. At this point they put a plate in my mother's hand. The mere sight of the chile en nogada overwhelmed her. Unbeknownst to me, I'd removed the patch from my eye, but she was still wearing hers, and her gestures, which on another occasion would have been normal, because of the one eye were tinged with a pronounced sense of mocking. She'd finally noticed Martínez's resentful and belligerent demeanor, and she wanted to appease him. When she saw that he was rejecting the plate of nogada, she said to him, with a wink that looked like a mocking gesture, 'Cheer up, my great Martínez! Dig in! Think, like the skeptics, that it will burn less going in that when it comes out!' And she let out a hearty guffaw. His reaction took us all by surprise. The lunatic jumped in front of her and began to shake her, to strike her, to butt her chest with his head, uttering all sorts of insults. Ida Werfel's plate fell to the floor. I started screaming, frightened to death. The lunatic stepped in the nogada on the carpet, jumping as he struck my mother. She tried to get up, but he kicked her, and, with a shove to her shoulders, made her fall again. Hands over here, legs over there! It all happened in the middle of the crowd, with bewildering speed. Several people tried to restrain him. Delfina's brother, the one married to Malú

González, managed to throw him out of the house. Ida Werfel was slow to recover. At that moment the drunken young man arrived and blurted out, 'Huehue! Where did you go? What's wrong with you? You're really pale and disheveled. Are you already drunk, Huehue? You're not gonna start with how you don't want go to the Leda anymore. No, no, no, no! I won't let you!' They had to take him to another room. My mother wanted us to leave, but they wouldn't let her. It would be better if she composed herself, went to the bathroom to wash, and rested a while in Delfina's bedroom. It was the only violence she suffered in Mexico, but it caused her to suffer a great deal. The neighbor said, as we left the room, that we shouldn't mention Martínez's illness in front of him or he'd lose control of his nerves."

"What illness was she referring to?"

"I suppose to his insanity. That woman's name is Eduviges. She never liked us. One day, shortly before that party, she asked me to act as an interpreter for the boy who was killed that night. But that's another story . . ."

"And what happened to Martínez?"

"Apparently he didn't leave completely. He must have stayed to prowl around the building. A while later another row broke out. A drunk general insulted Escobedo, the painter. The party erupted in pandemonium again. I looked out the window and thought I saw Martínez in the corridor. I'm almost certain it was him. I believe that he whistled and left again. Some women, rather trashy, by the way, suddenly began to sing in the room. Minutes later the shooting occurred. You can just imagine the night we had, the depression of the following days, the feeling of insecurity that she suffered for the longest time. However, every horror has its countervailing bias. That incident put an end to the aberrant sympathy Ida Werfel felt for that clown."

"Did he ever bother you again?"

"No." She looked at her watch and let out a shout. She began to hurriedly put away the documents, without any order. She said she should already be at the university, that she had to leave immediately.

As they went down the stairs, Del Solar asked if she knew a German woman who used to live on the top floor of the Minerva, but she answered distractedly that she didn't know whom he was talking about, that many renters had lived there, Mexicans, Germans, people from all over.

They left in a rush; in a rush she got into her small Volkswagen and left.

CHAPTER 6

Who Sings and Dances

HE TOLD CRUZ-GARCÍA THAT HE'D committed to a new project. To try to do with 1942 what he'd done with 1914. An account of life in Mexico where the events, carefully selected and organized, explain themselves. An effort, he told him, that appears simple, but that in no way is. It requires a thorough knowledge of the time, a delicate touch to mix the spectacular, the surprising, the minimal, and the day-to-day. Numbers with poetry. Del Solar wasn't in a particularly good humor that day. He didn't understand why his book was delayed. The cover was printed, yes, he understood that, but in the end it didn't matter, the book hadn't come out. The delay in the binding was infuriating. As a special favor to him, they'd sewn three rather crude copies. The cover required yet another coat of glaze, Cruz-García told him, noting the lack of enthusiasm with which the author viewed his work. A sepia cover, filled from edge to edge with rows of Zapata-style hats; on top, in black letters, his name, and a little below, in larger type, the title: *The Year 1914*. Not only was he not enthusiastic in the least about the cover; he openly disapproved of it. He read the brief note on the back cover and ultimately said that the row of hats that ran from top to bottom on the cover had nothing to do with the book's thesis; on the contrary, it refuted it. In his book he sought to explain how the different currents (composed of a broad spectrum of nuances) that had participated in the Revolution emerged in 1914, only to immediately come into conflict—currents latent during the Díaz period and those that arose as a result of the very dynamics of the conflict—and how in 1914, although from the outside there was no sign of it, the institutionalist current had already triumphed, which for better or worse had shaped the country in which they lived.

Cruz-García replied that a handful of researchers or history teachers knew this; for a normal reader, the year 1914, or 1917, or even 1922 was reduced to hats and cartridge belts. The small groups of enlightened men mentioned in his book, the constitutionalists, the pettifoggers, certainly played an important role and were responsible for subsequent social reform, but at that time they were nothing more than faces drowned amid a vast country awash in sombreros. The visible poles were those that Diego Rivera, without dwelling upon nuance, had painted on the walls of the Ministry of Public Education: on one side, a blond man in English leggings and thin gold glasses atop a rapacious nose, and, on the other, the overflowing peasant mass that covered everything.

"Somewhat like," he concluded, "we're perceived in Europe, only in more modern clothing."

Perhaps it was true, but Del Solar refused to agree. And, as for "true," that had to be clarified; it could be in another context, but not in his book. What he set out to demonstrate in his research was refuted by a cover whose sole purpose was to stimulate interest in that product in the marketplace. Despite everything, he had to admit, at quick glance, such was the year 1914: sombreros, cartridge belts, bivouacs, executions by firing squad in the streets and, at the same time, mysterious meetings, quasiclandestine and visionary conversations around which a handful of men in the midst of that mass were attempting to forge a certain project of a virtually ideal society, which was undoubtedly promising but unfortunately lost, because it failed to find its way to create a different country, people and ideas that, at the time, were not able to save what still seemed salvageable.

"The glaze," said Cruz-García, redirecting the conversation that was beginning to bore him, "will add another relief to the cover; it looks neutral, but it will be different, you'll see."

Del Solar found the edition sad and dull. He'd find no pleasure in giving away those copies. One was set aside for Delfina Uribe, due to her father's participation in the events of that year. Licenciado Uribe had been one of the ideologues of Carrancismo. With the delivery of the book, he'd justify the questions he intended to ask her around the work that had excited his imagination: the events of 1942.

"I'm mulling over another book. I'm more interested, perhaps because of recent events, in the 1942 book," Del Solar had said at the beginning of the conversation, that is, when he arrived at the publishing house.

"Are you planning to specialize in annuals?"

"It wouldn't be a bad idea. At least they'd be useful, but it's not my thing. I'm planning to limit myself to a trilogy." At that moment the idea occurred to him for the first time. "I'll situate each book in a key year in the history of Mexico, those years when for some reason the country's direction or calling is defined. I find exciting elements in 1942 . . . The declaration of war on the Axis powers, the role of Mexico in the international sphere, the sudden cosmopolitanism of the capital, the national reconciliation of all sectors. President Calles returns. An amnesty is declared for the Delahuertistas. The Porfirianos return from Paris. There's also a flood of European exiles representing all leanings, from the Trotskyists (I need to verify if Trotsky's widow was still living here then), the German Communists, Carol of Romania and his small court, Jewish financiers from the Netherlands and Denmark, revolutionaries and adventurers from a thousand parts. Amid that avalanche it's not easy to know who was who. Do you know, for example, anything about Ergon Erwin Kisch? I recently learned, by chance, of his enormous importance in Central Europe during the interwar period. On the other hand, the securities provided to the capital already formed the country's new economic model."

"You sound like a textbook on socioeconomics, which is so popular these days. What a drag!"

"The radical right and the financial circles, which until then were one and the same, began to follow parallel paths that were sometimes very different, or so it seems. Guadalajara's wealthy, the old money, never ceased to encourage the peasants to cut off the ears of the rural teachers; by contrast, their children, when they came to Mexico City, went to the chic Casanova nightclub in the hope of seeing King Carol dance with his mistress, Lupescu. There are thousands of elements to be rescued, verified, hierarchized during that period. And I'm just beginning to track them down, to sniff them out."

"You've got a year to deliver the book to me. It looks like it's in the works, am I right? And after 1942, you'll bring me 1937, 1922, 1965; any year you can think of. Yearbooks always have a readership, you can be sure of that. People buy those books mostly for the photos."

Del Solar looked at the cover again, and it seemed even more drab. The year 1914 was too distant for him. He realized how deeply he'd planted his feet in 1942. For a moment, he faced facts about the failure of his attempts to gather oral testimonies that established the microhistory that interested him. The incident at the Minerva Building had him stuck. He suspected that he should look for background information in the archives, record and study the conversations with politicians of the time, with financiers and journalists, instead of listening for hours to the endless recitation of a pathetic little woman about her mother's sympathies and aversions or witnessing the insane scandalmongering of his Aunt Eduviges. The repeated comments of Cruz-García, who insisted on referring to his books as annuals, seemed to him to be in rather dubious taste. He said reluctantly that he'd apparently not expressed himself well. He wasn't interested in compiling a mere record of events and anniversaries. If he were to write a third and final book, he'd consider 1924 or 1928, because of its political importance; he still didn't know. He insisted that there should be only three volumes. Three significant moments that defined the country. Not to worry, he wouldn't bug him. If the year 1942 didn't interest him, no big deal. He didn't think it would be too difficult for him to find a publisher. That is, if he even wrote it, because he hadn't decided yet.

"Do you see how you're carrying on, damn it? Of course I'm interested! That's all I was trying to tell you. To start with, 1942 was one of the years of my youth; for that alone I'm interested. I'd been in Mexico City for three years and was studying law. Whether I wanted it or not, my father's reputation opened a lot of doors for me. Let's see, in 1942 I must've been in my first year of law. I'd written five or six poems by then. Don't laugh. They're lost somewhere in the magazines of that time. They were horrible! And don't get any ideas about looking for them! By then I must've met my wife . . . No, no, that was later, a few years after. The city was small then, but a lot more fun than it is now. Every week a new place opened. You have no idea what Ciro's was. A review of the nightlife from the time alone would merit a beautiful edition. No hats or cartridge belts!"

"One day I'll come and interview you in earnest. When I have a better grasp on the material. By the way, do you know someone named Balmorán?"

"Balmorán? Rubén Balmorán?"

"Pedro Balmorán!"

"The one and only, who sings and dances! Of course I know him and that his name is Pedro. I don't know where I got Rubén. He wasn't ever anyone big. Why are you interested in him? He used to be a reporter, but I don't think he was any good. A really mediocre type. And a troublemaker, watch yourself. I don't think he'll help you very much with those years."

"I've been told he sells rare books and papers. He interests me from that perspective. I want to get pamphlets and other information from the period. Synarchist leaflets, for example."

"I haven't seen him in years. He used to come by every once in a while. Maybe he's gotten worse; it was really hard for him to get around; his body's a wreck. As for me, I stopped collecting things. It was a pain in the neck! You're not going to believe it, but I don't even buy paintings."

Miguel del Solar asked his editor to introduce him to Balmorán. He could tell him, he suggested, that a friend of his was interested in some publications, and that at that very moment he was around the corner from his home; ask him if he could go and see him. Cruz-García seemed unwilling. Del Solar insisted; he'd been told that the eccentric bookseller wouldn't receive anyone without a recommendation. A secretary made the call, communicated the request, and then informed him that Balmorán agreed to receive him in half an hour. Del Solar took his three copies of *The Year 1914* and got moving.

He didn't enter the building immediately; he reached the garden facing the building, at the roundabout, and sat on a bench, the only one there. He tried to collect, once again, the scattered memories of his childhood. He was convinced that as a child he'd noticed something that at the time escaped the notice of others, and he didn't know what it was. On the other hand, he was radically opposed to accepting the official report he'd recently read. That simplistic version in which the owner of a car had killed a young foreigner for simply having confused his car with a taxi. He might know something, he insisted, that others either refused or didn't think it appropriate to remember. He tried to arouse and organize his memories. Images, as usual, flooded over him, contradicting each other, overlapping and, most of all, refusing to stop at the moments that interested him—the connection between Pistauer's death and his stepfather Arnulfo Briones's disappearance. He was surprised that everything, no matter how banal his recollection of the several months he lived in his aunt and uncle's home, was somehow connected with the war. The adults' conversations, the games in the central courtyard, mere skirmishes between Allies and Germans, the delight of the blackouts, the drills that darkened the city, during which his aunt forced Amparo to rehearse her Chopin by candlelight, scenes that seemed melancholic and romantic. At that moment he imagined a bombing, the ensuing destruction of the building, the corridors and stairs on fire, which he would manage to descend with his fainted cousin on his shoulder. What else? The familial strain when it was discovered that Arnulfo Briones was married to a divorcée, whose husband appeared suddenly in Mexico; the fact that the Brioneses regarded almost all the foreigners in the building as enemies; his aunt's comments against Delfina Uribe, against the Werfels, and especially the most violent ones against Balmorán; the daily visits of Arnulfo Briones, his black glasses, his hesitant gait, his silver-handled canes, his yellowed mustache, his rotten teeth, his walks with the skinny man who accompanied him everywhere like a bloodhound. The siblings discussed, relentlessly, issues he could barely comprehend. He picked up snippets, phrases, and words here and there; they sometimes shouted, although, in general, they were hushed conversations, amid whispers, like conspirators. The day of the grand spectacle, when his aunt delighted in giving voice to every word that might hurt her brother for having introduced a divorcée into the family.

At the end of long mysterious conversation about the couple, his aunt gathered the three kids in Antonio's room to make them swear that they would never talk to Balmorán because he was a degenerate, that they should not speak to him or return his greeting. He also remembers moments of joy when his aunt imitated her neighbors while he and Amparo burst into laughter, until the impersonator, infected with laughter, was forced to suspend her performance.

He remembers thousands of minute details: however, he doesn't know how he ended up in Córdoba: if his parents came to pick him up, if they sent someone for him, if his uncle took him, or if, and this seemed most likely to him, they'd put him on a bus, entrusting him to the driver, since ten was more than old enough to travel alone.

•

He got up after jotting down a few cryptic notes in his notebook. He crossed the street and entered the building. He stopped at the entrance in front of the directory to look for Balmorán's apartment number. Once he found it, he went up to the top floor.

He found a hunchbacked man in his sixties. A gaunt face, his hair cut almost to the scalp. His head too big for his rickety body, which was little more than a heap of shriveled tissue tied in knots. On his face, a kind of lump protruded from his nose. His right side was an array of deformities: a shrunken leg, the foot twisted inward, an immobile arm; a dead hand resting on his chest, over his heart. His body's puniness hadn't prevented the growth of a pear-shaped belly. At first sight, the invalid gave off a look of filth, but after a few minutes that effect disappeared. His village-cut clothes were as clean as everything in his apartment, which was larger than he imagined those on the top floor of the Minerva to be. Miguel del Solar was struck by the somber, contracted, discordant charge that the battered body emitted.

The hours he spent there formed a chain of tedious and irritating moments made bearable only by his patience and interest in the case. What a flowering, what a jungle, what yawning roots of megalomania, frustration, and resentment! An element of exaggerated contrivance made his monologues intolerable. A repertoire of grimaces, winks, silences, and dramatic pauses, accentuated by the incessant nervous twitch of his left hand, seemed to anticipate the importance of a phrase about to be uttered that always resulted in unbearable banality. From time to time he'd repeat the same refrain: the undersigned, Pedro Balmorán, the one and only, who sings and dances tangos, the one and only, who sings and dances the most enchanting waltzes in this world, the one and only, who sings and dances the frenetic mambo, hadn't aged, didn't feel his age, didn't even know how old he was, wasn't bitter, practiced happiness as if it were a daily exercise in health, when the truth was it would be difficult to imagine such an atrocious image of decrepitude as his, a vision of man transformed into a mere sack of bile and resentment.

The historian showed Balmorán one of the copies of his chronicle of 1914. He tried to provide a sense of his research. He explained why he was proposing to write a book about 1942. Cruz-García had recommended that he consult him about the bibliographic possibilities of the subject.

He was interested in obtaining the foundational books on the Mexican radical right, the Cristero novels, for example, and the political literature disseminated through the sacristies. He needed advice on these topics. He'd been told that during that period he'd conducted extensive literary and journalistic activity. He would be very grateful if one day he would allow him to consult his work.

The bookseller listened to him without any pretense of friendliness, but rather distance and condescension. At first he seemed only to measure the business relationship he could establish with an eventual customer. He said that in a few days he would formulate a small bibliography and would then see what he could find for sale and for what price. He made his way to the interior rooms covered with shelves and filing cabinets. Everything in the house, except the occupant, had an exacting professional appearance; there were no dusty books, no yellowish newspapers piled on the floor or stacked on the furniture. It was obvious that he was well organized. He showed him some expensive editions, of questionable taste, that compiled texts by European travelers in Mexico, illustrated with nineteenth-century images, and clarified that his main task was to prepare those editions for a club of bibliophiles. He commented sarcastically that Cruz-García refused to recognize him as a colleague and referred to him instead as a used bookseller, because in his youth—that is, at a certain point in his life, because he refused to acknowledge ever having stopped being young—in difficult times he'd been engaged in the business of buying and selling rare books, especially old editions of Mexican history, a task he continued to perform, as was evident, as an ancillary, almost vicarious job.

At the mention of his journalistic work, he replied that the nature of his articles was literary and had only rarely dealt with current affairs. He wasn't and had never been a journalist of the type to which Cruz-García wanted to reduce him. Not because he wanted to situate the writer above the journalist. Nothing of the sort; for him, any profession, any activity, even the humblest trade, was highly respectable.

"Yes, señor," he continued, "every profession can be honorable, even the literary, if one can call that a profession. Honorable! Unfortunately, most men of letters aren't. People who have no love for a trade! The only thing they seek is whatever power their photographs confer on them when they appear in the press. When I fill out a form, it never occurs to me to fill the space dedicated to profession with such a silly word as 'writer,' not even 'editor,' but rather 'bookseller.' I consider it, you see, a nobler and less polluted endeavor. As a rule, the bookseller doesn't hate his fellow booksellers. The writer does. He moves heaven and earth to stand in their way. He devotes himself to disparaging them, to plunging them into seas of filth, vats of scum, pails of slag. Vile garbage, señor, if one must in the end call things by their name! People are afraid of them. The publishers of magazines and literary supplements, the editors in chief, copy editors, all live in fear. And what do you have to say about the frightened editors? Didn't Cruz-García tell you that I was a simple bookseller? A secondhand bookseller! I can hear him. A journalist, no. Much less—oh no, never that!—a writer. And it's not that he doesn't consider me as such, I assure you, but that, the rat coward that he is, he fears the disrepute that the mafia can bring to his publishing house. I laugh. I've always been independent. They wanted to bring me down; they even tried to destroy me physically. Just look at what they did to me! But they haven't been able to beat me, I haven't allowed it. I laugh in their faces, and I continue to do what I do. One day, very soon, I'll reveal what I've accomplished during these long years of apparent silence. I'll show them my work amid a roar of laughter."

"What do you write?"

"What genre? Is that what you're asking me? How

important can literary genres be? I write, that's all. And I publish books for connoisseurs. I live! The activity, if you don't already know, that's most important to me. That's why I consider it an obligation to laugh at the whole world."

He let out a frightening hyena-like laugh.

Then he got up and left the room. He returned with magazines in hand. They were publications from twenty or thirty years before. Among others, copies of *The Prodigal Son*. He showed him the table of contents. Some articles and several bibliographic notes he'd authored.

"I also," Del Solar replied in a casual tone, and as if sharing Balmorán's positions, "endeavored to do my work on the margin of groups, which is largely why I decided to live abroad for a few years."

"Really? Does it make you feel better to live in the United States?" the bookseller asked, staring at him with an irksome grimace. "Does your mind feel clearer after a juicy bowl of cornflakes?"

He decided to ignore the sudden outburst of hostility. He patiently clarified, trying to express himself with the greatest casualness, that he didn't live in the United States but in England, where he taught Mexican history at a university.

"I don't believe I'm superior in any way," he concluded. "Why should I? It seems to me, however, that I worked better, freer from pressure. Nevertheless, I plan to stay in Mexico. I hope to be able to devote less time to teaching and more to research. If I write the book I'm proposing I'll have to live here to consult archives, review the press of the time, interview a great many people. By the way, I spoke to the doorman of this building to see if there was an apartment available. There's not. Have you lived here long?"

"Quite long; seems like all my life. I used to have a small

studio, on the same floor. When this one became available, I moved immediately. Books reproduce like mushrooms. I'm not a bohemian; disorder makes me ill. Soon I'll need more space." Balmorán got up. He raised his good hand with a theatrical gesture and smacked himself on the forehead. He had forgotten the coffee, which the stove had surely consumed. He'd make another pot, or would he prefer a drink? He could only offer him tequila or rum.

They ended up drinking a bottle of rum. From the third drink, Balmorán's resentment acquired a hulking violence. They'd tossed him aside, he repeated endlessly; they'd spared him no violence. He'd been too close to the miracle, to the revelation, and that, he knew, would cost him. They thought they'd defeated him. Who? Beautiful question! Society, of course, every arm the octopus had at its disposal, and the mafia, the eternal conformists, the petulant writers, the detestable mediocrity. Everyone! They tried to take away his youth, the only thing left in his life, but without success. He continued to work, unaware of any outside circumstances, with patience and joy. The grasshopper and the ant! Two sides of the same coin.

"It seems," said Del Solar, pointing to the table of contents of one of the magazines the other man had put in his hands, "you're interested in Mexican symbolists, a group of writers about whom so little is known."

"As little as the romantics and modernistas. Little is known about everything. In the end, nothing. People have stopped studying, they scarcely work, and those who attempt to do so seriously not only encounter closed doors, but . . . Good God! Why continue?"

It was easy to steer the conversation, thanks most of all to the rage that occasionally overcame Balmorán. The historian gave him the last word about everything. He attempted at first to talk about his own work, his first book, about Dr. Mora, but the knotty bookseller had no patience for listening to anyone. He made disarticulated gestures. Tremblingly, he tacitly demanded that he continue to be his audience, not to interrupt him for pity's sake, not to deprive him of sympathy. To refute him would have been fatal. But listening to him at times became torture. He gesticulated too much. He contorted, twisted, tied himself in knots. He paused for what seemed like an eternity with his arm in the air, outstretched, trembling, impatient, signaling that he'd not yet finished saying what he was determined to say, that he wouldn't yield the floor, that the verb about to emerge from his lips was so extraordinary that his listener would lose his breath upon hearing it.

He learned unnecessary things. About two failed marriages and several love affairs that carried an implicit charge of sordidness, about his many businesses, his periods of economic comfort, also about episodes in which he was forced to give up even his writing. Del Solar successfully steered him to several topics that interested him. He attempted to get information about the German woman who'd lived locked away in a wretched apartment for many years, without getting anything. Balmorán shut down:

"I'm dumb as a post! I know nothing, I see nothing, I hear nothing. I've never exchanged words with that woman, nor do I care to. She can live as she wishes! If she likes stench, let her enjoy it! Respect for the rights of others is peace! Eternal glory to the All-worthy!"

Del Solar noticed that if he wanted to know something, and above all he was interested in the account that had so alarmed his Aunt Eduviges, he had to proceed with extreme caution. That abhorrent body was equipped with an armor of thorns. Any misstep would cause him to lose valuable information.

The topics Balmorán was working on at the moment? Various. Poems, works of scholarship, including three or four biographies of brave, curious, extravagant characters, whom society and its prejudices had ripped to shreds. The conversation, without Del Solar knowing how, jumped to a Mexican castrato who'd ended his days as a fakir in Naples. His heart skipped a beat. A castrato? Could he perchance be the libertine related to Eduviges Briones?

"A castrato? A castrato poet?" he asked in a hopeful voice.

"No, señor, that pitiful being was a soprano. Perhaps a poet too, though, in his own way. A soprano assoluto! That was how the insatiable baroness who corrupted his body and led him to ruin dared to introduce him in Rome. A classical castrato in the musical sense, or at least that was what was claimed at the time. *Il più che melodioso rosignolo messicano!* A very curious story, an exceptional document. An apparently typical biography of the time: product of the Intervention and the Empire. Deep down, however, something more majestic. Silence! I'm shutting up! The castrato recounted his memoirs in old age, on the brink of the grave, to an Italian friar who, I'm afraid, added a thousand anecdotes of his own invention. The memoirs arrived in Mexico among many other curious books and documents. I had them!" he shouted, his cry akin to a foal's whinny and a pig's squeal at the moment of slaughter. "They were mine! They were mine, your undersigned servant, the one and only, who sings and dances furious polkas in time to a cancan! Three hundred pages, of which only forty were saved!"

"And the rest?"

"How would I know?" he shouted again in a newly adversarial voice. "I never knew if they were destroyed or not. You ask a lot of questions! At the time, there were several versions. All I know is that forty pages were saved from the carnage. They were taken to be examined by a woman whom I considered at the time a serious and eminent polygraph, and who turned out to be the worst, most cunning huckster to ever set foot on Mexican soil. She, the distinguished scholar, didn't understand the exceptional value of the tale. She had the insolence to tell me that it wasn't serious, that it was neither socially nor literarily interesting, but in a different way, with ambiguous phrases and praise so weak, so tortuous that they were tantamount to an expression of contempt. She lived here. She went so far as to say that the text wasn't in Italian. Yes, here, in this very building. A philistine of the worst sort! A clever fool who sailed under the flag of genius until the day she died! Of course, I keep the pages that survived in a safe place. They can come and search everything; they won't find a thing. One should never—this is the only advice I will allow myself to give the world—be caught short without precautions. I lost the movement of my right leg and arm," he said, pointing with a reproachful, almost repulsive look at his useless side, "because of that priceless document. They can do whatever they want to me, they won't find a line. One day, when it's least expected, I'll publish it. If my life has been an example of anything, it's resolve, stubbornness, if you want to call it something. Balmorán, the hardheaded! You see, I haven't given up; I still have a few salutary surprises to share with the world."

"And who would be so interested in the appearance or disappearance of the memoirs? The family of the castrato? When do you say he died?"

"In 1896, in Naples; I already told you, of starvation, madness, syphilis, abandonment. With only rats to gnaw on his desiccated cartilage for a while."

"So someone objected to the story being disseminated?"

"What have I been trying to tell you! A little slow, aren't you, my good historian!"

"Who would be opposed? For what reasons?"

"That's the $64,000 question! I don't know. Well, I suppose I know who they were, but I'm not sure why. I've asked myself a thousand times, and a thousand times I've given myself a different answer."

Miguel del Solar began to feel lost. The castrato couldn't be the relative of Eduviges Briones. The dates didn't coincide. Nor the death in Naples. A singer who ends up a fakir! It was too distant from that boy imprisoned in perpetuity at the back of a Porfirian house, mentioned by his aunt.

"Perhaps," he ventured again, "the castrato's relatives were frightened by the memoirs becoming public."

"The castrato's relatives? But what are you talking about? Can you please tell me? What family could the poor castrato possibly have? His earthly cover was that of a Tarahumara Indian, an Apache, what do I know . . . I didn't study to learn about Indians . . . He lived in San Luis Potosí, where a pair of adventurers filled his head with smoke. They prevented him from fulfilling the purpose for which he was destined. An evil woman, the widow of an Austrian baron, and a French lieutenant took him to the capital in secret, hid him for a while, and then she, the shameless baroness, took him to Europe. I won't reveal to you the mystery of his personality. His mystical sign. Could that creature have redeemed the world? I believe so, but he was prevented by the greed and wickedness of those into whose hands he fell at the wrong time. The pope could have rescued him, but he lacked intuition, generosity. I don't want to say any more. I'm dumb as a post! The only thing I can assure you of is that it wasn't a family matter. By no means. Just think about it, a few illiterate Indians who more than a century ago lost track of the character." He tilted his head back, stroked one of his sideburns, and shouted drunkenly, "Enough! On to something else!" He said something about the weather; then, with the greatest fickleness, he returned to his soliloquy: "I can assure you that for a while my life was a nightmare. This building became, if you'll pardon my pleonasm, the most hellish circle of hell. Concealed interrogations, inquiries, traps. A shower of anonymous vulgarians that, by the way, has recently resumed. Thirty years later, and the language is the same. One day I found my apartment, not this one but the other one, the one next door, where I lived then, ransacked. My books on the floor, the furniture torn to pieces. They'd ripped the mattress, like in B movies. And my papers, gone without a trace. The story about the Mexican nightingale, that hideous castrato from San Luis, had been snatched from me, along with the thesis I was about to finish, and my notebooks. The forty pages I have were saved because, as I told you, I'd temporarily put them in meretricious hands. They took everything. There were papers of incalculable value, notes on the Jesuit missions in the Sierra Tarahumara, for example. I never graduated. For a while they managed to discourage me. Then I recovered, determined to prove that my life was joy, constancy in joy. Waltz of waltzes! They believed they'd broken me, and, as you can see, they were wrong. To have rewritten the thesis would have been to admit that they were right. I showed a greatness of spirit that I myself didn't expect. I rubbed in their faces that not only did they not harm me but that they'd done me a favor. I've been an eternal student ever since. Permanently young! I still am! At first it wasn't easy for me to react properly. I lived in fear. They weren't content to seize my work; shortly after, they tried to kill me. I was shot. They didn't manage to kill me, but look, they left my hand and leg crippled. Bastards!"

"Did it happen a long time ago?"

"I can tell you the exact date. November 14, 1942. That day marks a milestone in my life. It serves as a before and an after for me. Even in my dreams I see a calendar and a date circled in small flames: November 14, 1942."

He shouted that date repeatedly with the face of a demon, as he struck the ground with his cane.

"*Nineteen Forty-Two* is the title of the book I'm planning. I was with Licenciado Uribe's daughter, Delfina; perhaps you know her. Delfina Uribe, from the art gallery. I told her about the book I intend to write. It deals with internal tensions inside Mexico during the first year of war with the Axis powers. Don't laugh! Delfina told me that a party of hers ended with a horrific shooting in which her son was wounded, and that the date also represented a milestone in her life, marking a before and an after. It's funny, but I think she used the same words as you."

Balmorán was by that time very drunk. He looked at his interlocutor, his eyes bulging out. He placed his cane upright and stood up with a theatrical and complicated act of balance. His whole body shook as if an electric current had passed through it. Del Solar feared he would attack him. The mad, he recalled, often possess tremendous strength.

"So you're a friend of Delfina Uribe?" Balmorán shrieked.

"I know her. I'm more of a friend of her niece," he replied calmly. "They say that in her day she was a very attractive woman. And to some extent still is. She told me that her son was mortally wounded at the end of that party. According to her, I should focus my research on that gathering. There, apparently, in all their cruelty, the contradictions that I'm interested in studying revealed themselves. That night coincided with a spate of currents that, when taken to the extreme, could no longer coexist. That radicalism shattered the structure that constrained them."

Something seemed to reassure and infuriate Balmorán at the same time. Talking about the subject seemed to bother him, but, at the same time, it represented an irresistible temptation. He collapsed again into the chair from which he'd managed to get up with such difficulty before.

"I can see her perfectly. The quintessential protagonist of the Mexican Revolution! An absolute diva! History as a family chronicle! Her father, the round, red sun of the era! I'll tell you one thing only: if Delfina represents anything, it's only herself, her infinite pettiness, her desire for power, her boundless rapacity. You'd be amazed if I told you what close friends we were. I was completely wrong about her. One of the prerogatives of youth, in their healthy attitude toward life, is to believe in the good faith of others. Young people are generous; they are willing to discover virtues where they don't exist. Even in that Werfel woman, which is saying a lot! Three or four years ago Delfina invited me to dinner. The last time I saw her! Do you know her house in San Ángel? A kind of mausoleum. Icy spaces, in keeping with the corpse she's become. There were four or five people there who smelled just like her, like cadaverine. A servant wearing white gloves served us drinks. They mumbled some incomprehensible language to simulate communication. The truth is, they spoke only to perform a ritual, with a sole purpose, to say nothing. I stayed a while. Delfina asked me about my editions. The only thing that interested her, I'm sure, was how much I made and what kind of painting she could sell me. Or perhaps making sure that she'd done well by inviting me or, on the contrary, if she'd committed a faux pas. The stench of high finance was unbreathable. If they talked about a painter, it was to brag that such and such painting had sold for I don't know how many millions of pesos, that a Rivera had cost I don't know how many hundreds of thousands of dollars and a Tamayo another such amount at an auction in New York. When we sat down to eat, I was afraid the waiter would tell us the price of the shrimp

dish and the pepper steak. I ate only the soup; I couldn't take
it anymore. A guy I barely knew by sight, a publicist, assumed
a familiarity that wasn't there, using my first name, and in the
diminutive: 'Look, Pedrito, if you aspire to eat arroz con pollo
every day, you must be dialectical, and do this and that in life.
It seems, Pedrito, that I'm committed to including you in the
synthesis. One has to be very careful. Always demand that
one order rice, that it be served with chicken,' and continued,
'Pedrito' here, 'Pedrito' there, as if we were friends. I got up
and said I didn't feel well, that something had given me indiges-
tion, perhaps the conversation, that they'd offered me arroz con
pollo several times, but what they wanted to serve me was arroz
con culo. A skinny, shriveled-up woman, who looked like a bull-
fighter wearing a tie of lights, whom they had stuck me next to
looked at me as if I were trash. The others pretended that they
hadn't heard my words. I asked the skinny woman where the
bathroom was; I told her I needed to go urgently, because I was
about to burst. Delfina, out of mere form, got up, took me by the
arm to the living room, asked me if I needed anything, if I would
like her car to take me home. For the first time she also allowed
herself to call me Pedrito. I stopped her cold: 'I'm a young man,
not a baby, Delfina. So please don't use diminutives to speak to
me.' I added that many things had brought us together, perhaps
the most tragic things one can imagine, but the past was just
that, the past, that she should understand how impossible it was
for me to continue sitting there, in that beautiful villa next to
her guests, that I felt as if I were eating carrion. I bolted out and
never saw her again. And, at one time, I'm telling you, it was difficult to find two better friends than the two of us. Did you know
she used to live in this building too?"

Del Solar looked at him with an empty stare. He didn't
answer. The other man seemed to interpret this silence and

neutral gaze as a demonstration of astonishment. He seemed to like the effect. He bulged out his eyes, made an endless display of faces, ready, apparently, to make a final statement, stretched his left hand out, and began to shake it madly to prevent any untimely comments from his guest.

"Yes, señor," he continued, "that's the way things are." Her Royal Highness lived in this building in 1942. She didn't tell you, of course. She must find the experience of living with other people dishonorable. This isn't her palace in San Ángel, nor the fiefdom they tell me she owns in Cuernavaca. 'The Land Belongs to Those Who Work It,' I imagine it's called or, perhaps, 'Land and Freedom.' You know, the natural-born agrarian can't live without her catchphrases. The party that she and I have referred to, listen to me closely, took place on the second floor of this building. Because we're both talking, as unlikely as it seems, about the same event. November 14, 1942, was a date that changed both our lives, mine for the better, hers for the much worse. A gathering filled with shameful incidents. Not all, it must be said, attributable to her. In the end, when we were on the street, the shooting occurred in which a foreigner died, and where Delfina's son and yours truly, the undersigned, who at this point was singing and dancing to the national anthem itself, were injured. I, more seriously. A bullet injured my spine; partial paralysis, almost death."

Balmorán savored the interest he'd generated. He had become a hero, the absolute protagonist. He began by talking about the climate of distrust that reigned in the building in the months prior. A family linked to German interests had created that atmosphere. People whose nature was to live surrounded by thugs. He'd made the mistake of contacting them. In particular, a demented and ignorant woman, niece to none other than a certain Gonzalo de la Caña, a decadent poetaster of negligible stature, about whom he'd found only one or two scattered and contradictory details.

"A primitive symbolist. His poetry was a true perversion but diminished, of course, because of the milieu in which he moved—Baudelaire drowned in his cup of thick chocolate! They slammed the door in my face. Riffraff completely alien to literature, born and raised in the Dark Ages and intolerance. Following that visit I felt watched, persecuted. The story of the writer as an enemy, an abominable being whom it was necessary to drive from the castle, was repeated. One morning I was introduced to a pissant shyster lawyer, a fixer, a nasty character with a stench of chicanery, whom, as I later learned, the whole building knew as 'the lunatic.' He didn't know how to start the conversation. He asked me, as if testing the waters, about my relationship with the neighbors, especially with the teacher Werfel, that master of imposture. His pretext for approaching me was banal and yet credible. He came to inquire about someone who could help the daughter of a friend of his write her university thesis. He became interested in my financial situation. He said I was burning the midnight oil studying to earn a pittance; it was true. He referred to the injustice involved; others, without doing anything, were rolling around in gold dust with their paramours. The person had repulsive manners. His presence, his paternalistic tone, began to make me uncomfortable. I've always been very sensitive to slovenliness, and his greenish teeth disgusted me. Every time the stench of his mouth reached me, I became dizzy. I replied that it was unthinkable that I should help anyone else when I myself was about to graduate. 'Yes, I know,' he said with a furtive smile that hinted at complicity. 'Rumors have reached me that you have certain papers about the life of a famous invert and that you're preparing to publish them.' I didn't understand; I began to explain to him what romanticism was, the subject of my thesis, and what its effects were in Mexico. 'Oh, yes, how romantic it must be to reveal the life of a degenerate bastard who fled his country to live a life of faggotry in another!' I repeat, I didn't understand what he was talking about. There was a mis-understanding, but I couldn't figure out where. At last I began to understand; he was talking about the castrato, about my project to write and publish the mystery of his prodigious life, but he con-fused the story with others. I asked him plainly if he was refer-ring to the castrato. 'Who the hell do you think, oh wise man of my soul?' His little familiarities stuck in my craw. He came out with something about someone willing to pay a rather respect-able sum for the papers, that the transaction could be carried out as long as I agreed to pay him half for his services. I replied that his proposal was absurd, that I wouldn't sell the papers for any amount of money. You fail to understand that there's an ongo-ing conspiracy at work to prevent the miracle from taking place, to cause the material to blindly destroy the mystery. Please don't get restless on me! Relax that face! When I publish my version you will understand everything. Finally the shyster pencil pusher left, but from then on, they bothered me night and day, relent-lessly, on the phone, through anonymous persons, as much as possible. One afternoon, two boxer types jumped me in the mid-dle of the Parque España, pretending to be drunk. I escaped by pure chance. The persecution resulted in the theft of my papers. They lured me to Cuernavaca with a very attractive proposi-tion that's not worth talking about at the moment. It was all a trap. I returned, furious, to find my house looted and my papers stolen. I didn't see the lunatic again until the day of Delfina's party. He shunned me for a while, taking refuge in the Werfels' protection. A raving lunatic. Suddenly, while I was talking to a friend, he approached me and blurted out that I'd been an idiot, that if I'd listened to him at the time we'd be rolling in dough. I

was petrified. I could expect anything except that he'd come out
with that. He ran off. Then I saw him strike Ida Werfel's volumi-
nous body. Between Bernardo, one of the other Uribes, and me,
we managed to stop him. There were a lot of people, more kept
coming in. Somehow unbeknownst to us he slipped through our
hands again. I went out into the hallway, to the stairs, but he was
gone. I went down to the courtyard; there was no trace of him.
He might have snuck into an apartment, or hidden in one of the
building's many nooks and crannies. Late that night I saw him
again. He was motioning through a window at the German boy
to go out into the corridor. The time had arrived to settle the
score with him. I didn't care what might happen. I was strong
then, and he was a weakling. I'll make him talk, I said to myself.
Today I'll find out where my papers ended up, and, if I don't
succeed, I'll at least give him the beating of his life. At the door I
stumbled upon Ricardo, Delfina's son, who had just arrived, and
asked him to come with me; I needed a witness. We hurried outside. The lunatic was already in the roundabout in front of the
building. The German boy was running toward a car when the
scuffle began. It seems that they were shooting at us from several directions. They left us for dead. I had three surgeries. One
of the bullets, as you know, hit my spine, another left my pel-
vis shattered. It's a miracle I'm alive. It was a long time before
I was able to walk again, to recover. I've had setbacks in my life,
but without selling out to anyone. I haven't grown bitter, as you
can see. One day the story of the *spaventoso castrato messicano*
will come to light. It won't contain all the details of the original,
but the essential elements will remain intact. I'll end up recon-
structing it. During his ill-fated appearance in Rome, those who
wished him ill spread rumors that just hearing him was painful to the ear. Poor soul, he failed even as a fakir. His moment in
the spotlight hadn't come; his appearance was premature. His

appearance in the end was so frightening that only vermin dared go near him, and the rats, as I've already said, that little by little went about devouring him."

It was about four in the morning. Balmorán got up to open another bottle, but Del Solar stopped him. He spoke just as he walked, in circles. He'd repeated exactly, using the very same words, some passages from his story. He accompanied him, doddering, to the door, and promised to look for the bibliography that interested him. He should return, to see the books he'd published, to chat. There was a tacit plea in his voice, in his gestures, in his defeated look of drunkenness. He could tell him much about the year 1942, he swore. He could tell him things he'd never confided in anyone. He'd make an exception for him! He must return as soon as possible. Tomorrow!

CHAPTER 7

In the Garden of Juan Fernández

"MY GRANDFATHER HAD A GROCERY STORE in Paraje, Veracruz. Just imagine! Grocery store is merely a euphemism. A rinky-dink store in a down-on-its-luck town in the tropics is a more apt description. My father was born and raised there. As a child I visited the family two or three times. A very sad place, I assure you; I'm afraid it hasn't changed. Next year I'll return with Bernardo and Malú to celebrate its hundredth birthday. They're going to call it Paraje de Uribe," Delfina said on a Sunday at mid-morning in her garden in Cuernavaca. "There was a beautiful natural spring nearby; otters abounded. In the house we had two or three coverlets made from pelts that the farmers gave us. Also some archeological objects. They may have determined my brother Bernardo's vocation. If I'd asked my father for them, rest assured he'd have given them to me, but as a young girl, unlike my brother, I wasn't interested in the pre-Hispanic world or the visual arts. I was in love with literature. It's possible that the objects were Totonac, although the distance between Paraje and El Tajín must be considerable; I couldn't say. Every time I ask Bernardo he gives me a different answer. You can't imagine the fits of snobbishness I suffered during my youth," she burst into a dry laughter. "It was my gallery, my work, my dealings with painters, that brought me back to reality. My passion for my father was total, and, in return, he adored me. I asked little of him compared with what he insisted on giving me. I was his only daughter, after four sons; only Bernardo and I are still living. I had a privileged childhood and adolescence, and yet I felt, and I swear it's true, decidedly revolutionary. I was moved, I'm still moved, by my father's life. His efforts to study; his decision to escape from an environment as reductive as what Paraje must have been at the beginning of the century; to complete first a teaching degree in Xalapa, another degree in law here. But you, historian, know that perhaps better than I. When I heard him talk about the moment he decided to take up arms, his journeys on horseback around the country, the revolutionary conventions, prison, I was so moved that I seemed to share all those experiences with him. I felt as if I were in the Sierra Madre on horseback or by his side in prison. In exile I was even more radical. I attended public events, university and trade union rallies. But the power—imagine a house where ministers and generals dined, and sometimes the president of the republic!—must have made me dizzy. Deep down, I also wanted to be the best-dressed woman in Mexico, the most attractive, the most dazzling. For the Porfirianos to tell me that they'd been dying to dance with me while I recounted the dinner Papá had given for Rubinstein or the Picasso exhibition I'd seen in Paris. For their sisters to ask where I had such and such dress made so I could tell them that it was an original Schiaparelli. I studied literature in England and France, spoke the languages well, traveled extensively, and, after my divorce, lived in New York. It was natural that I should feel I was the most educated woman in Mexico; however, in secret, I desperately admired some of the women from the vanquished world. Eduviges, for example. Without resources, by fashioning old dresses that had belonged to her mother or some aunt, she was able to be as elegant in her way as the best-dressed woman in Paris or Rome. Class! Wouldn't you say? The way things are!

Our relationship didn't last long, but it was very intense. I'll try to explain it to you. We lived in the two best apartments in the Minerva, side by side. In the morning she'd call me at the gallery; in the afternoon she'd pick me up, and we'd have coffee, drive around the city in my car, and then go back to my house and talk nonstop until dinner, when she'd return to her apartment, and I'd dress to go somewhere. At one point I thought about making her my associate. Her connections could have been very useful to me, I thought. I'd take care of dealing with the painters and with a certain sector of our clients, politicians and foreigners; she, the bankers and people from the old families. But her ignorance was colossal, not to mention her indiscretion. Our partnership would have ended in utter failure. I was able to see it in time. It wasn't friendship, despite the intensity with which I speak of her, that united us; it was a very mismatched relationship, with disparate needs, a sort of disease. Eduviges knew nothing about modern art; it simply didn't register with her. Instead, she'd go into an antique dealer's home, take a vase, isolate it from the tchotchkes surrounding it, and turn it into an extraordinary object. She was going through financial difficulties, even though her brother Arnulfo had made millions. Upon entering her home, the first thing one noticed was the taste with which, despite having little or nothing, it had been decorated. Naturally, there were difficulties; one fine day, her whims and tantrums began to show themselves. We'd planned to go to Guadalajara to see some furniture that some of her aunts were considering putting up for sale. At the last moment, the train tickets purchased, the suitcases packed, she decided not to go, giving me some trivial excuse. I was offended to an extent that I still can't explain. From that day on, our relationship became increasingly strained. I hated her brother, but I tried to be prudent, never to broach the subject. She, on the other hand, at a certain point, began to provoke me. At first, they were little mosquito bites, in keeping with her intelligence; later a wasp's; if I'd allowed it, a viper's. I imagine she was bothered by my lifestyle, which allowed me to get along so well that I could go to New York for a few days to buy a coat or a couple of hats, for example. One day I commented in front of her how happy I was that my father had begun to publish a series of articles in which he retracted some positions critical of the expropriation of oil. She responded rudely, nastily to be frank. She began to recite points of view that had to have been her brother's, whom, months before, during the brief summer of our friendship, she'd regarded as a relic of the past. I don't know if you know: at that time a commission had been created to confiscate enemy assets; it was headed by Don Luis Cabrera. My father was invited to sit on it. He didn't accept, because his illness, of which everyone was aware, made it impossible. But Eduviges commented on his decision with an evil phrase, which she surely deemed ingenious but served only to demonstrate the magnitude of her stupidity. Once again, she hung up on me. By then, we were speaking to each other only occasionally and had stopped seeing each other altogether. You're probably wondering why I invited her to my party, then. The truth, however unpleasant, however distasteful, is that I did it to offend her. To show her my world. To show her that I rubbed elbows with the intellectuals and artists of the time, with people who'd returned from exile and also with European nobility, whether fake or real, who'd flocked to the city as the war spread through Europe. Titles dazzled her; they made her giddy. A party that was designed to ruin someone's night was bound to end badly. Violence begets violence, as they say." She attempted to laugh again, but stopped herself. "I planned to expose her lack of culture to the whole world, turning her into the boor of the

Minerva, the fool of Mexico, the laughingstock of the moment; to cause her to know, above all, to whom she was presuming to compare herself. The disaster wasn't long in coming, and the only one punished was I. I'd just opened the gallery a few weeks earlier with what turned out to be a magnificent reception. I had no reason to repeat the act in my home. The idea of doing something to celebrate both Julio Escobedo's exhibition and the return of my son wasn't necessarily a success. What did it matter to Ricardo that the minister of education or the director of the National Museum was present at the party I was throwing for him on his return home? That should have been another party, or none at all. In short, there would be time for those once he settled back into the country. Such a gathering didn't make sense to Julio either, I imagine. Those people had already been at the gallery. Only his closest friends should attend a gathering at my home; that's what we agreed, but everything turned out differently. At first one might believe that this was an allegory of the country's reconciliation. In those days, owing to the war, there was much talk of national unity; on the night in question, my home looked to be where that unity would be realized. At least at first glance. Mere appearances! There's never been a more disastrous party. As an appetizer, Ida Werfel was beaten by a deranged man. Then, General Torner, who'd become Matilde Arenal's protector, attempted to punch Julio because he thought he'd humiliated the actress in a painting . . . Were you able to see her in any of her last appearances? No, of course not, you weren't old enough. She wasn't that bad, despite being rather unintelligent. When Torner married her, he didn't allow her to return to the theater, not even as a spectator . . . You see, the general, who had a reputation for being self-possessed, who claimed to love me like a father, caused one hell of a scandal that night, as my nieces say. He tried to punch

Julio. It was dreadful! And then, the real tragedy, the shootings, the dead man, my wounded son, all very serious."

"Balmorán told me you went with him to file a report," Del Solar was finally able to interject.

"Pedrito Balmorán? Did you meet him? You realize, of course, that he's crazy. He's been living in his own reality for a long time."

Miguel del Solar described his visit in great detail. He underscored Balmorán's claim that his persecution had begun when it became known that he possessed documents about a nineteenth-century Mexican singer, a castrato to be exact.

"Can't he get that out of his head? Doesn't the fool realize that all he's doing is playing Eduviges's game? Who the hell cares about those documents? It's possible that it's a case of revenge, and he's persisting in concealing the reason. That, for example, he'd acquired those documents improperly and their real owner showed up to retrieve them and, in the process, decided to take other things. It's all very far-fetched, either way. Why would Ricardo go with him if he didn't even know him? And why did he go down to the street that night? Did he tell you?"

"Yes, he said something. Apparently, Martínez, Ida Werfel's aggressor, had told him some time before that a third party was interested in buying the documents about the castrato's life. Do you see? They must have been of some value to someone. That night, Martínez insinuated that he knew who'd broken into his apartment and taken the papers. After beating Ida Werfel, he was thrown out of your home. However, Balmorán says that he reappeared a while later in the corridor, calling for Pistauer. Then, possibly in his cups, he mustered the courage to call him out. He demanded to know who'd looted his studio. Among other things, they'd taken the thesis that he'd written for his degree. When he left, he stumbled upon your son and asked him to accompany him. He wanted to have a witness to his conversation with Martínez."

"Don't believe a quarter, not even a tenth, of what Balmorán tells you. Take my word for it: he's an irredeemable mythomaniac. He has been his whole life. No one surpasses him. He very likely fabricated that story over time and must believe it to the letter. At the hospital, Ricardo told me that Pistauer asked him to accompany him. He barely spoke Spanish and wanted my son to explain to the taxi driver how to find his house. They had met that night; they must have been more or less the same age. When they got out to the street, a car parked in front of the building met them with gunshots. Ricardo didn't even notice that Balmorán had followed them. He was also injured; did he tell you? Hence his deformities and undoubtedly his mental imbalance."

"Could it not be possible that the attack was the work of the people targeted by that newly formed commission, who feared the seizure of their assets? Perhaps they wanted to warn your father; thus the attack on his grandson."

"Miguel, don't allow yourself to be seduced by melodrama. No! I repeat, no! If I'm sure of anything, it's that the attack had nothing to do with my father."

"How can you be so sure?"

"For one simple reason: I believe in facts. It was no mystery to anyone that my father was very ill; a few weeks earlier he'd been on the verge of death. He recovered, fortunately, but at the time, we didn't know what would happen. The newspapers reported that, because of his health, he hadn't agreed to be a member of the Council on the Intervention of Enemy Assets, as it was known. Licenciado Cabrera presided over it, as I told you, and, as far as I know, no one ever shot at his children or grandchildren . . . Look, it's always good to speak plainly; the goons were waiting for Pistauer, Arnulfo Briones's stepson. One of them got out of the car to finish him off. Balmorán and my son were hit by stray bullets, as they weren't the ones being targeted. If what they were trying to do was make my father nervous, then why kill the stepson of Briones, a man with long ties to the Germans? He had, or had had, important business interests with them. How odd! Balmorán never told me about Martínez's reappearance to get Pistauer out of the building."

"Perhaps he also fabricated that detail and now repeats it mechanically," Del Solar said, tired of the intensity that had emanated from Delfina since the start of the conversation.

"You don't need to tell me about his mythomania, I'm the first to have suffered from it, but he might have told the truth once," she replied incoherently, and then asked, "What exactly did he tell you?"

He repeated the details of the episode. Martínez's presence, the immediate departure of the Austrian. Balmorán's request to Delfina's son to accompany him to the street as a witness.

"Come, let's go to the garden and cut some flowers!" exclaimed the hostess suddenly, as if she'd grown tired of listening to nonsense.

They walked to the hollow in the back of the garden. They went down to a stream bed. She was carrying pruning shears. He couldn't say if she was nervous, but she was distracted. Beside the stream she fell onto a bench and motioned for him to do the same. She then called to a boy who was placing stones on a sort of homemade dike, a primitive dam; she handed him the scissors, told him to cut some birds-of-paradise, but first go to the kitchen and ask for a couple of whiskeys.

"Perhaps I'll have a coffee," Del Solar ventured.

"I don't think it's strictly the time to begin drinking, but with this heat one can allow oneself certain flexibility, don't you think?" Delfina replied. Then, with the same sullen, refocused air, in a dry voice that reminded him of the end of their first encounter, she continued, "Perhaps the incident will never be cleared up. My son's lung was pierced, as I told you; he died when he was just twenty-two. He was never able to recover; for those couple of years he lived as an invalid. One would assume, then, that I would be the first person interested in the facts being cleared up, and in the culprit or culprits, if they're still alive, being punished with the full weight of the law. However, that isn't the case. Why dig deeper into this? My father was of the opinion that in politics, when a battle was lost, it was best to bury the past and immediately start fresh. It's been so long! Why stir up these stories when you know beforehand that nothing will come of it?"

"You think it's impossible?"

"As do you."

"I'm not so sure; rather, I don't know. I'm simply trying to investigate an era. As I told you at the beginning, I read a series of documents that provided a starting point for my new book; the dossier on the activities of German agents in Mexico alluded to crimes that took place in the building where you lived at the time. I'm very aware of the grotesque nature of what must seem like a parody of a police investigation. I hope you'll forgive me. When I read that dossier I didn't find your name; I'd completely forgotten that your son was one of the victims. But if I must be honest, if I'd known, I still would have imposed on you."

"Thank you for saying that. But as I've already told you, in my son's case, it was a mistake," she insisted, churlish, as if talking to a child who was determined not to understand something easy. "The crimes to which that dossier certainly refers were those of Pistauer and Arnulfo, Eduviges's brother."

"Do you also think he was killed?"

"Of course. And look, I'm sure the case must have been

solved. My father told me not to lift a finger. The authorities had all the leads they needed. If there were culprits, they were certainly punished."

"There were bound to be culprits. You just told me that Pistauer and Arnulfo Briones were killed."

"One sometimes talks just to talk . . . But yes, you're right. There were crimes, and there were criminals; the latter were surely punished in due time. Why try to investigate the case thirty years later? I don't intend to cover for anyone. That's all I need! I just want to tell you that the situation was very complicated. There were very complex interests at work. The world in which Briones moved was decidedly dark; those people were doing crazy things; they were capable of anything out of desperation. I consider myself someone capable of acting in cold blood. Few things rile me, I mean, upset me." She took a deep breath; her eyes lit up. She seemed to be searching for the words to confide in him, but she stopped in time: "Yes, yes, several currents were at play, some very murky. That Martínez, to whom you alluded, worked for your uncle."

"For whom?"

"He worked for Arnulfo Briones."

"Briones wasn't my uncle. Eduviges was my aunt, yes, but only by marriage. Her husband was my mother's cousin." Delfina let out another of her usual guffaws, a short, dry croak.

"I'm delighted that you find that relationship vexing. Look, I'm very easy-going. But we were talking about Martínez, weren't we? I also met him. One day he appeared at the gallery, at the request, he said, of someone very important who at the time preferred to remain in the shadows, to choose a painting to present to some big shot whom he couldn't name. He wasn't authorized to do so, he said. I didn't have the slightest interest in asking him anything, which apparently baffled him. It's possible that he thought that with all the pretension and mystery I was going to give him preferential treatment, dance to whatever music he was playing; in short, I don't know what he expected of me. I could tell within a few minutes that he had no idea what painting was; what interested him least was seeing the paintings I'd begun to show him. He asked me one or two rather absurd personal questions. For a moment I suspected that creepy little man was trying to woo me. He waved his arms incoherently as he spoke. He was a mess. At times he seemed unable to hold his gaze; at others, he stared into my eyes, as if to hypnotize me. Look, Miguel, I was truly lucky to have a father who one day was a cabinet minister and the next had to pack up and go into exile, and vice versa. Don't forget that I grew up in very turbulent times. Living in that environment as a child, whether I wanted it or not, sharpened my sixth sense. Within five minutes of dealing with that clown, I was sure I was standing in front of a dangerous type, certainly in the service of someone. There's a certain type of man who's unable to act on his own. He was one of those. I told one of my employees to take care of the client, I said goodbye as naturally as possible, and I locked myself in my office. I ordered my secretary not to interrupt me that morning for any reason. But Martínez was a leech. He returned two or three times, perhaps more. He befriended the girls who worked for me. I also began to run into him in the building where I lived, the Minerva, as you know. It was always the same, he wanted to strike up a conversation, but I would avoid him, perhaps with a little more haughtiness than usual, to make him feel that we weren't from the same milieu, and to show him that he didn't frighten me. I asked my chauffeur, a man who had my brother Andrés's strictest confidence, to follow him. I learned that he worked for Briones, that he visited the Werfels, Balmorán, the doorwoman, who spent part of her time in Eduviges's apartment, where Arnulfo had his office. I tried to warn Ida, who refused to listen to me, determined to consider him a fiery Latino driven mad by her white bosom. You already know the outcome. He had to be removed from the party when he lashed out at her. Imagine my surprise when I saw him sitting, pretty as you please, in my living room. No one had invited him. It would never have occurred to me! He showed up when there were already people in the house. I couldn't afford a scene; otherwise I would have sent him away from the start. You must know the kind of atmosphere that reigned in the building around November of 1942, with that kind of riffraff always hanging on our coattails."

They had brought the whiskey. Delfina ordered some canapés and coffee. She never asked, apparently, what others wanted. She had remained silent, as if lost in her memories. She took an art magazine out of her bag and handed it to him, opened to a page with photos of a recent painting. While Del Solar read absentmindedly, the hostess, glass in hand, went to talk to the gardener. He saw them walking along a path at the edge of the stream, gesturing, pointing to some climbing plants with tiny yellow flowers, disappearing; after a while she returned alone to the bench, without a single hair having moved, her skirt wrinkled, or her makeup smudged. She knew the secret of being impeccable. She walked toward him with a serious air. The severity of a tribunal that contrasted with the garden's rich colors. She seemed surprised at how quickly someone had placed a plate of taquitos, cups, and a coffee pot in front of him. As she served him, she spoke again:

"You're a historian, not a novelist, that's why I can talk about matters I don't usually air. I know to whom I can talk. As you can see," she said with her tidiest smile, "I haven't lost my sixth sense. I detest talking about my personal tragedies, but I must tell you that the death of Ricardo, my son, was the hardest blow I've ever suffered in my life; shortly afterward, my father's followed. I feel guilty about both, not for having caused them, of course. They are the two people I loved most, the only ones if I may be so bold. They were in fact the men of my life, and I failed them both."

Del Solar listened to Delfina's story, which she detailed in a dispassionate voice, as if emotion, if it existed, always lingered in the background, laggard, despite certain emphases produced rather by adjectivization.

She had been the only woman among five brothers. The youngest. Her parents and siblings loved her dearly. This always made her feel very powerful, but at the same time bound by an iron frame. She could never go out alone; she was controlled by friends, places, schedules. When she left the cinema, the theater, a party, there was a car and driver waiting for her. Because of this she was already married before turning twenty. And within a week she regretted it. Cristóbal Rubio, the man she had chosen, turned out to be a real lout. He kept her even more locked up than when she was single; he treated her badly, even rationing her books; he read her diaries and commented on them, laughing and telling lurid jokes. He got her pregnant almost immediately. He saw her as a business, a good investment, and he didn't hide it. This was perhaps what offended her most: that her body represented for him a kind of profitable enterprise. After three months she couldn't take it anymore and talked to her parents. She wanted to return home. Cristóbal insisted on living with her. They gave him a room in the back, where the garages once stood, a servant's room of sorts that he accepted without the slightest dignity. They didn't have relations again. When her son was born, they registered his birth and then separated. Her father and brothers took charge of the divorce, and

she, in the meantime, moved to New York, where her cousin
Rosa's husband had set up a business. She spent almost two
years with them. Rosa had at the time a nine- or ten-year-old
son, Gabriel. She became interested in studying again; she led
a very intense life—theater, music, galleries, parties of various sorts, what she'd hoped for when she decided to marry, the
conquest of a space where she could develop her personality,
not a descent into the grave. She returned to Mexico in 1926.
Shortly afterward, her father broke with Calles, and she accompanied him into exile. She spent seven years in Europe. Upon
her return she settled into a house belonging to her mother in
Colonia San Rafael. In 1934, a divorcée living alone was always
surrounded by an aura of scandal. She took the risk. She was a
friend to everyone who was truly worth it. With minimal effort,
she become one of the city's most stylish women. Saying it gave
her obvious delight. Shortly afterward, her mother died, and
her father began to decline. He developed a very painful kid-
ney ailment. He then went on a business trip to Chiapas and
Guatemala from which he returned with a very rebellious myco-
sis; the doctors detected microscopic fungi under his scalp. At
first it seemed easy to cure and caused only slight discomfort,
but the infection eventually developed into a malignant disease
that spread throughout his entire body. When the disease began,
Dr. Muñoz, his physician, recommended an English clinic spe-
cializing in tropical diseases. They set sail again; both alone
for the first time, which had been the dream of her childhood
and adolescence, and she began to call him "Licenciado," just
as her mother had. In London he was immediately admitted to
the clinic, where she visited him daily. During a dinner at the
embassy, she stumbled again upon Cristóbal Rubio, the father
of her son, whom she scarcely remembered. She would never
quite understand, she said, what madness had overcome her. As

an unmarried woman, when she chose him with absolute indifference as her husband, she'd felt little more than superficial attraction to him. He was handsome, well dressed, and well spoken; that was all. But on the night of the encounter in London, she returned to her hotel troubled. Once they went to the theater and again to a dance; less than a week had passed when he had proposed a quick trip to Venice. She'd fallen in love with him; she was unable to say otherwise. She invented a thousand lies to be away from her father for a few days. She told him that some former classmates were getting together in Italy. The Licenciado said nothing; he never offered the slightest reproach nor alluded to those days when Delfina left him alone in a hospital. All he asked of her was that she not call him "Licenciado," as her mother had, because it saddened him. She returned from that journey shattered. In Paris, Cristóbal exacted revenge for what he called the mistreatment she and her family had inflicted on him a dozen years before. He spared no humiliation. She never saw Venice; she decided to interrupt her trip and return immediately, more distraught than ever, to her father's side. She told him that she'd cut short the outing because she couldn't bear the idea of leaving him in mercenary hands. He offered no comment, but the change in their relationship was irreparable. He died shortly after her son, Ricardo. After returning to Mexico, they saw each other frequently. She lunched at her father's home once or twice a week; he, on the other hand, stopped visiting her and did so only after the attack on Ricardo; he always apologized, alluding to his ailments; he frequented, instead, her brothers' homes. He promised to go to the opening of the gallery, if only for a few minutes. But at the last minute he called to beg off. His health didn't allow it.

Delfina poured out the words with exactness, without haste or alteration. She seemed to be reading someone else's story.

However, Del Solar thought he perceived a genuine current of emotion. A current that led nowhere, without any desire to establish communication, preferring instead, like everything else in her, to remain locked up, steeping.

"Did he find out with whom and where you spent those couple of days?" Del Solar asked, as if emerging from a hypnotic trance.

"The greatest mistake of my life!" Delfina said, not answering his question. "My flight to Paris. A couple of days with fatal consequences! Even now I feel like I'm still paying for it. When we returned to Mexico, Ricardo was about fourteen years old, in full adolescence. Then I met a Colombian and began to toy with the idea of marrying him. I'd lived alone for a long time and was starting to grow bored. But Ricardo was at the worst age to understand certain things. We'd spoiled him too much, I, of course, but also my parents, my brothers, his nanny. He was tied to my apron strings; it seemed that he hadn't developed his individuality as he should have; he began to become jealous, to act out violently. We'd recently experienced a family tragedy that I still recall with horror. Rosa, my mother's niece, with whom I lived in New York after my divorce, had just died. The way Gabriel and Rosa devoured each other still makes me shiver. After she was widowed, the poor woman did nothing but foolish things. Her husband had left her a lot of money, and she decided to move to Mexico. After three or four years here, she found a suitor. Gabrielito, her son, went crazy. He spied on her, blackmailed her, said horrible things to her, and then, when Rosa broke down in tears, he threw himself at her feet, hysterical. He even attempted suicide. The suitor got fed up, fought with my cousin, and finally broke off the engagement. Rosa came to tell me the news with a radiant air. She understood that the marriage would have been impossible. She didn't want to get married, she told me, she'd allowed things to go on by inertia, perhaps just to give Gabrielito a father, which he'd shown he didn't need. Canceling the wedding, she claimed, almost shouting, made her feel free, happy. I wasn't as convinced. There was an excessive fever in her words; her eyes sparkled too much; she gestured with an exaggeration more suited to the circus. Soon after, Gabriel came to pick her up. He seemed genuinely happy. Proud and modest at the same time, without gloating too much in his victory, but without hiding the happiness it gave him either. They'd opted for a change of scenery, a trip to Europe. They would set sail in a few days from Veracruz, bound for Cherbourg. They deserved that trip, Rosa said; both of their nerves were frayed. Later, in the years that followed, I saw very little of them. They returned two or three times, transformed into a terrifying couple. Rosa was a skeleton; they said she was injecting morphine. The immense greenish circles under her eyes had reduced her to a caricature; a tragic doll, operated by a string mechanism, so unconscious and somnambulistic were her gestures. All she did was talk about her son, how happy she'd been with him, the wonderful future that awaited them, his intelligence and sensitivity, how happy, she repeated over and over, she'd been during her time abroad. A tango was playing on the radio; Rosa got up, turned up the volume, and began to dance alone; she doubled over, looked to be at the point of falling to pieces, straightened up, then took a few long steps: an absolute image of insanity. At the end of the tango I went to the radio and turned it off. She sat down next to me again and continued to talk about her son. Gabriel had taught her to enjoy Venice, where they usually resided. Thanks to Gabrielito she was able to appreciate the Giorgiones, the Crivellis, and the Tizianos. Thanks to Gabrielito she'd learned to love, above all things, the baroque music of the Venetians and also Stravinsky, whom they often happened upon during their walks. Gabriel behaved with his usual modesty. He listened to his mother with a sort of veneration, though at all times he asked her to speak about herself and not about him. But when her son wasn't present, Rosa could only talk about her lovers. Perhaps fictitious, nonexistent, who knew! Italian gigolos with whom she said she spent whole days dancing tangos; German boys who'd introduced her to the most rakish pleasures; Black men from the Sudan who, like panthers, licked her body before devouring it. Over time, her monologues became more and more lurid, surprising, insufferable. She'd pause suddenly, get up, put a foxtrot on the phonograph, and begin to dance, always alone, her left hand outstretched and her right against her abdomen. She'd sit down again, continue to talk about viscous liquids spilled on her thighs, describe her true discoveries in Mexico, as she called them—that is, her encounters with chauffeurs, soldiers, doormen, bricklayers—with a verbal delirium that became increasingly alarming. One morning my nephew called to let me know that his mother was very ill, that the doctor thought her death was imminent. I rushed to her home. The boy was distraught. Although he was responsible for all of Rosa's manias, I was very fond of him. He was the image of innocence, helplessness, and even health in the face of my cousin's ruin. She could barely speak. Rosa, in fact, was in her last moments. She'd woken up without recognizing anyone; the doctor repeated that there was nothing he could do. When I entered her bedroom, she half sat up: a gaunt, emaciated old woman with a ghastly appearance. She looked for her son, and when her eyes found him she began to insult and curse him. It was a horrific moment. Gabriel listened to her without moving, without speaking, blinded by the revelation of the fierce and animal hatred, by its inconceivable magnitude. She said the filthiest, most disgusting things to him, things I could never repeat. She died with a curse on her lips. It was the worst scene I've ever been forced to witness. I took Gabriel to the home of my brother Bernardo, the archaeologist. He spent a few days there in a state of near unconsciousness. Later he returned to Italy. We heard little about him, but almost always ugly things. He'd resolved to die, I imagine, although it took him several years to do so. That's why, when I started dating my Colombian beau and noticed the tantrums that Ricardo took pleasure in, I decided to make a clean break. I was terrified that history would repeat itself. I wasn't Rosa, of course, but I wanted to take the necessary steps. I sent him to study in California. We saw each other once and even twice a year. I married, and the marriage didn't last, but for reasons unrelated to my relationship with my son. Ricardo was a magnificent boy and then young man. My father adored him. I went to see him, and he came to visit us during vacation. In 1942, when he returned for good, he was almost twenty. Permanently! He wanted to be an architect. He would be fifty now. How dreadful! I can't imagine him at that age; it makes me dizzy. To think that such a radiant young man would have begun to grow old! The very idea seems monstrous to me. I still haven't recovered; sometimes it seems as if I'm not going to make it," she said with sudden violence. "What would I gain by knowing who shot him? The reason, I know, I've already told you: it was an accident. The stupidity of chance. Punishment, I tell myself sometimes, for failing my father when he was ill, for abandoning him in a hospital in a strange land. Punishment for sending my son abroad and separating him from me when he needed me most, all so I could love at my leisure a Colombian with emerald eyes who in the end didn't even turn out to be my type. I'll tell you, I did it for his sake; I didn't want to repeat, even if it were on another level, what happened to my cousin and to Gabriel. Ricardo was very sensitive; he was capable of becoming too attached to me. My security could have destroyed his."

A young man appeared to let them know that the guests had begun to arrive. Delfina came out of her trance. They got up, climbed the hill, and headed for the house. The terrace began to fill with people. Malú, Delfina's inescapable sister-in-law, her two nieces, the Vélezes, Julio and Ruth Escobedo, and many, many more people were there. The hostess began to circulate, to offer her bare cheeks for kisses, to chat with the guests, to show them the new plants.

Lunch came and went. Miguel del Solar would have liked to speak to Escobedo and his wife, but they were seated at distant tables and left before the others had finished eating. After a while he retired to his room. He read for several hours a book by Dickens, *Our Mutual Friend*, which he took from a shelf in the living room. He thought of Ida Werfel, about the comments he heard Emma, her daughter, repeat about *The Garden of Juan Fernández*, a play by Tirso de Molina where no one was who they claimed to be, in which the characters unfolded continuously, adopting the most absurd masks, as if it were the only way of living with others. The same thing happened in Dickens's novel. The same impersonation by characters, false names, fictional biographies. He remembers the first time he lunched at Delfina's house; she talked about her thesis on the split personality in the Victorian novel. That is, concealment, the mask, the confusion of true identity. Why did that theme always come up? Where was it pointing? Who was pretending to be who they were not? Someone knocked on the door to tell him that they were about to serve dinner. In the kitchen he found only Malú Uribe and Rosario, Delfina's niece; the rest of the guests had gone. Delfina, they told him, had gone to bed; she was tired and had a migraine. He barely spoke; he was also tired, and the two women were discussing something about taxes that he neither understood nor was interested in understanding.

SERGIO PITOL

He returned to his room. He continued to read Dickens and
then slept for a few hours. He'd told Delfina that he'd return
to Mexico City in the morning. He wanted to eat and spend
that Sunday afternoon with his children. He still wanted to
ask Delfina several more questions. In reality, all of them. The
superintendent of the Minerva had alluded to an old German
woman who lived like a vegetable in an apartment on the top
floor. Perhaps from among the group of German refugees in
Mexico. Perhaps a witness to the underground struggles that
took place in the building. That morning, before saying goodbye,
when Del Solar attempted to talk to Delfina, she seemed like
steel. She made him repeat the first question twice, pretending
not to understand it; she then answered him with a curt smile.

"How would I know who lives in a building that I haven't
set foot in for almost thirty years? I've already told you; I know
very little, nothing, about what was going on there. The only
thing I can tell you is that some people were committed to making the air unbreathable. You, Miguel, and you must forgive me
for saying this, have chosen the wrong interlocutor. I am, if I
may, an extremely limited woman; I involve myself in very few
things: my gallery, my painters, the health and happiness of a
small group of friends and family. I could not care less about anything else. Talk to Eduviges; she's always been in the middle of
everything; she'll tell you who is who, who lives in what house,
who works in what office. I concern myself with other matters."

Miguel del Solar returned to Mexico City. As he drove
his car he remembered Delfina's air of withdrawal, a kind of
physical selfishness, a refusal to surrender emanating from her
body, and wondered why she'd invited him to spend the weekend in Cuernavaca. Other than the two women in her family, only he'd enjoyed that privilege. To talk to him exclusively
about her personal life? To show him that behind that grim and

ascetic exterior, blood had once coursed, and passions had once taken refuge and ignited? Her father, a pair of insignificant husbands who seemed like interchangeable profiles in her biography, friends, a son. Why did she seem to know everything and refuse to say anything that might shed light on what happened in her home one night thirty years ago? Why would she want him to abandon his inquiries?

On that beautiful spring morning it was more than obvious that he'd lost time and even his way in his determination to solve the Minerva affair. He was lost among the trees, and they were hiding the forest from him.

He was certain of only one thing. That day, when he arrived in Mexico City, he would write to England, inform the university of his decision not to return. He would terminate his contract, as he'd decided to stay to work in his country, and two hours later, standing in front of his house, it occurred to him that Delfina had acted in a more than Machiavellian way, and that she hadn't attempted to make him lose interest in the Minerva affair; with her elusive manner and the various smacks to the head she'd given him, she'd only managed to pique his curiosity. Her words were meant to direct him toward certain clues, inviting him, above all, to return to the family, to question Eduviges.

CHAPTER 8

Portrait of a Diva

"I WAS ONLY AT TWO OR three of Ida Werfel's talks for society ladies," said Ruth Escobedo, with an expression of absolute skepticism, "and I was also able to be present at some of her happenings on different occasions. My experience is different from Julio's for the simple reason that her dealings with women were different. There were those who fell to their knees before her. Ida followed a kind of ritual: she'd arrive to the room, look for the center chair, and survey her surroundings. She'd smile, she'd nod slightly, and everyone acted as if a particle of the immense wisdom dispensed by that Sophonisba had touched their soul. Is that how you say it, Julio? Look at him!" she said in a screeching voice to Miguel del Solar. "When he doesn't want to listen to me, he tunes out. I'm afraid one day he'll stay that way, in his own world . . ."

"What are you mumbling, Ruth?"

"Nothing . . . After directing a courteous look at the audience, Ida would begin to speak to the people closest to her. Until the moment when, without having to turn up the volume, the only voice that was heard was hers. Her presence always seemed improbable to me, her manners, her wardrobe, her interaction with her daughter. When she noticed that everyone was listening to her, she slowly raised her voice, and began to reel off her stories: 'Allow me to reflect on a scene I had the good fortune to witness. Setting: Munich. Protagonist: the consul of a South American country, whose name I hope you will allow me to omit.'"

"No, Ruth, no, please! Are you really going to tell it again? It's not possible! I've heard that story at least a dozen times, and I have to say that each time it gets worse."

"'Yes, my friends,'" she continued undaunted, "'a consul general of an American country. I frequented an eatery near the university, where I was in the habit of taking a light snack after my morning classes. The consul would order in a stentorian voice two glasses of beer, which he then began to consume at a leisurely pace. It was always two glasses, which he demanded be brought at the same time. After finishing the first, he'd begin with the utmost meticulousness to ingest the second. He needed to have the two steins in front of his eyes. One day I approached him and said, "What is that about, my dear Consul General? Why do you order two steins of beer in advance? Why not one and then, if you still want the other, ask for it in due time? Perhaps at that moment you will no longer want it. You might prefer a soft drink; a glass of magnificent white wine from the Rhine, or simply a cup of fragrant coffee." He looked at me in astonishment, as if I'd said something outrageous, a sacrilege, as if I'd wounded some deeply held conviction. That day the life of our illustrious consul underwent an interesting turn. He began to examine his attitude, analyze it. Two steins of beer every afternoon in both winter and summer! "Why?" he wondered in astonishment. Did drinking them, by chance, provide him any pleasure? He wasn't even sure about that. He'd acted in this same blind way in all other matters of his life. He had to learn to choose; to know why he opted for one thing and not another. He had to learn to be human, to discover the man inside him. From that day forward a new destiny began.' To me, those kinds of stories," Ruth continued, "were nothing but a joke, but people left agog, trembling with emotion. They'd heard the goddess Minerva herself draw back, through apologues and allegories, the veils of an enigma, touch the essence of knowledge, things like that. She made a tidy sum by edifying well-to-do ladies and introducing them to the pleasures of Góngora and Berceo. The funny thing is that she was always on the verge of scuttling everything she'd gained, because of a bizarre, overwhelming passion—purely verbal I hope!—for certain abdominal functions and their consequences. If anyone so much as uttered a word that had the slightest connection to the intestines or their effects, Ida became lost; her burst of laughter could be heard as far as the sidewalk out front. Now that I think of it, that was her greatest pleasure. In her later years, her closest friend was Licenciado Reyes, from the university. They'd die laughing as they altered well-known proverbs. Reyes was very witty: 'No, Ida', he'd say to her, 'a picture's worth a thousand turds,' and from that moment on they'd both go off the deep end with proverbs: 'Actions speak louder than turds,' he'd shout; 'A shitting crow starves,' she'd say; 'Like farter, like son,' both at the same time. Ida celebrated those verbal feats with joy, she savored them and then repeated them at the slightest provocation."

"There you have it! An oversized kid with a fondness for shit!" Julio shouted. "Ida was all that, I admit, but also a lot more. It's difficult to pinpoint her; any definition is reductive. Her work's also uneven. At the end, she just repeated herself; she'd stopped thinking."

"That night," Ruth continued, "they arrived at the party in costume. Do you remember, Julio, what they dressed up as?"

"A lot of people went. It was and wasn't the group we'd decided to invite. Friends were walking around lost among so many different predilections. The gathering turned violent.

Someone was responsible for planting sticks of dynamite in advance. As a matter of fact, the first one exploded in Ida's hands. I never knew if the intention was to entertain or confuse us. The last explosion was the decisive one: the gunshots, one dead and others wounded. The attack on Ida was both beastly and absurd at the same time. Like a harpooned whale, just that dreadful. But, of course, nothing compared to the death of one of the guests."

The discussion of Ida Werfel had been incidental. The meeting with Julio and Ruth Escobedo happened as follows:

Del Solar hadn't seen the painter in recent years. As a newlywed, he often ran into him at the home of an aunt and uncle of Cecilia, his wife. During Delfina's luncheon in Cuernavaca, he was sitting at a table that allowed him to see him from the front, bathed in sun. He must have been sixty-five but looked twenty. The first impression he made was that of a fado singer, his face so dramatic, his expression so sober and dignified. Cuernavaca's dazzling light highlighted his paleness, his perfect bone structure. A gentleman perfectly dressed for a country house: linen pants and jacket, with slight wrinkles where appropriate. Upon seeing him talk to Ruth and the other people seated at his table, it seemed as though his gaze possessed an obsessive, manic fierceness, like that of a rapacious animal, a gopher for example. But his other features belied that gaze. What passions could arise from that tension established between the ferocity of the eyes and the placidness of his other facial traits? He remembered that Cecilia had shown him certain characteristics of his painting that might correspond to those he was observing on his face at that very moment. His paintings suggested a Dionysian world with a sudden note of untamedness and severity, a shudder without which the painting would be purely decorative.

As the luncheon ended, when he attempted to approach

Escobedo to talk, he discovered that the couple had gone. A few days later he phoned him. He reminded him of their meetings from several years ago. He told him about his recent residence in England, about Cecilia's death, about his firm decision to stay in Mexico. In passing, he told him about his desire to begin working on something new concerning 1942. He'd seen him in Cuernavaca, at Delfina Uribe's house, but when he looked for him he'd already left. He'd like to talk to him, if he had no objection, not only about the painting of that period, but also about various aspects of life in the city, and he spoke to him very vaguely about the project. They made an appointment.

A few days later he was in Coyoacán. A house full of objects whose pairing made them appear unusual: very simple antique furniture, almost conventual, and a world of strange, cheerful, and bright objects that ran from the elementary to the most sophisticated. Small handmade toys, shiny spheres, enormous wineglasses of Bohemia crystal, and carts overflowing with old multicolored hardware, baroque angels, Talavera from Puebla, various exceptional paintings, almost all his.

As he approached to greet him, Del Solar felt a flash of panic. The stark face, the razor-sharp profile, the precise facial bones he'd admired in Cuernavaca, the Luso-Arabic dramatic quality, each had been transformed into something else, its opposite. The face in front of him was soft and not only showed the painter's age but added years: an old man with a lost gaze who slurred his words as if his dentures were loose.

"It was a true movement; he was inspired by a great truth," he said. "Unlike the muralists, most of us had traveled little; we did so later, once we were known, when we began to have a little money to spare. We had little knowledge; we desperately wanted to expand it. What saves much of the pictorial work of the twenties and thirties, early forties, is its conviction, its sense of play, and a lack of complacency with what has been achieved. Our sense of curiosity was very much alive. I can say this without equivocation: it was the finest moment of Mexican painting. We painted, we had fun, from time to time we fought. We had a great time."

"I'll say we had a great time," Ruth said suddenly, a slight, gaunt woman, dressed in an old Chinese brocade robe. "We didn't have two cents to rub together. When we did come into a little money, we didn't even get to enjoy it. We had to use it to pay duns. Our rent was only forty or fifty pesos—a pittance!—and yet we didn't even always have that at the end of the month. But we had a lot of fun. There wasn't a single night that we didn't tie one on."

"The merit of painting during that period," the painter hurried to interrupt, as if he'd taken advantage of the time his wife was talking to collect his thoughts, "although to be honest I don't know if it's a merit or mere accident, was that it attempted to focus on the visual from other strongholds. Not just from the political; that was our fundamental difference from the previous generation. Poetry was for many artists of my time the real starting point. It was painting charged with literary allusions, and yet for good artists the result was painting, very good painting. Did you tell me you're interested in 1942? If I'm not mistaken that was the year of Tamayo's dogs howling at the moon, wasn't it? When the painter attempts to yield to reality, he turns it into an enigma. That's much clearer now."

"Ah, the blissful perspective that comes with age!" Ruth said in a voice soaked in alcohol and unexpected sarcasm. She was returning to the studio just then with cups of coffee. "I prefer those times, from before we became cosmopolitan." Then, addressing Del Solar as she passed him a cup, she said in a more reasonable voice: "Nothing makes me as happy as when

Julio returns to his old subjects . . . If you compare a painting from today with one of his earlier ones, you'll think he hasn't changed."

"What? Only Ruth could think of something like that! I haven't changed? How can you say such a ridiculous thing? Talking about one's own work is almost always a fool's errand. The artist is the person who sees it the least, he's too close. One experiences differently what he did and what he's doing. I can't turn my head and look back. Of course, I can; what I mean is that I gain nothing from it. All I know is that a few things, who knows why, turned out to be true, and the rest, who also knows why, fell by the wayside. One is the least suitable to talk about his own work. If one says stupid things, imagine his wife. I've tried several paths, without necessarily intending to. I'm not one to say: today I'm going to paint an abstract, today I feel expressionist, today I'm going to become the Goya of our time. No, those are a fool's tricks for a fool's consumption; things emerge differently. I've returned to many of my initial themes."

"That was the same thing I said, only that I did it in just one sentence and you in a bunch of mumbo jumbo that was neither clear nor amusing."

"Why do you always have to insist, Ruth? I'm saying something entirely different from what you said. My painting can't have the same spontaneity as thirty years ago. If I'd continued to paint what I was painting then, my paintings would seem dead now. Those of today seem the same as those from before, but that's only achieved through patience, working daily, seeing other artists' paintings, reading, conquering one's own freedom. It's not easy at all. I'm going to show you something. Excuse me . . ." He got up, went to the door, didn't open it, took a few steps back, went to a large bookcase but didn't take anything out; he turned to where Del Solar and Ruth were, and from the center of the study he stared at them, as if waiting for instructions, his legs apart, his head fallen to one side, his mouth half-open . . .

"Don't stand there like an ostrich! Are you looking for your catalogs? Remember, they're in the bottom drawer, at the very bottom." And in a hushed voice she whispered to the historian: "Do you see? Some don't believe me when I say it; they have to see it. What Delfina is doing to him is unspeakable."

"No, I don't need to look for them," Escobedo said and returned to his seat. "Del Solar isn't particularly interested in painting, but other things that happened at that time. The book you're preparing isn't just about painters, is it?"

"No, although painting will be an important part of it." And he repeated again, with some variation, the introduction he used to present himself to the various people connected to the subject that interested him. He emphasized the dossier he had in his hands and spoke of the crimes that took place in the Minerva Building, the implications of which very likely extended beyond the national sphere. He spoke of Delfina's party and the shooting that happened at the end.

Julio and Ruth Escobedo listened to him with an almost childlike fascination.

"At one time I suspected something and told Delfina," she said. "A case of pure intuition. I used to go to that building often. We had several friends at the Minerva. One of the few places where everyone knew what everyone else was doing. Well, the same thing must happen in poor neighborhoods. The strange thing is that it also happens in an affluent building. And the Minerva was chic. Do you know it? A beautiful building with five or six stories and a central courtyard. To enter any apartment you have to walk along the corridors that surround the courtyard. A glass house. I went many times, sometimes with Julio, others alone, to visit my friends. In addition to the Mexicans, who were probably the minority, there were exiles from Spain and other countries, and the occasional diplomat. A friend of mine had a very good apartment; her name was Ruth, the same as me. Ruth Kerves. Who knows what became of her! She was a biologist, a very fine Hungarian. She lived in Mexico for several years; I don't remember when she left or to where. Costa Rica, I think. It's horrible the way one makes friends and then they just disappear. I spoke to Ruth every day, asked her what I should read, what dress to wear, what medicine to take for my stomach and sinusitis, and I don't even know if she's still alive. I think about her, and I'm overcome with a fit of affection and, you see, she's a ghost. It's been years since I even remembered her existence. She must still be alive. She was very young when she arrived in Mexico. I don't know what her politics were. Liberal, I imagine. She was afraid of everyone. She lived alone with a small son. Her departure from Europe, she told me, had been extremely difficult. She spent a fortune, everything she had, to be able to get the necessary papers. When she got here she started from scratch. I used to love the Spanish refugees' dustups; they were so raucous. She, on the other hand, was tormented by them; they racked her nerves. She couldn't understand why they'd insult each other at the drop of a hat. She was consumed with fear. 'You're going to make yourself sick, Ruth,' I'd tell her. She was terrified of foreigners as well as nationals. To make matters worse, sometimes a character closely linked to the Germans would show up in the corridors of the Minerva. A politician, it seems, who was always down in the dumps. He'd been an apostle of the Cristero insurrection. He even had to leave Mexico for a while. He'd appear and disappear from the country. Ruth lived in terror. The guy, she told me, had intervened to get the Hamburg consulate to deny her brother-in-law a visa. Everything was so mixed up in those days that the guy who'd prevented a Jew from entering Mexico turned out to be married to a German woman whose former husband was Jewish, for whom he obtained documents when it was next to impossible to leave Germany and travel to Mexico. Ruth, like many refugees, I imagine, was understandably a part of a network of communicating vessels. She had to manage a thousand things: whom to be careful of, who could harm her, who could protect her in a desperate situation. The poor woman lived in terror. She left after Ida Werfel arrived in Mexico. If I'm not mistaken, she was the one who got an apartment for Ida in the Minerva. In the beginning I thought Ruth Kerves was seeing things; then I began to notice that it was true. Something queer was happening in that building. I told Delfina about it . . . out of pure intuition."

"It was precisely that party, which I mentioned a moment ago—the one thrown by Delfina Uribe, and at which a young Austrian, Erich Maria Pistauer, was killed—where Ida Werfel was present. I discovered that it was on that occasion that she was attacked by a virulent anti-Semite."

"It was a party in honor of Julio, in case you didn't know. Yes siree, a madman attacked Ida Werfel, and Julio was harassed by another guest, a jealous madman, which is worse. And to think it was a party in his honor!"

Del Solar realized that it was time to begin organizing the information in a certain way: to add that the first husband of Arnulfo Briones's wife, if Ruth was right, was Jewish and therefore the young man who was murdered as well. He needed to collect information and then discard characters, situations; to begin to classify, reconnect with the same informants, and direct the conversation toward those still-obscure points. He noticed how little he'd learned about the starting point of his research: the activities of foreign agents in Mexico during the war. In large part because he hadn't taken it seriously. When his book on 1914

finally came out, he'd begin to work methodically. He'd consult
the official documents, talk with the functionaries and important men of the time. For the moment he could consider his initial meanderings a mere amusement. He was convinced that all
the talk of parties, rags, and rumors would allow him, at the right
time, when the work required discipline, to preserve, even if it
were nothing but a reflection, this tapestry of manias, tastes,
aversions, and sympathies that imbue a place at any given time
with a certain coloring different from others.

"Twenty years before Delfina opened her gallery, we were
already friends," Escobedo said suddenly. "There've been
some difficult moments; every relationship has them. I've told
Ruth more than once that anything can happen, but we're not
going to fight with Delfina. You know her; she can be unbearable; of course, we all have those moments, but hers occur more
frequently and are more intense. In the end, we're old friends,
and sometimes friends become the cross that we bear until the
end. Anyway! Delfina—poor woman!—she is how she is, and
that's how we accept her. Now she's preparing—did she tell
you about it?—an exhibition in New York. She's working with
an American gallery that's not half bad, and, to be honest, she
couldn't have made a more arbitrary selection of paintings. If I
had to give it a name, I would suggest 'A Tribute to Whimsy,' or
even better, 'A Tribute to Nonsense.' There are people alongside whom it's not possible to exhibit; not because I believe
they're worse painters or because I consider myself better. Not
at all. But because exhibiting next to them lends itself to all
kinds of confusion. A work is enhanced or diminished according to those next to it. Albers said something similar about colors in a painting. Canvases can't be hung at random. They must
be paired with others that allow them to exhibit themselves
in the best possible way; if not, they're ruined. It's hard to

believe, but something as simple as that, a question of common sense, Delfina—and remember she's had the gallery for thirty years!—still doesn't understand. I don't know if you noticed the other day in Cuernavaca; she was walking around with her tail between her legs; she refused to talk to me about it. That's why we left before the others."

"We missed the desserts, and hers are always the most delicious."

"If we'd stayed," he said, taking back the floor, "I'd have ended up saying something to her that she wouldn't have liked. As I've told Ruth, we're not going to fight with Delfina. Although she pretends not to understand completely, she's become a burden . . . What can I do? Sometimes I feel like washing my hands of her."

"She told me that she inaugurated her gallery with an exhibition of your work," said Miguel del Solar, trying to return the conversation to that legendary party in 1942.

"She told you that? Did you hear that, Ruth? Yes, in fact, she opened the gallery with an exhibition of mine. She talks as if she'd launched me, as if I owed my prestige to her, when the truth is that by then I'd been painting for more than twenty years. Look . . . Ah, now I remember what I was looking for . . ." He got up, went to a walnut desk, opened a small drawer, and took out a letter, which he handed to him. "This year marks my fiftieth anniversary as a painter. They've asked me to make a statement for a kind of national celebration. I wasn't even seventeen when I exhibited for the first time. So, you tell me, what do I owe Delfina for that showing? I'd already made a name, and I lent it to her. I've known her since she was a little girl. I did it gladly, and I must say that she organized the exhibition carefully, even with a certain emotion."

"Delfina's relationships with men," Ruth said, "have

always been difficult, because at some point in her life they've all been in love with her."

Escobedo put his hands over his ears in a theatrical display, as if he didn't want to hear inanities.

"The party was intended to celebrate the success of the exhibition, wasn't it?" Del Solar insisted more than anything to break the pettish silence that followed Ruth's comment.

"More or less," his voice had returned to normal. "Delfina had already thrown a party on the day of the opening. She went all out. The second celebration was supposed to be different. We wanted to bring together a group of our most intimate friends, ours and hers."

"She was also celebrating her son's return . . ."

"That's what she says now. Yes, yes. A story she invented to make the outcome even more pitiful. She's come to believe it. She's absolutely convinced that it was a party at which a model mother was welcoming her son. Poor thing! The truth is, we wanted to invite a group of friends to dinner and drinks, because we were happy. The exhibition was very well received, and almost all the paintings sold. Already by then it was obvious that the gallery was going to be a success, and, it must be acknowledged, how well she was able to organize it. We'd worked like crazy, Delfina on the material aspects, I with the paintings, and we wanted to celebrate the success with our friends. Yes, Ricardo, her son, had just arrived, and it's also true that she was very happy because of that; she wanted to introduce him to her friends. She'd sent him to study somewhere near San Francisco from a very young age, and he returned all grown up. She was very proud of him, and understandably so, because he was a nice, smart kid. I did a portrait of him during one of his vacations. By the way, I don't know where it is; I haven't seen it in years. His death wounded Delfina deeply. It was a very hard year, as a few months later her father, the passion of her life, also died. We were afraid she would fall apart, but she beat it; if she has anything—when you know her better you'll appreciate it— it's a remarkable animal force. You see the person she puts on display, delicate, exquisite, as if a single harsh word were capable of crushing her, but the truth is she's made of steel. That year we took her to New York with us. Unstoppable! So eager to know new places, to see others again! She moved around the city like a fish in water. She'd lived there several times. We went more or less to encourage her, but she was the one who energized us. Of course, she was living at the expense of her nerves. Her personality suffered for it permanently, that can't be denied. She had a very hard time, terribly hard; the press attacked her with unspeakable viciousness. That's why we tolerate so many things from her."

"I didn't know that it was just a celebration of close friends."

"Because it wasn't. It was supposed to be, but a lot of other people crashed the party." Ruth took the floor. "That was the first strange sign. Someone had invited those people to ruin our night. The first thing I saw when I arrived at the apartment were the Bombón sisters, a very fashionable duo at the time. I think their last name was González. A pair of divine fat women, perfectly tacky. As it turns out they were geniuses; that's what people say, and it must be true, because when I listen to their records I become paralyzed with emotion. They've been vindicated, but at that time they looked like the height of vulgarity, and, of course, in many respects they were. Good God, the way they dressed! In pastel pink and blue, with butterflies embroidered in gold sequins. They were the first ones I saw when I arrived. They were sitting on the sofa in the middle of the living room; I thought I was on the wrong floor. They were wearing orchids on their shoulders and tiny hats with a half veil of chiffon that were divine. Someone had invited them, and they were elated, surrounded by adoring admirers. There was no way anyone could tell them to leave, that it'd been a mistake. There were several cases of this sort, among them a woman, what a disaster, Matilde Arenal, who'd been led to believe that she was the great tragic actress of the time. She arrived accompanied by General Torner, who would marry her later, one of those types who goes around with an air of an éminence grise, and no one ever knows if they're really important or poseurs. That night he started a ruckus with Julio, did they tell you?"

"Very vaguely."

"I'll tell you about it. First, let me tell you who was there."

"Ida Werfel and her daughter," Del Solar said.

"Yes, but they were invited. I was referring to those who'd been invited to ruin the party. Ida was a friend of us all."

Miguel del Solar recounted that he'd recently visited Emma, her daughter, and that she'd given him the impression that she failed to appreciate her mother's role. She'd told him a load of nonsense, emphasizing aspects that weren't necessary. He couldn't say if she'd told him about a genius or a fool.

"Because, if I may, Ida could easily be both," said the painter. "She was a big bag that contained everything: talent, rapacity, discipline, refinement, generosity, vulgarity, even genius. Few people can store all of those qualities inside without exploding from time to time. We learned a lot from Ida. To read, to enjoy what we read, to reflect. She was a woman who caused those of us who knew her to change."

"At times to me she was an outright calamity. In that regard, I agree with Delfina. Yes, she knew her subjects well; she was diligent. There's no doubt about that! But she could be a bore. There was a time when Julio wouldn't miss her lectures."

"I didn't go just to hear her but to see her. She was a

consummate actress. What was truly remarkable was that her immense body never managed to get tied up in knots. She transformed—I don't know if it was because of the belts, corsets, special rods—into some kind of Gothic aspiration. From one moment to the next it looked as if that white whale was about to take flight. Yes, it was a pleasure to listen to her, especially to see her. I never managed to paint her; when I started to draw her I noticed a parodic element that caricatured and diminished her, and that wasn't what I was interested in capturing in her."

"Pirates! They were dressed as pirates! With a black patch on their eye." And then Ruth related the anecdote of the South American consul in Munich whose life Ida transformed through a simple conversation about two glasses of beer.

"The person I least imagined running into that night was Arenal and the general who later became her husband," said Escobedo, who until then had been drawing nervously in a notebook. "Arenal! I dreamed of her! Sinister nightmares! I was afraid of her! The matter of the portrait was from beginning to end an alarming stupidity. I can't understand how Delfina and I could fall into that. A former lover—not General Torner, but an insignificant little mouse, a common rake—asked Delfina who could paint a portrait of the actress, and Delfina recommended me. He even gave me an advance. I had no idea what trouble I was getting myself into. That whateverhisnamewas's plan was very naive. He wanted to organize a kind of promotional campaign in which Matilde Arenal would be presented with a portrait painted by a more or less famous artist. It wasn't a personal gift, but a tribute rendered by the nation's first sons. The cost would be underwritten by the most prominent men in the country. He made lists of important men. He acted as director of the campaign and was probably planning on keeping some of the funds. The only thing I understood from the beginning was that it was all nonsense. Letters were written. It was announced in the press that a group of Matilde Arenal's admirers, which included Mexico's most prominent men—bankers, newspaper publishers, intelligentsia, writers, industrialists—would defray the costs of her portrait. I can't tell you how much the publicity annoyed me! I was interviewed by some small-time reporters who had no idea who I was or what I'd painted. My photo appeared in the most idiotic magazines. It was ridiculous! As for Arenal, every time they asked her about her portrait, she'd give the name of a different painter; she never managed to name me. Deep down she felt humiliated. She wanted Diego Rivera to paint her, or, in the worst case, some famous socialite portrait painter. She posed reluctantly; she didn't do what I asked of her; she constantly got up to see what I'd painted and criticized it. I couldn't take it anymore; I decided to suspend work, to which the patrons responded very timidly. Two or three illustrious men, when interviewed, told the press that they knew nothing about the matter, that they had never given their consent. Others, who'd believed that the picture was going to be raffled, demanded their money be returned when they learned that wasn't the case. As a consequence, the love affair deteriorated and the guy disappeared with what little money he'd collected. I stopped. I'm sure Matilde Arenal must have been happy. Obviously, she didn't want to confess how much she'd been hurt by the lack of response on the part of the important men or by her lover's stinginess. She declared that she didn't intend to acquire the work, despite the fact that our paintings were selling for very little money back in those days. I think they were going to pay me two thousand pesos, more or less, in the end—a pittance.

"The deal fell apart," Ruth exclaimed emphatically, "and everyone ended up on bad terms. The actress with her beau. Both of them with Julio and Delfina. The only ones who remained friends were the last two. They made a deal. Julio wouldn't return the advance, because he'd more than earned it for having to put up with that silly woman's foolishness. In addition, he got to keep the painting, but he had to modify it so that no one would recognize that it was Matilde Arenal."

"I began to redo it. Its name was *The Diva*. There was a slight resemblance to the model, which was natural. I accentuated the gestures and style of a *monstre sacré*, certain grotesque forms. I was certain that no one would recognize Arenal in the figure that finally emerged. A piece-of-shit newspaper, one of those committed to narrating the sad lives of our actresses, played a dirty trick on me. It published a photo of the painting with a note proclaiming that it was an act of ridicule of a well-known actress. It caused me a lot of headaches, including a lawsuit by General Torner, one of the admirers of the true diva, with whom he unexpectedly arrived at Delfina's house that night. The incident wasn't funny in the least. When that man insulted me, I was about to answer his challenge. Fighting a general has a certain suicidal quality!"

"Who'd invited him?"

"A blackmailer," replied Escobedo, without hesitating for two seconds. "A pitiful little man, the same one who'd played the newspaper prank a few days before. In those days I went to the gallery and to Delfina's house every day, which was very close. We worked on my exhibition and the overall organization of the gallery. Delfina bought works by several artists and sometimes asked me to advise her. I don't know how that guy managed to wiggle his way in there; what's certain is that several times I found him talking to the gallery's female employees, offering his opinion on everything. An inarticulate insect, a real galoot. One fine day he came up and greeted me with an unctuous servility that I found disgusting. All the paintings were on the floor, leaning against the walls. We were going to start hanging them. He told me that a person of the greatest importance would be there, if not on the day of the opening, he couldn't be sure of that, then during the first days of the show. He'd asked him to suggest one or two paintings he'd planned to buy, and he thought that the one titled *The Diva* would be the right one. That mooncalf was starting to get on my nerves. When he spoke, he gave me the impression that he wanted me to understand something else, that he was transmitting a signal to me that I didn't pick up. As I said, he was a real piece of work. The next time it became more obvious. He began to tell me about the portrait of Matilde Arenal, and I replied that there was no painting that had anything to do with her; what's more, the one he wanted, *The Diva*, wasn't for sale, because both I and the owner of the gallery had decided to keep it for the time being. That clown's information was full of holes about what'd happened. He seemed to give more importance to the incident than it really had. I imagine he'd found out from the staff about some of the circumstances surrounding the painting and had digested incorrectly the articles of certain tabloid columnists when the campaign was suspended." He paused, seemingly lost in the past, to visualize the anecdote. He turned to Del Solar and, surprisingly, asked, "Are you a hunter?"

"What?" Del Solar asked, puzzled.

"Do you ever go hunting?"

"No . . . Well, as a boy. Near Córdoba, in the sugar mill where my father worked. That was a long time ago. I used a BB gun."

"In an open field?"

"In the backyard. Sometimes from the terrace. I shot thrushes. And sometimes also in the canals, when we went to the river. But that's not hunting."

"I'm afraid to say it doesn't feel the same. When hunting

in a reserve, or in the middle of the woods, there's a time when, once the site is set, the weapon is ready, one begins to sense the closeness of the prey. The dogs become excited. All the senses are sharpened. The body is lying in wait. A magnificent moment. You should hunt again; feeling that moment of alertness in the body is one of the most stimulating sensations that anyone can know. Sometimes, very rarely, something akin to that happens in the middle of painting."

"Would you care to tell us where all this is coming from, Julio?" his wife interrupted in a voice that, for the first time, sounded genuinely distressed to Del Solar. "You were telling the professor about your problems with General Torner."

"I know very well what I'm saying, Ruth. I was talking to him about a blackmailer. I can't remember his name. What does it matter! The name is the least important!"

"Martínez!"

"Indeed. Martínez. How did you know? You couldn't have known him, he . . . How old are you . . . No, of course you didn't know him."

"I've heard a lot about him in recent weeks."

"He asked me if I was willing to pay a commission if he sold a painting of mine to a very important man. I told him that he needed to arrange that with the gallery. I didn't involve myself in sales. He looked at me all at once with hatred, contempt, and distrust. At one time, as I said, I often went hunting. In my student days. Later with Victorio Mantua, we went several times to hunt deer in the Huasteca and pumas south of Veracruz. I haven't been in years. One day I'll show you my guns."

Miguel del Solar began to grow impatient. Ruth approached him and said in his ear:

"Don't let him wander off like that. I'm afraid one day he won't come back."

"He wanted a sales commission?"

"I'm getting there; don't think I'm lost. Ignore my wife; everything's under control. Yes, it started there. He didn't become discouraged when I referred him to Delfina. I've already told you the feeling of the hunter when he feels the closeness of the prey. At that moment that idiot felt it. I noticed it suddenly. I almost fell down in surprise. He was living the excitement of the tracking dog when he catches the rabbit's scent, or that of the hunter when he learns he's close to the prey. That man was pursuing me. He showed his dirty horse teeth, stuttered, looked erratically around us, as if he suspected the conversation might be overheard; then he fixed his madman's gaze on me. I was puzzled. I had a psychopath in front of me. That was plain to see. But what was wrong with him? What did he want? I don't deny for a moment that I was nervous. One suddenly feels guilty in front of that kind of person about something he can't even pinpoint, guilty of everything, of breathing. Do you remember the young tradesman in *Crime and Punishment*, the one who in a moment of contrition confesses that he's the murderer of the old moneylender, whom, if I remember correctly, he barely knows? That moron Martínez approached me with a grimace that he attempted to disguise as a smile. He took me by the arm and said to me: 'What if you pay me something in advance? I assure you no one will bother you. I give you my word of honor.' I simply didn't understand. I told him so, and he blurted out something more or less like: 'That's very cautious of you, very delicate! Refined and romantic! No? But what about when it's a matter of tarnishing a person's reputation, stabbing a lady in the back? Because to me, a woman, even if she's an actress, is still a lady. They've already set the prices; I saw the list. You pay me half in advance and nothing happens. A military officer is interested in protecting that lady; I assure you he won't ever find out.

I can come forward and swear that the woman in the picture, the famous "diva," is my sister; that's how far I'm willing to go.' I burst out laughing. For a moment I thought that clown was a comedian and that his talents were brilliant. I'd been alarmed at first. I was still laughing when Delfina came in with someone, I think with you, Ruth."

"Don't put me in your story. This is the first time I've heard these details."

"I've told it a thousand times."

"Sure, to Delfina. All I knew was that it was the same person who tried to strangle Ida."

"What do you mean 'strangle' her! . . . Yes, he was the one who headbutted her and would have struck her if Bernardo Uribe hadn't stopped him."

"He did strike her. I saw him headbutt her ample bosom. He kicked her too. No one knows why."

"I'm sure he would've attacked me too if Delfina hadn't shown up with someone else at that moment. I was certain it was you, Ruth. I noticed that my laughter had riled him. He was haggard. His physical disintegration became more evident than usual, his tics more pronounced. Under his breath, whistling the words, he told me to think about it, that he was giving me a couple of days to consider it. Three days later, he called me on the phone and, of course, I told him to go to hell. In an evening newspaper, a photo came out on the gossip page, where I was accused of insulting a respectable actress in a painting. I didn't see him again until the party. I wasn't amused to run into him there, let alone Matilde Arenal and General Torner. Oh, in the meantime, a few days earlier, some nasty articles had reappeared in the entertainment pages, and again the photo with a slanderous caption that tied *The Diva* directly to Matilde Arenal. Well, on the day of the party there was a moment when General

Torner, in a state of intoxication, insulted me, and I wasn't having it."

"You may think him spiritual, but my Julito is also a tiger," Ruth said and laughed buoyantly.

"I don't know how it would've ended. Delfina's brothers, everyone surrounded us. I remember someone grabbed me by the arm. A good friend who worked at the Ministry of Education took me to the dining room and tried to calm me down. They were shouting in the living room. Ruth sat down at the piano and started to play, and the Bombón sisters started to sing. Next we heard the shots, and that's it."

"At times, and Julio is exactly right about this, it looked like the scene had been contrived to distract us while they were killing that young man downstairs," Ruth concluded.

"Who knows! There are things that, no matter how many times you mull them over, reject interpretation. We've taken precious time from Del Solar, and I didn't tell him anything important about that year, the year of the dogs' howling at the moon, about Tamayo . . . And what about Lazo? He was a very good painter, very refined, and an excellent friend. Cardoza wrote somewhere that his painting was the search for an enigma. I don't know if he exhibited that year. 1942? I don't remember."

He was nervous, in a hurry, obviously wanting Del Solar to leave. He finally said he had to finish a job. A set design. He'd started working for the theater precisely at the suggestion of Julio Castellanos. He'd done nothing in the field for twenty-five years. He loved returning to the stage. Another day they'd discuss the painting of that time. They'd talk about Julio Castellanos and María Izquierdo. Both excellent. And where did he place Juan Soriano? They'd have to rediscover Manuel Michel, consider Olga Costa again. A much more original generation than people imagined. Almost all painters in Mexico had, at least on one occasion, worked for the theater. Gerzso did a masterful set design for Mozart's *Don Giovanni*. More research was needed. To do monographs . . . He shook his hand and hurried to his studio. Ruth accompanied Del Solar to the door.

"He's been like this for several weeks now," she commented as she said goodbye. "Such urgency, such desperation, such restlessness! Tell Delfina! She's got to know where his intransigence has led him! To be honest, this is no longer a life!"

CHAPTER 9

The Love Parade

"WE'RE LIVING IN A PERIOD OF TRANSITION; this is just between us, but I want to be clear. If my Aunt Eduviges goes on the offensive, she stands to lose. The moment may be ghastly, I won't deny it, not entirely. But neither is it necessary to exaggerate. Antonio, you'll forgive me for saying, Chatita," he said, winking at Amparo, "isn't a saint. We must try to act with a clear mind, without unnecessary illusions; otherwise one is lost."

Miguel del Solar had known Derny since childhood. He was the favorite nephew of all his aunts and uncles. They weren't related by blood. A man of almost fifty. A bitter aftershave that smelled very nice. A small gray-and-green plaid jacket made of marbled wool, and faded dull green trousers. On closer inspection, the age difference between them was no more than ten years. Del Solar was nine when he moved into his aunt and uncle's home, and Derny had begun or was about to begin his law degree at the Libre de Derecho in Mexico City, which at that time created a vast age difference. They hadn't seen each other in a while. He saw him in passing once, while visiting the home of mutual relatives. And a few other times at get-togethers of writer friends, politicians, professors of philosophy, where his presence was always baffling.

Del Solar had been trying without success to communicate with his Aunt Eduviges. It was almost impossible to get her to pick up the phone, and when she did she didn't talk about anything but her trials and tribulations. Antonio had disappeared, a fugitive from the law until his situation cleared up. The authorities harassed her with appraisals, financial statements, and incomprehensible documents. Disgrace. Wounded vanity. She didn't leave the house. She feared running into friends, old and new, having to offer explanations, or having to endure that kind of gleeful condolence with which they greeted her. Staying home made her anxious. She only did so because she had no other choice. But in recent years she'd grown accustomed to going out, to being everywhere. When he had visited her weeks before and had a conversation about the events of 1942 in the Minerva, Del Solar had found himself completely lost. He was fumbling his way through unfamiliar terrain. After interviewing several of the main characters in that drama, the dialogue, when it came time, would have to be different. But she always postponed the meeting. At times, when talking to his cousin Amparo, he again felt the tenor of another time. Del Solar managed to forget the harshness with which she had answered the phone shortly before. Amparo had been his first love. His love at nine years old. Amparo provided him during the call detailed reports of her mother's household affairs, her mood, and her nervous condition, which honestly didn't interest him. Apart from his cousin, he felt no affection for anyone in that home.

Amparo had been a kind of excrescence for her mother that wasn't always bearable. She was a couple of years older than Antonio, with a slightly deformed hand, smaller than the other one, which didn't stop her from playing the piano with a certain grace. It was only a matter of days after moving in with his aunt and uncle that he discovered his cousin's peculiar condition, and only because of his aunt. As a child, she acquired a special art for concealing the defect, of wrapping her arm in a scarf, for example, or carrying her hand casually in her pocket. In the afternoons he'd listen to her practice piano for a while, there where it seemed impossible to hide her physical deformity, but she created a kind of semidarkness in the room and made him sit in a place where it was difficult to see the keys. He remembers the day he finally saw Amparo's hand. His Aunt Eduviges, in a fit of ill humor, alluded to the defect, and not yet satisfied tore away the handkerchief that covered her hand. Del Solar felt almost dizzy, as if the deformity of his cousin's hand had occurred at that very moment before his eyes.

When he returned to Mexico City to study at university nine or ten years later, they began to see each other again. They went to parties together, moved among mutual friends; on Sundays they attended concerts. At that time he encouraged her to study history and was on the verge of convincing her to enroll with him at university. His aunt wouldn't allow it.

When he married, his encounters with that side of his family declined drastically. They moved in different circles. Cecilia, for example, could never tolerate Eduviges or her children. The few times he saw Amparo then, always casually, he found her unpleasant, full of pretension, of absurd verbal mannerisms, of a nostalgia for lost grandeur. Vulgar, stiff, ridiculous, prudish. Cecilia had been right about not wanting to deal with her. But it seemed that something had matured in her recently. Perhaps the blow to the family, her brother's public prosecution, made her more yielding and natural. Cecilia maintained at one time that both Amparo and her mother had settled on the idea of a cousin marriage, and that their marriage had put an end to those expectations, of which Del Solar was never aware. Perhaps that was the reason for the unpleasantness in her demeanor toward him at one time.

Once their relationship had returned to normal, she began

to call him. He told her that her mother had left Mexico City to recover, in order to adapt to the new situation and to be able to face it. She'd felt for several years like the mistress of the world, and the blow had almost driven her mad. A friend from another time, Lola Palacios, with whom she'd fought because Antonio hadn't resolved, as she'd hoped, a legal action that had been forgotten for many years, called her on the phone at all hours, day and night, sometimes in her real voice, other times feigning to be someone else, to insult her, to play crude jokes on her, bursting into offensive laughter and referring to the accusations that hung over Antonio with vulgar adjectives. She was at a country home somewhere near Puebla. She most certainly was spending her days reading and eating. She would take car rides, since, because of her weight, walking was too exhausting. The important thing at the moment was to calm her anxiety. When she returned, she would have a new phone number that would lessen the frequency of the ghostly calls that were a cause of such anguish.

His mother told him one day that Amparo had come to visit them. She wanted to meet the children, and she'd found them charming. They'd also been very delightful. She'd asked him to contact her. When they spoke that night, she extended an invitation to dine the following Sunday at Derny Goenaga's house. She asked if he remembered him. He had visited his home often when they were boys. He owned an advertising company, which he ran himself. On Sundays, he and his wife stayed home and received friends for lunch.

And that's why he was there that day, listening to Derny, who was providing lessons on political wisdom. He recalled that on one occasion, several years before, when talking to his mother about a layover he had in Chicago on his return from England for the purpose of delivering a spate of lectures at Notre Dame, which was relatively close by, his mother commented that

Derny Goenaga had studied in the same place, and went on and on about the brilliant career he'd embarked upon, the fortune he'd made in just a few years, the shrewd way he'd managed it, his gift with people, and so on. The kind of comments that always made him feel that his book publications, his lectures, his doctorate, the academic reputation he'd acquired weren't really worth the effort. That because he hadn't yet made a fortune, he was teetering on the brink of failure.

Derny's house reflected his fortune. Everything came together—the colonial furniture, the classical and contemporary paintings, the accent placed subtly, without pomp, on antiquity—as if to indicate that one couldn't afford to ignore modernity, that the inhabitants of that home were able to appreciate it and do it justice but that, in any case, its function was mere accompaniment, an accessory to the old viceregal carvings that coincided with the family's arrival to the country.

Derny welcomed him with a brotherly embrace and a wide smile that surprised him a little, as he didn't remember their ever having been friends in particular. And Eloísa, his wife, kissed him on the cheek. It was a family reunion. The couple; Arturo, a son in his twenties; his girlfriend; a cousin of Eloísa; a young woman, the widow of some other relative; and the two of them, Amparo and Miguel. A friendly conversation from the first moment, relaxed, despite Derny's obvious tendency to make his guests listen to him and above all to hear himself talk. At times his tone tended toward pontifical.

Del Solar commented how long it had been since they last saw each other. Since before Derny had left for Notre Dame. Derny looked at him in a special way, and Miguel thought he was surprised at how well he remembered his biographical circumstances.

"I'm lying," he corrected himself, "we saw each other

again on your return, the day that bore Herrera Robles graduated. Yes, do you remember? You'd just returned. If I remember
correctly, the party was at a large house on Calle de Durango."

"Exactly. At the house of his grandfather, Don Pablo Robles.
Who told you I was coming back from the United States?"

"You, I imagine. That would've been the most logical. Or
Amparo, or my Aunt Eduviges. Anyway, someone in the family.
It must've been you, that same night."

Derny put a glass in his hand and took him by the arm. He
led him to one end of the room, where a beautiful bronze sculpture stood on a glass table.

"I bought it last year. It's my latest acquisition," he said in a
rather matter-of-fact voice. "I later acquired some other things,
but none like this. I saw it, and I was in awe. I'd left the gallery and walked more than a block when I realized that I had
to go back, that I couldn't imagine life without this piece. The
expressiveness of these Benin bronzes is limitless. Do you like
this one?"

"Very much! I saw a few in London, and others in Vienna.
Two years ago I went to . . ."

"Look," Derny interrupted him almost rudely, "I have to
travel to New York often for work. I take the opportunity to visit
galleries, and sometimes I bring something back. As a young
man, I'd spend hours, days, in the Art Institute of Chicago.
There was no better place to spend a Sunday in winter. Chicago
was an hour away from school. I didn't study at Notre Dame; I
don't know where that confusion came from. Maybe Amparo
made a mistake when she told you. Women, my father used to
say, find one thing the same as the other. I was at a college, also
Jesuit, not far from Chicago. Hence the mistake. Several of us
were Mexicans. To be frank, the academic level was the same.
Jesuits, no matter where they are, are Jesuits. Except a college,

as you know, never has the social prestige of a university. If you ask me, what you're really paying for at Notre Dame is the prestige. The fact, for example, that it has a famous football team."

And he changed the conversation to talk about the Benin bronzes, which he'd seen in Mexico four years before in 1968, during the Olympics. They joined the others, and for a long while the conversation revolved around exhibitions and concerts, movies. Del Solar was impressed by the amount of information they all possessed. They asked about shows and exhibitions that had taken place in London, which he hadn't been able to see during his stay in England but that they had, in London or on some trip that might include New York, Paris, even Mexico City. They were all well traveled, cultured, elegant. They were living, Derny added, through an irreversible period, that is, merely transitory.

"... how hard it must have been for Antonio," said Amparo.

Derny wasn't a pessimist. They were living in a period, he'd already said, that wasn't eternal. Antonio would be back soon. They'd make him pay something, which is normal. If there were errors in the accounts he would have to take responsibility for them, even if his subordinates had committed them.

"We're living through the disastrous consequences of the previous sexennial," Derny continued. "It may surprise you that I talk about it in this way, but I think we need to start thinking in modern terms. It's our obligation to know how to foresee consequences. I haven't become a radical, I warn you. The results of the past administration are obvious. This distasteful rhetoric is its antidote. It's a good thing you live in England, where you won't have to experience the death throes. We have to adapt, equip ourselves in order to, at the appropriate moment, establish our conditions. If I am convinced of anything, it's that we are necessary. Even now, in this year of grace, 1973, at the height of verbal one-upmanship, they don't dare ignore us. They've had to admit that a culture isn't improvised, that good taste can't be reconciled, for reasons of a very different kind, with the majority, at least not in a mechanical way. Perhaps someday! Let's hope! Why not? Maybe in the future things will be different. But that, Miguel, is a while off. Look, people in the north are starting to wake up. They've decided to cultivate themselves. They used to go to San Antonio to go shopping, or to places near the border. Now they take their planes and go to New York to hear Nilsson sing *Elektra*, or to see a good musical. They dine. Have a fling, if possible. And the next morning, they're back home. They're in their offices by ten as if nothing happened. They're still very new, you might say. Yes, they are, but if they work hard, they can make it. Antonio is a smart kid, very levelheaded; that's always been his biggest virtue. He knows that in his situation all he can do is take the hit. He will. I'm sure he'll use the time to improve himself, update his readings, and prepare for his comeback. In time, his friends will smooth everything over so he'll be able to return without a hiccup. But it's essential, of course, Amparo, that your mother remain quiet, please, and not talk."

Del Solar commented that the day he visited his aunt, she told him about the persecution of the Brioneses since the start of the Revolution. According to her, the campaign had something to do with the murder of the young Pistauer, the stepson of Arnulfo Briones, and the attempt to remove Antonio from political life.

"Forgive me, Amparito; forgive me, everyone," Derny said theatrically, "but logic has never been my aunt's strong suit. There isn't the slightest connection between the murder of that young man and the indictment issued against Antonio. None!"

"Of course. Mamá isn't a model of clarity, I know. But think about it, Derny, they may be coincidences, whatever you want, but in some way what she says is true. Every few years the family receives a blow that leaves it teetering. And that's not a fabrication; I lived it as a child. Yes, I agree, the cause of that boy's death, perhaps even that of my Uncle Arnulfo, is different from the problem Antonio has had. And yet . . ."

"Dialectics, Amparo, is the highest product of German idealist philosophy," Derny said surprisingly in a professorial tone. "Hegel was its true architect, not Marx, as the masses believe. One must always emphasize this. There are those who become nervous when one utters the word *dialectical*, partly out of ignorance, but mostly out of fear of a political misunderstanding. Ultimately, it's the same thing. You never have to be afraid of concepts. That's my theory, that's my practice. Dialectics is a Hegelian concept. Thesis. Antithesis. Synthesis. As easy as that. Thesis? The Porfiriato. Antithesis? The Revolution. And the synthesis? The synthesis is all of us. Well, not everyone; that's not possible yet. The synthesis, let's say, is those of us who survived the disaster and those who have joined us. We make up, whether we like it or not, a new materialization of the concept of national unity. The synthesis is precisely those of us who are sitting around this table."

A strange noise could be heard. An awkward hum, close by. Arturo's girlfriend, a blond girl with short, extremely curly hair, was covering her mouth with a glass. That's where the hum seemed to be coming from. Suddenly the contents of the glass began to spill. Could she be gargling? Was she biting the glass? Arturo suddenly erupted into an overexcited laugh. The liquid from his girlfriend's cup splashed onto the tablecloth. The girl laughed as if she were the victim of an attack. Everyone immediately began to speak very loudly. Amparo imposed her husky voice and told a short and rather simple anecdote about a trip she'd made to Xochimilco with some Americans, one of whom had gotten drunk, and everyone present began to laugh uncontrollably. Derny glared at the young couple, especially his son.

"One of these days, Derny, you should speak to Mamá," said Amparo, now in a serious tone. You're one of the few people she listens to. Perhaps it would reassure her to know that the persecution Antonio is being subjected to is part of a dialectical process."

"There are phenomena that, at first sight, are very abstract; one scrutinizes them, and they begin to reveal their truth, their day-to-day clarity. I'm not going to insist insofar as dialectics. But think of our Uncle Arnulfo, whom you've all referred to, and, in the same way, I'd offer my father, to both of whom our life would almost seem like a crime. They made no effort to embrace the phenomenon in its whole, in its process . . . This, whether some like it or not . . . is a dialectical process. Look, we all, in one way or another, collaborate with the government. During their time, that would've been impossible. They were the frontal opposition. Ideas that are now unsustainable. Although I'm afraid attitudes are heating up too much, and there are people making the same serious mistakes again. Now more than ever it's necessary to keep calm, wait for the downpour to fall, for sunny days to return. We provide the government with the cultured, worldly image it so desperately needs, and, in return, it provides us with other services. A tacit pact that benefits us all."

Miguel del Solar wasn't interested in listening to Derny philosophize; he wanted instead to redirect him to 1942, when he often saw him arrive at his aunt and uncle's apartment and sometimes lock himself away (one of the few allowed to do so) with Arnulfo Briones in his office. He ventured that he'd noticed that a kind of historical compromise was being reached, unlike in the past. He said that on several occasions he'd heard Arnulfo Briones scold his sister because her husband taught at the university, which for him was akin to a betrayal. The personality of that man, who was so uncommunicative, with whom conversation was tantamount to an interrogation, was always an enigma to him.

"His black glasses," he concluded, "seemed to separate him from reality. He seemed like such a defenseless old man, so unconfident when walking, so fragile. Imagine that! Then I learned that he was a man of great power, much feared. It's hard to believe."

"The times are different. When you met him he was losing his sight. That upset him. Arnulfo Briones. Yes. He and my father were cousins, but they treated each other like brothers. My father must have been a dozen years older. When I was born, he was already old. After six children, none of whom lived beyond one year old. And I've never been sick a day in my life. I was the last and only one. *Le dernier* . . . On Sundays we were given military training on a ranch near Teotihuacán. We had to be prepared for when the cause required it. More than anything it was physical instruction and moral indoctrination. Now those would be an obsolete pair, veritable relics, an impossible anachronism. Pure thesis!"

"My Uncle Arnulfo had a special fondness for you," said Amparo with a hint of sarcasm. "He considered you his successor. He was determined to turn you into a true crusader of the faith."

"An extension of the thesis, no? I must confess that his theories moved me. He saw the world threatened everywhere. The true faith about to succumb. The family in flames. Sullied principles. *Give our life for them!* was our motto. *Die for Danzig!* What times, good God! National honor, class responsibilities, race. Even at that time that was somewhat barbaric and stale. But to many of us it sounded like bronze. You have no idea what a throng of followers we had. They were fierce! Despite being one of the leaders, Arnulfo Briones wasn't what one would call a popular man. He didn't have the makings of a leader. That's why he stayed in the shadows most of the time. Perhaps his blindness affected him. To conceal it, he behaved with excessive arrogance, which cost him sympathy. I have the impression that in the end, in the world of his ideals and interests, he had more enemies than supporters. Yes, there were those who hated him. In the end he stopped going to the training camp."

"I imagine that must have been the most radical sector of the right."

"You can call it that. It was a group that was entirely convinced that only an iron hand and conservative vision could save the country. People very close to Falangism. They distrusted the Americans because they considered them Judaizers. No, Arnulfo had no leadership skills. His voice, above all, cost him supporters; it was hollow and raspy. One day he gave a speech at the training ground; I was ashamed to hear it in front of my classmates. You could barely understand him. He had no gift for speaking; he repeated his sentences over and over, became confused, started over. A disaster! He must have had other virtues; the ability to negotiate, I imagine. He relied on his reputation of having been a formidable polemicist in earlier times. Either way, he was a figure from another era. Can you imagine if he'd understood our current position!"

Evening fell. They went for a walk in the woods. The youngsters took the opportunity to say goodbye. The other couple did so shortly after. Derny led Del Solar to his study.

"I'm glad to see you," he began again. "I know your books have been successful. Sometimes I've thought about writing, to elaborate on the views that I laid out. Unfortunately, the moment isn't right. Whatever I said, they'd label me a reactionary, attack my father's memory, my business would suffer. I don't work alone. I have partners whom I won't expose just to give me the pleasure of expressing my opinions," he paused; then he added, "In college I learned that perhaps the greatest virtue is prudence. Do you agree? My school might not have been Notre Dame, nor did it have a national football team, but I learned everything there I needed to negotiate the obstacles in this life. Why would I want more, can you tell me?"

Miguel nodded. He said two or three vaguely conventional phrases about education and its practical effects and asked if it would be possible for him to have another cup of coffee before leaving.

His request was received with warmth, one might even say with enthusiasm.

Del Solar began to lay out for Derny the research he intended to carry out on 1942. A mere look into the framework of microhistory. He commented, with all possible discretion and gentleness, that from the crime that had taken place in the Minerva Building—that is, that of Arnulfo Briones's stepson—a government agency had deduced certain movements of German agents. He commented that this seemed bizarre to him, as Arnulfo's sympathies must have been, given his background, his way of thinking, entirely on the side of Germany.

". . . although I just found out," he concluded, "that on his father's side the young man could be Jewish, and that Arnulfo Briones did everything possible to save the boy's father. Strange, don't you think?"

"Look, Miguel, I was very young," Derny commented. He began to speak normally, as if in the absence of the other guests his need for oratory had disappeared. "I was sixteen or seventeen then. And I assure you that there wasn't a more naive boy in Mexico. Imagine if I had been raised inside a bottle, wrapped in sterilized cotton. A ten-year-old boy today is more on the ball than I was when I got married. There were very strange things in the air. That period has become stifling and incomprehensible to me. You probably don't remember, you were very young, perhaps not even born, the religious persecution. We experienced all of that in our home intensely. We were, just imagine, a piece of the flesh of the martyred Christ, a drop of blood from the agonizing heart. With World War II, many other interests came into play. If you ask me what my uncle was involved in, I couldn't tell you, I don't know. He had an official office on Avenida Juárez, which belonged to his company that exported minerals to Germany. It provided him with a lot of money. The office staff took care of everything: exports, shipments, maritime transport, customs permits. He spent his mornings there. After the declaration of war he closed the business, but he continued to go to the office. In the afternoons I went to my aunt and uncle's house, yes, to the Minerva, where they had a room reserved for him. I often took him notes from my father. There he'd receive some people, dictate correspondence, transact business. One night I had to bring him an urgent document. My father was desperate; he'd tried most of the day unsuccessfully to communicate with him. He suddenly asked me to look for him at an address downtown. I had to go to Monte de Piedad first, check there if anyone was following me. Only then if I knew with absolute certainly that I wasn't being watched should I continue to the address given to me by my father: the second floor of a more than sordid building on Calle Brasil. I'm sure you can imagine! The number belonged to a seedy jeweler and watchmaker's shop. I was about to leave, bewildered, when an old man removed the watchmaker's loupe from one eye; he asked me what I wanted, and who I was looking for. I gave him my uncle's last name. The old man made no expression; he told me that he'd see if that person was in the offices next door, with which he shared the address of the business, and asked my name at the same time. After a while he came back to ask me to go with him. We entered through a corridor that led to several doors. The place had a nightmarish, unreal look. We entered through one of the doors and went up a flight of stairs. There was my uncle, sitting at a desk, in front of a stack of papers. It was a room identical to the one he occupied in the Minerva Building, with the same type of dark, heavy furniture. Black bookshelves with glass doors covered with white curtains; a mirror covered in fly dirt, and a medium-sized lightbulb covered by a thin film of greenish gauze. Everything was very tasteless, sparse, ugly. I think of that place that—I swear to you!—I hadn't remembered again until today, and I get chills. I handed him the envelope; he opened it, read the contents, then ripped it up. He asked me if I was sure no one had followed me; I nodded. He asked me to tell my father not to worry, that everything was in order, not to believe any rumors; it wasn't necessary to take him a written answer; it was instead enough to repeat what he'd told me, and tell him not to worry. He called the watchmaker, who led me out another door to another street. I raced home and gave the message to my father. It seemed to take a great weight from his shoulders. He made me swear that I wouldn't discuss the existence of that office with anyone. He explained that he'd put me at great risk given the extreme gravity of the matter. He'd never send me back; in the end there'd no longer be a need. He'd spent the two most horrible hours of his life waiting for me, but one day I would understand. And so far, Miguel, I swear I haven't understood anything."

"Was it after Pistauer's death?"

"Yes, after. I'm almost sure it was only a few days before my Uncle Arnulfo was killed. My father spent those days burning letters and papers."

"Apparently everyone knows that Arnulfo was murdered . . . For me, you know, that's been an absolute novelty."

"In my house, we always assumed it was a fact. My father and uncle had become estranged after the boy's funeral. Somehow the letter I delivered had reconciled them. Yes, I'm sure I paid him that visit shortly before his death."

"Do you have any idea what might have happened?"

"His marriage must have had something to do with it, but that's only my intuition speaking without any basis in fact. Adele was very beautiful, too much of a woman for him. I don't see how she could have been in love with that old codger. Come to think of it, a nearly blind old man with a carrot-colored wig. No, that doesn't add up. That woman married for money or to leave Germany. Doesn't it seem strange to you that shortly after they arrived in Mexico, the former husband showed up?"

"Who did he live with?"

"Not with them, that's for sure. The times didn't allow for that kind of eccentricity. I don't even know what happened to him. He was a doctor. If he were alive, he'd be about eighty years old now."

"And her?"

"She was beautiful. One Sunday we went to the sports club, and I saw her play with her son. A goddess! Not more than forty years old."

"What became of her? Did she continue to live in Mexico?"

"No, but I don't know where she went. My Aunt Eduviges should know. After her son's death, she wanted to leave immediately but wasn't allowed to cross the border into the United States because of a passport or visa problem. She waited in Ensenada. She finally had to return to Mexico City. That's when my uncle was killed. I think she managed to leave later. It seems like to Brazil."

"There's an old German woman who hasn't moved since she arrived in Mexico who lives in the Minerva Building. She doesn't talk to anyone. Could it be Adele?"

"Adele never lived in the Minerva. They had a very nice house in Polanco. I'm almost sure she left the country."

A servant brought them coffee. The oratorical effects had disappeared from Derny's language. In those moments he seemed like a pleasant, clear, honest friend in his attempt to help Del Solar illuminate the past. Del Solar served himself a second cup of coffee.

"Did you meet her first husband?"

"Adele's? I saw him at the cemetery. He didn't speak to us. Do you think they were having an affair behind my uncle's back?"

"It's possible . . ."

"On the other hand, my Uncle Arnulfo didn't pay the slightest attention to that beauty. Otherwise he would've stayed at home more instead of visiting his chain of clandestine offices."

"Did you go to Delfina's party?"

"I wish! I'm telling you that I didn't even have a key to my house until I finished college. They treated me like a child; I was a child. Just think: my son takes that airheaded girl he runs around with into his room. My wife and I couldn't care less if they listen to music, talk, or engage in less innocent things, which is most likely. Arturo has created his space, and we respect that. In my house that would've been impossible. My father would've gone berserk if I'd told him that a female friend was going to spend time with me in my bedroom."

"Are you in contact with Delfina?"

"Yes. Look, I purchased that María Izquierdo cupboard from her a few years ago. Some of the paintings you see in this house come from her gallery. Delfina, in a way different from us, also belongs to synthesis."

"What?" Del Solar asked, puzzled.

"The dialectical synthesis I was referring to. Delfina comes from a different social background. However, as you can see, she's been incorporated into us. It would be impossible not to treat her as an equal. By skipping stages she's achieved the synthesis. I enjoy seeing her, talking to her, having lunch with her. We're the same. Our importance, and this is what my son and especially his girl don't understand, is having created a model for people like her to expand their personality. I don't believe in classes the way some of our friends are adamant about them. Advertising has taught me a lot. It makes you shake off the cobwebs. One moment you age, and then you're lost."

"I lived at the time, I don't know if you remember, in the Minerva Building."

"I didn't go to the party," Derny said, cutting him off, "but of course I found out about everything. Who didn't? There wasn't a single newspaper that didn't publish the news. And at home, as you can imagine, the scandal was tremendous. The funeral was held with the most discretion possible. The mother didn't attend. But the German did, his father. No one spoke to him. He showed up with another guy. I think I saw them arrive at the grave, wrapped in worn-out black leather coats that no one in Mexico wore. From the family there were the two Brioneses, Arnulfo and Eduviges, my father, and me. Who else! Oh, and a sort of bodyguard who went everywhere with my uncle. It was a very brief service, out of mere obligation, without any affection."

"What was said in your house?"

"About the murder? My father told me that the boy had drunk a lot at Delfina's house, with Delfina's son and some hooligan, someone from the underworld who passed himself off as a writer and probably invited them to go out looking for whores. They stopped a car, tried to force their way in, and, in

SERGIO PITOL

self-defense, someone in the car shot them. My uncle suffered
from nervous depression. His wife no longer wanted to live in
Mexico. The poor man had no peace until his death. As I said,
they were estranged somewhat in those days. They didn't reconcile until the end. Until the day he died, which they spent
together. They went to dinner at Manolo, the restaurant on Calle
de López. Or was it in Luis Moya? Do you remember? They'd
arranged for papers so Adele could leave. I was about to meet
them for dinner, but at the last minute my father wanted me to
stay home to take care of I don't know what matter. That was
also the end for him. That night he realized that the cards were
stacked against him. He never got mixed up in politics again. In
anything. He took refuge in his home, in his devotional readings,
in prayer. The death of his cousin, without a doubt, foretold his
own."

"It's possible that both deaths, that of Briones and that of
his stepson, are linked. Almost certainly. Escobedo thinks that
the dustups that took place in Delfina's house were intended to
create a climate of confusion to distract those present while the
boy was being murdered downstairs."

"Everyone, just as in Pirandello's plays or in *Rashomon*, has
their own version of events," Derny said, taking the opportunity
to flaunt his readings. "In my opinion, the brawls that took place
at that party could've been perfectly coincidental. My Aunt
Eduviges was there. Did you know that the first fight was started
by that sort of hit man who was always with Arnulfo Briones?"

"Martínez?"

"Exactly! The great Martínez! Do you remember him?"

"No, but I've heard about him a lot lately."

"He had few friends. People thought he was a lowlife.
Delfina, for example, won't forgive him for sneaking into her
house without an invitation. And, well, no one finds it amusing

that someone comes in and starts beating a woman. That's exactly what made Martínez seem wonderful to me, his coarseness. I think I was his only supporter. I knew him well enough. He accompanied Arnulfo to the so-called military training practices. We also saw each other frequently at the Minerva. Delfina's right about one thing: Martínez was the king of vulgarity. There was no one like him! He called himself a lawyer, but it was clear that he'd barely completed primary school. He got the language right: spurts of the same kind of pompous language as the Brioneses, with a certain hint of street thug. 'My adviser,' my uncle used to call him with a paternal attitude or, sometimes, 'my consultant.' I can't imagine what kind of advice, or what my uncle would consult with him on; it was plain to everyone that he was a royal idiot. But I found him amusing. He tried to pass himself off as a ladies' man. According to him, he'd been born a ladies' man and a diplomat. 'A ladies' man and a diplomat! I swear to you, my good Goenis, the main event, the man with the golden baton!' he liked to say. 'People don't take me seriously yet,' he told me one day with some regret. 'Oh well, I'm not one of those people who was born with a knack for blowing his own horn. They're the real losers.' We were at the door of my aunt and uncle's apartment, yes, in the Minerva. Martínez squeezed my arm, and with the other hand made a wide gesture that seemed to take in the entire building. 'I was born to give joy, to bring peace to the world. Look at those who live here. All the secrets they keep have made them unhappy. They despise each other; they're afraid of each other; they distrust each other; they harm each other, they hurt each other. I could make them happy. The men would give me a little dough, according to their means, according to their possibilities. The women would pay me another way, less impersonal, more tender, and I, I swear to you, my little man, I'd introduce harmony into their lives. I was born with a talent for diplomacy for a reason. I'd solve their problems without their even having to know about it. From time to time, some Sunday, we'd bring a trombone and a drum, and all the tenants, without exception, would march to the music through these corridors. It would be the love parade, the harmony march, and I would lead the parade with a golden baton. But there's no redemption in this world: men, as long as they don't have to let go of a penny, prefer to live like wild animals. Wolves of men! They don't want to be anything else. Did you hear that, Richie Rich, I even made a poem.'"

"I've heard some less than favorable things about him . . ."

"He thought he had absolute control over women," Derny continued without even hearing him. "To be honest, as strange as it may seem to you, it was true, at least to some extent. Eduviges must know the role he played, what his work consisted of, since it was obvious that her brother considered him indispensable. He even took him to Germany once or twice. The celebrated golden baton. One of his biggest pleasures, almost a habit, was telling me about his ribald escapades in Hamburg and Berlin. You have no idea how much I enjoyed listening to him. I was a chaste prig. Listening to Martínez meant looking into the abyss, inhaling sulfur, bathing in a spring of the most forbidden sensations. The same, I imagine, as reading pornographic books for others. He told me about his endless experiences in Germany. His women had to be older and have a little meat on their bones. No little girls and no skinnies. 'An old hen makes good broth!' he'd say, or even, 'There's no pleasure that compares to swimming in fat!' and he'd lick his lips with relish. His life was darkened by a single tragedy: he suffered from hemorrhoids. 'My organism's cruel stigmata,' he told me one day. He was so stigmatized by the disease that he wouldn't even go to a pharmacy to ask for the remedies necessary to

treat them. He asked me once to buy them. He was overcome with grimaces, pretensions, complexes. My father couldn't stand him. He found him disgusting. An upstart, he said. You probably remember what a snob my father was. That's exactly why, knowing the way he was, I can't figure out why he sent me to study at a mere college and not at the university nearby. The mysteries of the human heart! Our destiny is to be children of the wild man of the Slavs, the dark Fedor. Tell me, why not Notre Dame? So, I was saying, my father was bothered by how close Martínez and Arnulfo were. Needless to say, I hid our conversations from him. It was in fact Martínez who went to the restaurant to tell my uncle that Adele had just left Bellas Artes, and that she'd broken her heel going down the stairs. Martínez was supposed to drive her home, but, according to him, she said she wanted to talk to my uncle for a moment. She was waiting for him in the garage, next to the Palacio, a hundred meters from the restaurant. My father waited. After a while he got fed up and returned home, which is where he got the news. My Uncle Dionisio called. Arnulfo Briones had been struck by a car while crossing Avenida Juárez at 8:30 p.m. That was the first version. It was a Sunday; at the end of the opera . . ."
He paused and stared at him intently. He was no longer the same Derny from before, the enthusiast of the laws of dialectics, the proclaimer of social synthesis that would redeem the country's future evils. Something had moved him. Suddenly, when he realized he was being watched, he let out an empty laugh and added: "The great golden baton! There aren't many people as memorable as he! A true Valentino. You should've heard the advice he gave me on how to seduce a woman. And he was able to do it, despite his horse teeth! At least he made people take interest in him, they listened to him, they smiled at him. I know for a fact. I saw him flirt with female employees,

waitresses, maids. They loved the way he approached them, I think. What he never imagined was that a woman he thought he had at his feet would humiliate him publicly, mocking his tragedy, the stigmata of his organism: his blasted piles. That woman was Ida Werfel. That's why he went mad with rage and despair at Delfina's party. He felt betrayed, as if they wanted to strip him publicly and expose to the public the thing that embarrassed him most. He felt like a mandrill who was being asked to show his yaws you know where. Days before the tragic party, my Aunt Eduviges called me. She was very nervous, distraught, on the verge of collapse. She was sure something very serious was going to happen. To be exact she feared a betrayal. Arnulfo, she said, walked through life blindly. And that man, Martínez, who'd made him believe he was his Lazarillo, was preparing to throw him off the first cliff he saw. She'd seen me talk to him several times. She asked if I'd noticed anything out of the ordinary. I recounted our conversations, omitting the subject of women, that is, almost everything we spoke about. To downplay the matter and make her relax a bit, I told her about Martínez's drama, the cruel stigmata of his organism. The medicines I'd purchased because he didn't want to risk the pharmacy employees' associating them with his ailments. I saw my aunt again a few days later, after Pistauer's death, and she gave me her version of the party. She told me, among other things, that Ida Werfel was aware of Martínez's secret, that she'd begun to make unambiguous jokes in front of everyone, referring to chiles and their pernicious effects on the disaster area."

They both burst out laughing. Eloísa called them from the upper floor to go upstairs, as the newscast was about to begin, and then they had dinner and later listened to César Franck's Symphony, a magnificent version conducted by Barbirolli, which Del Solar didn't know. He then took his cousin to Coyoacán; she declared that she was delighted to have seen him so happy at Derny's house; and he returned home dead from fatigue.

He thought that only in Mexico were such marathon visits possible, that Derny was much more pleasant than he'd imagined, and that perhaps the history of those crimes was simpler than it seemed. He needed to talk to his aunt. What was the relationship of the "golden baton" with the Briones family? Where had he come from? Where was he? What role in particular did he play in Arnulfo Briones's activities? He appeared in the accounts of all his interviewees. A blackmailer, a lout, a fifth-rate ladies' man. He seemed to recall vaguely the image of a skinny man, toothy, clad in a dark striped suit, with a hat whose brim covered part of his face. Martínez, ladies' man and diplomat! The great golden baton in the love parade!

CHAPTER 10

The Detestable Mexican Castrato

"THE STORY IS BIZARRE, I KNOW; outré, as the pedants say. There are people who have to live in the shadows, let there be no doubt. A cry rising from the suffering bowels of humanity! Another spiritual goal that had to be abandoned because the moment of redemption wasn't reached. There's an area of the astral plane (not heaven, not earth) that must be incorporated into our world. When that's achieved, the androgynous one will spread his message. Lingam will bestow his generative power to the Universe. If the astral conditions aren't met, we'll discover yet another failed experiment of nature. Deception doesn't pay! I've always maintained this. Baroness von Lewenthau, the handsome Lieutenant Giraux: a bunch of frauds, all of them! A company of high comedy as they claimed? Not at all! Comedians of the lowest sort, mixed with domestic and foreign rogues, riffraff lacking the slightest scruples. Filth! 'Wastrels of the world, unite!' That motto should've been tattooed on their forehead. Between them they ruined the project. No one wanted to be saved; no one, redeemed. Did you know, by the way, that José Zorrilla was the director of the imperial theaters of Mexico? Forgive me, I forgot that you're a historian and that you know everything. People today don't want to know anything. On the contrary, their ambition is to forget what little they ever knew. An efficient way to board the old-age bus. Oblivion and senility, amnesia and decrepitude; the concepts fuse or mingle. Those who run the world would like us all to have amnesia. Humanity? A band of forgetful and drooling old men. I don't plan to give them that pleasure. I'll always be young. I'll continue to remember. The adolescent Balmorán! Present, teacher! Yesterday, scarcely a boy with his blue satchel and big red balloon. And today? Behold! Look at him! He greets the world with a fresh and resplendent memory, always ready to grasp the messages generated by a fertile yesterday and a present, likewise. I'm still researching, be advised. I found a critical document in the notarial archives: the last will and testament of Baron von Lewenthau. Riches, to be honest, very few. The important thing is that the first name of his wife is recorded there: Palmira Aguglia, Neapolitan. Of course! Where else could she have come from?"

Balmorán had phoned several times over the previous days. He'd left messages saying that he urgently needed to reach him, that he had exciting developments . . . He returned the call, and they made an appointment. Del Solar had to postpone it several times, because once he decided to stay in Mexico, after he began to complete the paperwork necessary to return to the university, he discovered that it was taking longer and was more complicated than expected. The previous afternoon, when he again postponed the appointment for the following day, he perceived a shrill and scornful note in Balmorán's voice. He said to stop by his apartment whenever he wanted. He wasn't important and had never presumed to be. To stop by when he had time, when he felt like it; if he couldn't manage, no big deal; they'd see each other sometime. He wasn't entirely free either. He had things to do—appraise libraries, for example. Nothing as impressive as the ambitions of widows, he said in a disagreeable voice. They showed the prospective buyer a wall crammed with waste, garbage, cheap novels, papers only good for fermenting in rats' bellies. And they were asking for millions. What greed! What airs! What grandeur! Martyrology carved in their face! They didn't want the library belonging to the husband, that venerable national hero, to leave the country, and so they were offering it at a reasonable price. In Texas they'd pay twice as much, but as long as they were able, they'd prevent those treasures from leaving Mexico. His life consisted not only of seeing widows. He had to go to the printing workshop, oversee his editions. He had other occupations. He couldn't stay home forever, waiting for Godot. In short, if he promised to be at his apartment at five o'clock the next afternoon, he, despite his many endeavors, gave him his word that he'd wait for him. It would be, of course, the last time. He'd paid the utmost attention to the conversation they'd had the day he deigned to visit him. He'd looked for things, and he'd found them. In short, if Del Solar changed his mind, if he was no longer interested, oh well; he'd have wasted his time just as he had many times in the past. He'd appreciate if the client were at least kind enough to communicate his disinterest. Such was his profession; he accepted the occupational hazards of the trade. Patience! It wasn't the first time, nor would it be the last, that he'd worked in vain.

The meeting finally took place. The beginning was rather disappointing. When the bookseller had called him and insisted on his visit, the historian had thought he'd have new information that would shed light on the attack that took the life of Erich Maria Pistauer and where he, Balmorán, and Delfina Uribe's son had also been wounded. Miguel del Solar was convinced that if Balmorán and the other interested parties made an effort to remember, to intelligently connect one event with another, it would be possible to know what had happened, who had ordered those deaths and why. That instead of complicating the task, the time that had passed would make it easier. All they had to do was make a minimum of effort, to remember, to tie up loose ends, to discard easy solutions: the truth would eventually prevail. What specific interests ẘas Arnulfo defending? Why did he receive correspondence in several offices scattered throughout different neighborhoods of the city? Why instead of demanding clarification regarding his stepson's murder did he try to flee to the United States with his wife? Why did he fight and then reconcile with Haroldo Goenaga, his cousin, his best friend, days before he died? Was he killed? Balmorán hadn't made the slightest effort to review the circumstances that made up that puzzle. The developments he'd announced so emphatically over the phone were bibliographic: two tattered copies of *Timón*, the national socialist magazine sponsored by the German embassy, some clerical pamphlets on workers' issues, and two novels published in Jalisco on the Cristero uprising.

After a few minutes, he noticed that Balmorán had used those publications as a pretext. Just as he had, by the way! Neither of them lent the least importance to the printed materials that day. Balmorán wanted to talk about his work. He received his occasional client as a displeased father examines the behavior of his reckless son, whom he needs to return to the straight and narrow with an energetic and appropriate tug of the reins. With a severity that endeavored to show that it was just an act, a mere façade, the bookseller invited Del Solar to drink some wine and told him, with a certain degree of reproach, that he had momentarily feared that their beautiful friendship, which had arisen during the previous visit, had vanished into thin air. He'd felt the fluttering of a kindred (he should be forgiven for the hackneyed adjective, but, in his case, it was the only one that seemed strictly faithful) spirit. A kindred spirit! The rarest discovery in the world. Someone who naturally accepted a friend's youthfulness. It was obvious that he, Del Solar, wasn't one of those who sought the limelight of false heroes, who in order to remain on their equally false pedestal had to kill everything that pulsed within them that was truly human. He had a different personality, which was why he was sitting in front of him, Pedro Balmorán, with a glass of red wine in his hand and the calm and receptive attitude of someone who knows he's with a brother.

Since their previous conversation he'd worked day and night, nonstop, correcting and revising his version of the tragic misfortunes of the Mexican castrato. He hadn't touched that material in years. He'd devoted himself to other works, which he hurried to explain. He described himself as tireless and hard-working. He worked like almost no one else in Mexico. The book that would've made him famous thirty years ago, which he post-poned at one point, had risen from the deep lethargy in which it lay. A work beloved and hated at the same time. Because of it, he'd been mistreated and threatened, almost killed. They'd caused him to lose the movement of half his body: physically they'd turned him into an invalid. For long periods, he worked only very occasionally on that text. At first fervently, feverishly, then with lassitude, with emotional and intellectual distance. There came a time when he didn't even look at it. Much of the material was lost forever. There were missing pieces of information, dates. But also, on closer examination, the original material was noticeably imprecise. Memory wasn't the castrato's forte. The abbot, Morelli, who'd spoken to that monster of nature in the twilight of his life, must have invented many things. He describes, for example, the emperor and empress's journey to San Luis Potosí, where the castrato sang a Te Deum, celebrated in the cathedral, to great applause from their Majesties, receiving an ovation from the feverish multitude of local inhabitants who that night carried him on their shoulders around the city before depositing him in the inn where the Baroness von Lewenthau (née Aguglia, Neapolitan) was awaiting him. At the time Abbot Morelli interviewed him, the castrato was barely scraping by on a quay in Naples as a fakir. He says that he dreams all day long of eating and that in his homeland he ate little birds all day. When the abbot asks him what kind, what varieties, he answers totoles and zopilotes, the first being the Mexican turkey, and the second a species of vulture that in some parts of the Caribbean is known as aura tiñosa. The abbot explains to him that that can't be, that the zopilote isn't an edible bird, that its meat is disgusting; the castrato says yes, that he never ate zopilotes, that he ate little birds. Which ones, for example? Like the águila real and the totoles and the zopilotes. A dialogue that provides an idea of the difficulties of communication, on the one hand linguistic, and on the other due to the poor soprano's fatigue and mental deterioration. The entire story that Morelli recreates in great detail of the San Luis Te Deum, the musical success, and the magnificent banquets served on its occasion, is false. The emperors were never in San Luis Potosí. The closest cities visited by Maximiliano de Habsburgo were Guanajuato and Morelia, both more than a day's journey from San Luis. The Empress Carlota didn't accompany him on that or on any other trip through the republic, with the exception of her usual outings to Cuernavaca. On the other hand, given the scandalous way in which the character had fled the city, his return was completely unthinkable, even among the emperor's retinue.

Del Solar felt lost amid the abrupt appearance of the castrato, who had invaded the thoughts of the cripple. He tried warily to ask for explanations about the document. The bookseller looked at him with contempt, with a tang of his initial impertinence. He pursed his lips until his mouth looked like a chicken's butt, stretched out his good arm—the left one, that is—toward his interlocutor, as if officiating a ceremony of extraordinary significance.

"I noticed the other day," he continued, "your interest in this story. People died for it; the Austrian subject Erich Maria Pistauer, the young Ricardo Rubio, grandson of Don Luis Uribe, and yours truly, the lowly undersigned, who sings and dances, on tiptoes, if required, the *Danse Macabre* of Saint Saëns, and who, as you can you see, is physically broken. A story that, over the course of an entire century, has tried to emerge into the light, to make itself known, without success. Fate appointed me, for some reason, to undertake this task against all odds. When those 'Memoirs' were written, the poor creature could barely speak. All that about the little birds lingered over by Morelli, who was certainly a gluttonous friar, gives us an idea of his mental state: he'd forgotten everything; he'd even forgotten how to talk. The other narrator, Palmira Aguglia, the Baroness von Lewenthau, had been returned to her true status in Naples, where she tended a tavern in the port, becoming what she'd been before she met the old baron. Abbot Morelli claims to have met the baroness and the castrato in San Luis Potosí, and he happens upon them again by chance in the twilight of their lives. He doesn't hide the fact that the woman's current profession was reduced to carnal trade with sailors and common rabble. The wench had returned to her rightful place after attempting, by taking advantage of the military occupation, to make a fortune at our expense. Poor country! She assumed, it must be acknowledged, real sacrifices to allow the person to whom she'd devoted the best of her life, the castrato, to triumph. I clearly understood that I needed to return to the task. I had to finish the exploit. To make known the enigmatic existence of the prodigious nightingale. I was thinking of all that when the superintendent's wife, my dear friend, an angel who protects me from the blows of the world, handed over a letter to me, anonymous like those I received thirty years ago, before the assault, before the shooting, like those I've received almost daily for about a month, threatening me with violent reprisals if I dare to publish the obscene papers in my possession. The text may be different each time, but the content is the same. 'The devil's not going to do his deed,' said the first line of the first letter, followed by a string of incoherent insults. They don't upset me anymore; on the contrary, as I held that ignominious gob of spit in my hand, I felt my youth was acquiring another raison d'être. I'd kept in top shape—a young master at the height of his art!—to be able to finish the story about the fate of the hideous Mexican castrato. I have the feeling that I've described him to you in purely grotesque terms, but, I assure you, he's much more than that. He could have redeemed the world, let there be no doubt; I'm absolutely convinced of that. 'Yes, the devil will do his deed!' I shouted, over and over again throughout the morning. In the afternoon I began to write. I removed the papers from their hiding place, read them in one sitting, and I've done nothing since but work day and night. I can assure you that within three months, at the latest, I'll have the story ready for delivery to the press. Tremble who may, fall who may, the castrato, the character known in the Old World as the Second Mexican Nightingale, later as the Aztec Fakir, will go out into the world to live his second existence, his long-awaited resurrection!" Balmorán spoke like a madman, waving his hands, gesticulating, returning to the winks and gestures that demanded calm and patience from others, that intended to imply that the most important thing was yet to come, that they kindly not wrest the floor from him at that moment. "Yes, yes, I have worked tirelessly and made much progress. I'll read you passages, whichever you want, except for the ending, which is the true surprise of my book. You'll be dumbfounded when you read it; you'll know how profoundly demonic human existence can be; you'll see that when speaking of man, absurdity and madness know no bounds. It's all just appearances. There will be a time when the astral plane will be transformed into a single plane that will include heaven and earth. Perhaps the duration of this meeting won't last more than an instant. But it is possible that at that moment redemption will occur. Will there always be an ad hoc figure awaiting that moment? I wonder. Will he arrive? Forgive my digression. There are passages in which the clumsiness of style is still evident; there are holes; there are wrinkles, but the work to perfect it continues its course. The most important thing was to arrive at the words THE END. And those words have been written."

"Do you have any idea what happened to the rest of the original document?"

"What you say? Me no understand. Me no understand. Me just want to dance the cha-cha-chá."

"The pages that were stolen from you . . ."

"Forgive me, Horatio, but there are things that are much, much more interesting than your mercantile philosophy. I have an idea about the character's personality." He closed his eyes and exclaimed in a kind of ecstasy: "About his physiology! You'll read the text and will know everything. I will indicate in a brief prologue that for years these papers have been persecuted, seized, that the life of its glossator has been in danger, that even now he's threatened with anonymity . . . Let the readers draw their conclusions! Why is the interest in keeping the circumstances of this life hidden so strong? I'm sure many will agree with my conclusions. This isn't a mere hypothesis. It is the definitive illumination of the mystery."

"You mean . . . ?"

"Not so eager, my friend! You and I will continue to talk. I want you to be the first to read my story. In a very short time I'll have it ready for printing. Do me a favor, read it first! The pages were saved because they were in the possession of Frau Moby Dick, who of course couldn't appreciate them and had the nerve to declare them forgeries, that the Italian was incorrect, unlike the maestro Rafael J. Santander, a modest man whom today no one remembers, a zealous paleographer who also read part of the text at the time; I'd asked him to give me his opinion on the authenticity of the manuscript brought into question by Dr. Lardina Werfel. When he returned those pages to me, Don Rafael assured me that I possessed a treasure of incalculable value. The original pages, I mean. They'll be included as an appendix to the work, giving due credit to Abbot Morelli, who collected the testimony from the castrato himself and the Neapolitan woman. The rest will appear as my work. I've been its custodian, its glossator, its quasi creator. The work will appear under the name of yours truly, your attentive and assured servant, who tirelessly sings and dances the cha-cha-chá."

"Aren't you interested in knowing what happened . . . ?"

"To the characters whom Morelli couldn't interview? Magnificent question! I should like to die in such a manner from a single shot! I haven't neglected them, don't worry. I've tracked them as far as I could. The Lieutenant Giraux, the other protagonist, a small-time crook, succubus to the supreme wench, deserted the army and remained hidden for some time, until the triumph of the republic and the normalization of civilian life. He married a rich Jarocha merchant who kept him hidden in a warehouse in Veracruz. There was no way he was going to reunite with his former accomplice. He refused to return to a life of exploits, and, as we can see from the trail left by the other two, he had all the reason in the world. Perhaps he lived and died happily beside his devout and obliging wife, taking over the administration of her business, advising her on how to grant credit to some and deny it systematically to others; teaching her to appreciate certain new qualities of materials and products with which to expand her business, which slowly raised the quality of the establishment. It's possible this was the case, although it could also be the case that he ruined the shopkeeper, and that after a while he found another, and then another, and, in the end, fleeing from Tyrian and Trojan women, managed to leave Mexico and settle down in Martinique or Guadeloupe to cure his malaria or other even more unwelcome maladies, among people of his own language, until at last, reduced to human dregs, he began to go deaf, blind, and mad, and one day his ravaged corpse would appear in a piggery, to the great excitement of the rooting pigs. Who can know what his fate was! All that we know for certain is that the handsome Lieutenant Giraux didn't accompany the couple to Europe or share their final dizzying collapse. That at least can be deduced from Morelli's story.

Balmorán went on to recount the story grosso modo to his new friend and restive listener. The journey of a merry gang to San Luis Potosí, where Palmira von Lewenthau had set out to found a company of players that would conceal other activities—gambling, a house of assignation, etc.—in order to fleece the rich hacendados and miners of the region. The discovery of the voice in a deserted church visited by the baroness in the company of an Englishman, a mining engineer, who attempted to explain to her the peculiarities of local architecture, especially the use of the pilaster as a foundation of the Mexican Baroque. The baroness's astonishment at the sound of that angelic trill was crushing. "*C'est un ange!*" she exclaimed in ecstasy. "I want to touch its wings! I want to kiss its burning eyelids!" A wave of mystical inebriation took possession of the baroness. She was so bewitched that when at last the owner of that "golden voice," a novice with a coquettish expression, came down from the choir, the baroness didn't notice his ugliness, according to Morelli, which bordered on the monstrous. "He's the most beautiful angel I've ever seen in my life!" she exclaimed to the appalled English engineer, who was observing with disgust the protruding lips of the person in question, his eyes almost closed and squinting, so far apart that they gave him the appearance of a wild boar more than of a human.

"Like the golden angels of Bohemia! Like the most beautiful angels in my native Italy! Let me hear your voice again! Sing, Mexican angel, sing, please! Your humblest servant, on her knees, implores you!" The English engineer, who knew little or nothing about music, was so impressed to see the tear-soaked face of the elegant noblewoman prostrate before that angel of horror, that that night he commented in the salons of the Lonja that he'd heard a celestial voice sing, and added that the Baroness von Lewenthau herself, a lady of immense musical culture (which was false, since, with the exception of the Neapolitan tarantellas, an easily retained aria, and pieces of dance music, she knew nothing), had listened to him on her knees, her face bathed in tears.

The next day, all of San Luis was telling the story—except the angel, of course, still unaware that fate's gaze had come to land on him. The young castrato lived, his anomaly hidden beneath monastic habits, in a convent where an aging lay sister taught him to sing villancicos and motets ("and to eat little birds," he'd repeat in old age). That afternoon, at the hour when the nightingale was doing his daily vocalization exercises, while the old nun extracted with heavy parsimony music from the organ, the church began to fill surprisingly with gold braids, feathers, swords, sumptuous robes, jewels . . . the highest of San Luis society, which in terms of attire rivaled that of the Court,

French and Mexican officials, the high curia of the city, presided over by Archbishop Arozamena. At the end of the first motet there was a standing ovation, which was repeated at the end of each piece. With the archbishop's consent, the young soprano went down to greet his audience. The baroness embraced him passionately, and, away from the crowd beside a small chapel, they were able to exchange a few words. The soprano understood in broad terms what the baroness was proposing to him. A common language wasn't necessary. The incentive to vanity often works miracles.

That night at the inn, the baroness and the lieutenant reached an agreement. Still dazed, she managed to convince her lover that luck had smiled on them. "Fortune has placed a treasure in our hands. That prodigious voice belongs to a castrato. It's not a maiden, it's not a novice. He is a young indigenous boy from the sierras in the North, despoiled in childhood of his manly attributes. Only three or four people, in addition to the nun who has raised him and taught him music, know his secret."

"And you, how did you find out?" the idler rightly asked her.

"It's a complicated and rather long story to tell. The dear Madame Arteaga had told me something in Mexico City. But I didn't imagine I'd be so fortunate as to stumble upon this prodigy so soon." And she went on to explain the great venture that lay ahead of them: representing the Mexican nightingale in Europe. Beyond his musical talents, there was his exoticism. She didn't understand why the soldier spoke of a disgusting physique. She thought, though it was an attack on herself, that Giraux knew nothing about women. And she began to imagine a costume that would highlight the natural grace and voluptuousness of her protégé. The couple took care to bribe servants, promising promotions and privileges to those in charge of checkpoints in San Luis and the carriage service. In short, they managed to snatch

the castrato from the hands of the old nun who had protected
him since adolescence and move him to Mexico City, dressed as
a soldier, under the care of one of Giraux's pages. The couple
stayed a few more days in San Luis, pretending to grieve, shed-
ding tears, offering rewards to whomever returned that golden
voice to his divine cage. The devil's impostors! He was kept hidden in a house on the outskirts of Mexico City, which the baroness visited almost daily, fascinated by her acquisition. An old
singing teacher came to teach him the operatic repertoire with
which Palmira von Lewenthau dreamed of making him the toast
of the world. Sweet moments, gentle swoons: Pygmalion, in a
woman blinded by love, contemplated his ungainly body and
at the same time imagined his figure bathed in the glow of foot
lights on the most opulent stages of Rome, Palermo, Venice,
Vienna; in palaces of Seville and Stockholm. But he would have
to fight; the musical knowledge of the prodigy of San Luis was
elementary, good enough only to sing motets and villancicos
(and eat little birds, Morelli would add). He barely knew solfège,
he couldn't move with grace; they'd have to start from scratch.
And she insisted that her discovery become in a blink of an eye
Norma, the Sonnambula, Rosina, on transforming that piece of
crude clay into Monteverdi's majestic Poppea. She thought it
would be a matter of a short time, months at most. It would be
necessary to work night and day to overcome the indolence of
that languid fruit of the desert, who didn't seem to share the
optimism, the enthusiasm, much less the cult of action professed
by the baroness, but preferred to spend as much time as possible in bed, sleeping or savoring sweets (little birds). It's possible that Palmira wanted to live a series of scenic experiences,
unknown to her and forbidden by her age, through the castrato.
All she seemed to care about was that the world recognize his
gifts. By then she loved him to the point of delirium. Giraux

began to look with unapproving eyes on the bedazzlement, the giddiness, the anomaly. From the moment he saw the castrato again, he noticed with absolute clarity that he'd joined an enterprise destined to fail. Professor Carrara confirmed it without any hesitation: "That figuretta, at best, could only perform in circuses." The lieutenant refused to continue the folly and didn't stop at that, but began to treat his lover differently, put another way, to extort her vulgarly. One could say whatever they liked about Frau von Lewenthau, but, above all, one had to recognize that she was indefatigable and tenacious. She took money from wherever she could to maintain her way of life, to educate her charge, and to please her former lover. Lieutenant Giraux increased his demands more and more. He mistreated the castrato, hurled harsh insults at him and the baroness, increasingly scabrous allusions to the relationship between them, whom he called, sometimes cheerfully, other times with a demonic humor, "Capon and Caponnette." Once, after having gone drinking, he overstepped the bounds of propriety with the nightingale of San Luis. In the end, Palmira (not for nothing Aguglia) accused the officer before the authorities of two or three crimes of supreme gravity about which she had information, evidently firsthand. But first she made it known by an intermediary that he was about to be arrested. And just like that, she got rid of him. That indefatigable woman had to engage, during those days, in more than one roguish act to dress her pupil, rescue part of her pawned jewels, and buy the tickets that would take her to Veracruz and Europe. There was, then, no triumphant return to San Luis Potosí, that Morelli described with such care, nor any trip made by the emperors to such a prosperous city, nor a concert by the castrato in their presence. In France, the baroness published announcements in some newspapers to publicize the arrival in Europe of that extraordinary character. The empire seemed to be vanquished one day and saved the next. In the meantime, whatever news that came out about him still produced a certain sensation, and she knew how to exploit that climate, as she was a woman with imagination, ability, and resources. That's why the final downfall is so inexplicable. She'd appear in a box at the opera with the *rosignolo* at times dressed as a woman, at times as a young dandy, to general anticipation. She made him declare to the press that at the moment, despite the offers received, he wouldn't sing in Paris; he'd formally promised the first fruits of his voice to the Holy Father. He would sing in a Vatican chapel. And through his singing he would implore God for eternal life for the Mexican Empire and happiness for their Imperial Highnesses. The arrival in Rome, it goes without saying, was triumphant. The castrato was unrecognizable. His ugliness had been transformed into something mysterious: an opulent bird, a corpulent orchid, from the primordial world, a languid animal species formed on the first day of Creation, all this swathed in feathers, satins, wigs, jewels, and brocades. That pageantry was contemplated by his small, cold eyes, always closed halfway, with indifference, with contempt, as if everything were small in relation to what he deserved. The mere fact of existing, of raising an arm in the morning, of immersing himself in a tub of perfumed water, he conceived as a favor to humanity. He had debauched himself: it was obvious that he could no longer save the world. Even if the astral plane merged with the material one, the experiment was lost. There would be no redemption, not yet.

The night before his long-awaited performance, a retinue of officers arrived at the hostel to invite the castrato to dinner. They apologized to the baroness. They would have loved for her to attend, they said, but the presence of ladies wasn't allowed in the chambers where the little banquet would take place. It was a simple matter of protocol. The castrato wasn't returned until well into the next morning. The baroness didn't sleep a wink. At dawn she began sending messages to the Holy See. No one understood them. The castrato had apparently not been there, much less stayed overnight. She feared it was a kidnapping; she summoned the police, and two inspectors listened intently and, in the end, responded with jokes, double entendre, and vulgar gestures: "*Ah, i castratti, i castratti, fanno sempre lo stesso guaio!*" Finally, around ten, the missing character got out of a carriage in deplorable condition. His clothes disheveled, his velvet shirt-front covered with vomit, his eyes reddened, and a greenish color on his cheeks. He was missing a shoe. He didn't understand anything. He collapsed in the lobby and had to be carried on shoulders up to his room. They put ice packs on the back of his neck, bathed him. The baroness, in an intermittent crisis of hysteria, reprimanded him in the harshest terms. At last, shortly before six o'clock in the afternoon, perfectly attired, he went to face his fate. When he opened his mouth and let out the first notes, horror gripped the crowd. Cardinal Chioglia, of exquisite musical training, put his hands over his ears as if the cartilage of the labyrinth had been crushed, and all but ran from the chapel, certainly to inform the Holy Father of the concert's disastrous results. Abbot Morelli points out that the sounds the creature made that night were so infamous, so tense, that for a moment one might have thought that a flock of crows had penetrated the holy grounds. The castrato, with his eyes blank, apparently didn't notice the effects his voice had on the audience. At one point, the conductor of the accompanying chamber orchestra rushed out of the temple. A furious hissing was heard in the venue, and if there were no insults, it was out of respect for the chapel. The moral blow was tremendous. The soprano seemed not to understand what was going on. He tried to sing again without musical accompaniment, but the audience wouldn't allow it. Some strapping men, among whom Aguglia thought she recognized one of the revelers from the night before, rushed the platform, grabbed him without hesitation, by the arms, pushed handkerchiefs and other rags in his mouth, almost suffocating him, and with great force pushed him down and made him leave the chapel. The couple crossed the square very differently than they had imagined. There was no procession, no retinue, no ovation. Not even a rose. They met only angry faces, wisecracks, terrifying fists. At the first turn, after leaving the square, they took a street that led to the hotel. The next morning's newspapers were even more merciless than the public. They warned potential listeners against that Luciferian voice: *Fa male a l'orecchio; é un suono da vero cattivaccio, anzi pericoloso!* A pregnant woman, upon hearing the monster, was in danger of losing her child. Maximiliano's execution must have aroused new outbreaks of animus against the poor castrato. Someone remembered that he'd dedicated his first concert to the long life of the emperor and the answer had been his execution. Ergo . . . There began his via crucis . . .

"Incredible!"

"Yes, yes, of course. But what I'm interested in discussing with you is the esoteric aspect. That's what matters. The earthly phase is just an anecdote, gossip. The astral, on the other hand . . ."

There was a knock at the door. The superintendent's wife came in with a stack of freshly ironed shirts and a letter. She put the shirts in a bureau drawer. Balmorán opened the envelope, read the paper, and showed it to Del Solar, who had listened to the story with more interest than he'd imagined.

"Do you see? Another anonymous letter. They'll continue to come until I publish my work. They are connected to the existence of the book. They accuse me of divulging secrets that are not mine to tell. But this time the devil indeed will dare. He's already done so, ladies and gentlemen, he's already dared. Read it for yourself . . . You'll see that I'm not lying . . ." Then he asked the woman to make them some coffee. Del Solar took the opportunity to go to the bathroom.

When he came out, he found the bookseller with his features distorted and the look of a madman. He picked up his papers with desperation and placed them in the seat of a chair. The woman was shouting for her husband from the door.

"Get out of here! Get out of here immediately or I won't be responsible for your life!" Balmorán howled. "Get out of here! If I see you around this house again, I'll take justice into my own hands. If something happens to me, hear me, if my papers disappear again, people will know in advance who's to blame. At this very moment I'm going to write to different agencies denouncing what has happened. Get out! You thought this was Troy, that you'd managed to infiltrate, that just as before you had the material in your hands. But that's not the case; this time I was the one who toyed with you." Balmorán remained standing, leaned his body on the back of a chair, and hoisted his cane with his good hand. He threatened him, shouted at him, expelled him, but at the same time prevented him from withdrawing because he was standing in front of the door. Del Solar didn't want to expose himself to a blow of the cane from that raving lunatic. "What did you say? 'I deceived the unwary Balmorán again, isn't that right? I'll introduce the horse into the square and when he least expects it, I'll have conquered it.' No, señor! I repeat. This isn't Troy! This is, know it well, Sparta! Get out!"

At last the doorman arrived.

"Please take his cane!" Miguel del Solar shouted. The doorman approached Balmorán, took him by the arm, asked for his cane, and made him sit down. The woman brought him a glass of water, which he refused to drink. He seemed catatonic.

"I don't know what happened," Del Solar said. "I don't know where he got that I wanted to steal his papers."

Balmorán didn't answer. He was shaking, contorting, grimacing repulsively. He began to drink the water and spit it out.

"Has he had these attacks on other occasions?" Del Solar asked from the door.

The superintendent spoke quietly to his wife. In a downcast tone he said:

"He's a bit anxious. He's a learned man. A kindhearted person. He's never been like that before."

"Call the clinic next door; he needs to see a doctor. Try to calm him down. Tell him I didn't come to steal anything from him," Del Solar said as he walked with the superintendent to the stairs.

"He got that way when my wife told him that you'd lived in an apartment on the second floor."

CHAPTER 11

Crabs on the March!

"IN THAT REGARD HE WAS ALWAYS a very odd man. It would be impossible to find anyone more mysterious. Especially if, with distance, you begin to think about his peculiarities. For years I assumed that some religious vow prevented him from marrying, that he had made a pact, given a promise, or something like that. These things happen; more so then than now, fortunately. Arnulfo wasn't in any aspect of his life an open book, although in those marital hazes he went too far. Did you know that before the German he had another wife? You didn't, did you? And yet the marriage was completely legal, except we hardly knew about it. Felipa, Hermenegilda, Chole, I don't even remember her name, only that it was a maid's name. It was back when he worked in a sugar mill in the Huasteca region of Tamaulipas. A frightful woman, with oriental features, who barely knew how to talk. It pains me to say it, but that was Arnulfo Briones, if you must know. In his better years, he could have married anyone he fancied. To think that being the most conservative of conservatives, a sworn enemy of any project that might seem even remotely egalitarian, had fallen into the hands of that devil! I can't even imagine the in-laws, cousins, and other relatives he had to cope with back in Tamaulipas! Fortunately, I never met them. We came to know about the existence of that woman at the end of her stay in Mexico City, almost by chance . . . He never

brought her to our home, nor did he invite us to his; I'm grateful for that small gesture. If they hadn't gone to Germany, we
probably wouldn't have even found out about Chole or Chona,
or whatever her name is. The poor thing died during her stay
in Hamburg. I imagine because she didn't eat crabs on Fridays
or because she didn't know how to fix chilpachole. It was the
first time Arnulfo had left Mexico. And it was only on the eve of
the trip that he introduced her to us. We went to Torino, a rustic restaurant on the border between Colonia Roma and Colonia
del Valle. What times! A rustic restaurant where Colonia del
Valle begins! No one would believe it. There she was, the little maid, so demure, with her half-Indian, half-Chinese face,
between human and thrush. There were things, my goodness,
where Arnulfo was out of line! If you only knew what I've had to
endure over the years! Everything about him, if you think about
it, from the very start, was little more than a series of mysteries
and demands and arrogance and pettiness. He barely exchanged
words with my husband, who was his best friend in their youth.
He treated him with more contempt than his own bodyguards. I
didn't invite you here to talk about that, but these are things that
still hurt me. Well, he invited us to Torino. Chole, the woman
with the chilpachole, was wearing a hat with a half veil and a pair
of gray foxes tangled, literally tangled, around her neck. A laughingstock! The poor thing suffered throughout the entire meal. Of
course, how could she not suffer in that getup? She didn't even
recognize herself in those clothes; she didn't belong in them.
And Arnulfo didn't support her; he left her to her own devices,
which were none. I saw her desperately squeeze a tissue, a nap-
kin, I think even the edge of the tablecloth. 'Poor thing!' I said
to myself, 'she doesn't know where to put her hands or what to
do with them!' Frightful hands, pudgy, like little tamales, with
short fingers. 'Poor thing.' But, come to think of it, why poor

thing? Why should I pity her? She must have sucked out his brain to be able to hook one of the best catches in Mexico, perhaps she used those herbs that weaken a man's will. Now I don't believe in any of that. Arnulfo didn't need herbs; he was odd all his life, although we didn't realize it, so odd that his second marriage, to the German, still baffles me."

She talked without stopping, reclining on a large gray velvet couch. They were sitting in the living room on the ground floor of her house in Coyoacán, the one where the maid had paused briefly, he believed, to allow time to admire the home's treasures. A less private space than the room where she'd received him on his previous visit. What an exhausting accumulation of objects! On one wall descended a squadron of baroque angels of various sizes and designs; the mere sight of them produced vertigo. She explained that her daughter-in-law had brought them recently and hung them against her will. People had given so many things to Antonio, and he couldn't refuse. Well, now the objects are there, safe. Otherwise, they might have been seized. There were things in heaps: ivories, crystal, porcelain of different kinds, some very delicate pieces, but most of them of atrocious taste. Big oriental urns, bronzes, gilded wood. She wouldn't have half that junk in her home, she explained. All those horrors had been gifts, she repeated; they were there in transit, temporarily. Eduviges Briones stood up, moved with difficulty among the excessive pieces of furniture, pointed to several of them, and began to rail against the bad taste of the time, and in particular her daughter-in-law Gilda's. She was wearing one of those long tubular dresses that he associated with magazines from 1914, stacks of which he'd reviewed during the previous years. Only his aunt was capable of wearing those clothes so casually. A satin dress that touched her ankle, like a long tube that contained her corpulent body, and, as the only adornments, a border of lilac and maroon glass beads and, as a symmetrical complement, a bouquet of flowers of the same material around the shoulders. A splendid art deco dress. Coiffed, made up: a civilized person and not the exaggerated madwoman of the previous visit. Del Solar gave her a copy of his book, one of the three that Cruz-García had given him. She leafed through it, read the dedication, and with a downcast face asked him to please humor her, to write a few words to Amparo, who always read his things, who never missed his articles nor his interviews in the newspapers. She'd devoured his book on Freemasonry in Mexico. Mora, no? She'd be understandably offended if he refused, adding that her conversations with him, her Sunday outings, had restored in her a bit of confidence in life, which she very much needed.

"She's not young anymore. At heart she never was. When she was a child I always had the impression that I was dealing with a grown woman. She's very responsible. She started working very young; she had to interrupt her studies to help us. That's why she couldn't finish her degree. One day I asked Joaquín Granados to take her to Italy; I told him that a more loyal and hardworking employee he'd never find. It would be good for her to learn another language, to be a bit more worldly. You can imagine, because of her defect, how important it is to provide her with security. There's nothing better than travel. Too bad I started doing it so late! Your cousin didn't want to go. My husband had already become ill, and she didn't want to leave him. She's a very responsible girl. One day she'll marry someone who wants to settle down, who likes to work in peace. She loves children. Her leaving will break my heart. Do you realize that? I'll be completely alone. But I'll be glad to know that she'll have an independent life, that she'll be happy and make others happy."

Shortly after, Amparo arrived. Her mother handed her the book. She read the dedication; she went up to Del Solar and kissed his cheek. Certain insignificant acts—the way Amparo greeted her mother then sat down, the sudden conspiratorial tone—led Miguel del Solar to believe that the pair was plotting his incorporation into the family. They seemed to be performing a play. They spoke to each other in an unusual way, between sweet and ceremonious, which was very disturbing. To break the atmosphere, he commented on the book he was planning. A book about the famous year 1942, the year of the declaration of war on the Axis countries. Mother and daughter were reluctant to talk about it at first, preferring to talk about Juan and Irma, Miguel's children, whom Amparo would pick up from time to time to take them for a walk.

"The other day I saw Delfina Uribe, Aunt," said Del Solar as soon as they moved to the dining room. "She told me she's always envied your elegance." And he repeated the phrases Delfina used when talking about Eduviges's personal style of dress. "According to her you were one of her idols when she was young."

"Now that's queer! I would never have imagined that such compliments would come to me from those quarters. Not because it's not true; but because she's always been reluctant to recognize any merit in others. Queer indeed! Delfina Uribe had all the money she wanted to travel and keep up with fashion. She dressed well, but impersonally, as if she were shopping at Sears. At one point I ran out of money. I was content to continue to wear clothes that I knew were beautiful, with minimal adaptations. At one time, when I could buy whatever I wanted, I realized it was too late to change. I held fast to my style, and here I am."

And so, between fabrics and hats, without the two women noticing, they reached the year 1942. Del Solar asked about the way Briones's wife dressed. Was she elegant? Did she wear

French fashions? And it was then that his aunt commented on Arnulfo Briones's queerness, his rapacity, his harshness toward his sisters. Not only did he control the hacienda of their parents, who, no matter how far they'd fallen, still had something, but he left neither her nor her children a cent, contrary to what he'd always led her to believe. He hadn't made a will, or if he had, he didn't file it, so anyone could have destroyed it. Everything about him had been queer. His long bachelorhood. His first marriage, to that woman from Tampico with the fox coat with whom he sailed to Hamburg; the death of the poor woman on an operating table while her appendix was being removed, an illness from which no one died anymore; and his second marriage with its spate of surprises. He'd been married in Berlin. This time they'd received a proper invitation.

"Did anyone go to the wedding?"

"From the family, you mean? Who do you expect should have gone? The only one who could travel was Arnulfo. Because of his association with the shipping lines he could have gotten a pair of tickets on a German liner. Not even one for me, his sister. I thought Arnulfo was another kind of man, let's say, an idealist. During his lifetime, I was convinced of it, I would have sworn to it. Out of loyalty to him I fought with many people. Now, however, I'm no longer sure of anything. If you think about it, even then his ideas were a thing of the past, anachronisms. Dionisio tried to make me understand it many times, but the fact that he was my brother, the eldest, led me to admire him. One goes about learning things in life. The hard way. The first thing that strikes me when I think of him is his pettiness, his selfishness. He kept the family property; it was in ruin, I know; he improved it and from those spoils he built his fortune. Gloria, my sister, and I received no help. She, fortunately, didn't need it; I did. Dionisio, and you know this well, sometimes worked eighteen hours a day; at night he translated law books, and that was just to get by. Arnulfo's help consisted of paying the rent for our apartment, where he received his mail and had an office where he received occasional clients . . . and what people one had to put up with in return! And the risk he put us all in! Dionisio ended up losing his government position. But nothing that happened to others mattered to him. He was selfish, fractious, intolerant. And mysterious, which is what I found most shocking. His whole life was mysterious. Dionisio knew him best. At least as a young man, at a time when boys tend to be sociable. For me, he was always an enigma. Even now, there are a thousand things I don't understand. Antonio once told me that it was better not to understand or worry too much about the past. One had to make a cut, to leave everything behind forever. Sometimes it seems that we never get out of it. 'Let the dead bury their dead!' your cousin used to say. But the fact is, it's us they're burying."

All her elation was shattered. She remained pensive; she looked as if she were about to burst into tears.

"Derny believes the same."

"What?" she asked half-heartedly, no longer interested.

"The same as Antonio," Del Solar interrupted. "That every age has a physiognomy, and that it's not always wise to judge one by the laws of another."

"If it becomes necessary to judge an era, it would be best to apply the laws of dialectics," Amparo added.

"Where did you learn that gibberish, Miss Know-it-all? Can you tell me that?" said Eduviges with sudden fury, coming back to life. "One may or may not agree with him, but it seems that Arnulfo couldn't live anything except that kind of queer, isolated, twisted life that was his. That's all I've tried to say."

"As a conspirator."

"I don't discuss politics; I don't care to; I don't like to be misunderstood. I'm just talking about his personal life."

"So he married a woman from Tampico first?"

"Yes, she was very common, like a little monkey. When he introduced her to us, he'd been married for who knows how long. I'd thought, as I told you, that some religious organization had imposed chastity on him. Rubbish! He took her to live in Hamburg. She wasn't even able to go home to die, which, according to Martínez, was the only thing she asked of him. Once I asked Dionisio if Arnulfo had been a carouser in his youth, and he told me that when he was a boy neither of them was a womanizer, because their confessors were very strict. 'But he must have had someone, I don't doubt,' he said. 'He paid a visit to a woman somewhere.' They both married old. He must have been almost sixty when he set sail with that horror of a woman who ate with her foxes on and did nothing but push up the little veil on her hat so the spoonsful of soup wouldn't get it wet. He returned to Mexico City a widower, stayed here for a short time, and returned to Germany. He moved his offices and settled in Berlin. He did the right thing to live somewhere other than Mexico. The political climate was bad for him. That's why he had to escape to Tamaulipas before leaving. He stopped writing for the newspapers; people would call and insult him on the phone. Delfina Uribe told me that it wasn't true, her father had told her, that they'd taken away his newspaper column on orders from the government, but because the newspaper didn't like traitors, that he'd left many people in the insurrection in the lurch while he washed his hands of it. Now, I took everything that came from the Uribe family with a grain of salt because they were venting their pain. Anyway, once, as Arnulfo and I were leaving Sagrada Familia, some strangers came up to him, grabbed him by the lapels, and insulted him. All that, of course, made him very nervous. When he came back, after he was widowed, his situation was better. I think in large part thanks to the efforts of Haroldo Goenaga; so when he settled permanently in Mexico City he was already reconciled with his former allies, or so it seemed to Dionisio. The rooms he had in my apartment were meant to confuse his enemies. Another thing I don't forgive him for! The apartment in the Minerva Building was just a disguise. The authorities, his enemies, those who were interested in following his movements, believed that it was the place from which he was acting clandestinely. That wasn't true. It was designed for that purpose, so they wouldn't monitor other places, one of which was the real location of his activities. Wait, wait, don't interrupt me," she said, seeing that Del Solar already wanted to ask questions. "When he was about to return from Germany, one of his employees began to visit me, one of his 'advisers' as he used to call certain collaborators. He'd worked with him in Germany. But what was the point of all this, Amparo?"

"You mentioned an employee who started visiting you."

"What were those activities that had to be done clandestinely?" Del Solar took the opportunity to ask.

"One of Arnulfo's employees? Yes, I know that, I don't need to ask that; but what was the point of it? Well, I think, Miguel, I told you about him the other day, I'm not sure; a disgusting type. I ended up distrusting everything about him. He started showing up at my apartment, asking about my brother, the date of his arrival, the name of the boat. He wanted to go to welcome him in Veracruz, or in Tampico, wherever he was arriving. He said he had very important and urgent things to tell him. He'd worked with him in Hamburg. He told me about his life in Germany. He'd come into my house and look at me with a clairvoyant's eyes and make strange faces. Only Arnulfo, who was very much an imbecile, could trust such collaborators. He made me nervous, among other reasons because his gestures never matched his words, at times they meant the exact opposite. He'd say that something was very small and open his arms to show that it was as big as the world. Insignificant things, if you like, but things that concealed an anomaly. And the way he looked at me was very disrespectful, no matter who was present. In part for conversation, but mostly out of curiosity—which is natural for a sister, wouldn't you say?—I asked him about Arnulfo's life in Germany. I imagined him lonely, devastated, after the death of that crab woman. 'Not as alone as you might imagine; you've nothing to worry about in that regard,' he replied with a rather fresh wink. I didn't understand, so I asked him to clarify his remark, and he began to tell me that in Berlin Arnulfo met with his partners, his clients, and coreligionists, but also with one or two less than solemn friends. 'Don't forget,' he said, 'your brother is in the prime of his life, and Berlin is the vice capital of the world. My good lady, one day I'd like to tell you two or three tasty little things!' Very fresh! Don't you agree? That thing he said about the prime of life is a lie. Arnulfo was already an old fogy, and he looked older than he was. He was always pale, shriveled. 'Droopy,' my aunts used to call him. 'Yes,' that smooth talker insisted, 'don't think he's being neglected,' and then he talked about the women at the zoo. On more than one occasion I had to cut him off. One day I told him with absolute curtness that perhaps he didn't need to come to the apartment anymore, that he should leave his phone number with me, and I'd give it to my brother when he arrived. He'd call him when he had the opportunity. He had to be reined in, to learn limits. Once I ran into him on the ground floor of the building. He seemed to be waiting for someone. Suddenly Ida Werfel passed by with her daughter, and that vulgarian took me by the arm, forced us to move toward them, and said to me, 'Please introduce me to the lady.' When I realized what he was doing, it was too late. Until then I'd never spoken to that woman. His tactlessness left me flabbergasted. On that occasion when I cut him off, Martínez hid his tail between his legs; he was a sly one, a fox, but also a chicken; worse, a rat. Over time I came to know who he was."

"Who had knives out for your brother?"

"Aren't you listening to me? I'm telling you about the scum Arnulfo was mixed up with. Martínez disappeared for a while, then he reappeared, more sober in appearance, more cautious . . . but little by little he returned to his former self. It became necessary for me to put a definitive stop to it. Fortunately, Arnulfo arrived. Dionisio and I didn't go to welcome him in Veracruz. He did. A few days later my brother showed up at the house, sporting a reddish-gray wig. He looked worse than when he was bald. Older and more ridiculous. He told me that, when he finished settling into his house in Polanco, Dionisio and I should stop by to meet Adele, his wife. He should have brought her to visit me; it would have been the proper thing to do, don't you think? But—do you see?—Arnulfo was one of those people who knew nothing about manners. It was a manifestation of his selfishness, of the contempt he felt for others. He told me that his wife, the German, had a child from a previous marriage who had traveled with them, and she needed to get her documents in order, which was quite a complicated matter given the international situation. 'The fact that she's Austrian and not strictly German will help,' he told me. I assumed that he'd married a widow. Keep in mind, from a very young age, he'd moved almost exclusively among priests and sacristans. It would have been easier for me to imagine him living in common law with the boy's mother than for him to marry a divorcée. He didn't explain anything to me about her family relationships that day. He wanted to see the apartment, the room where we kept his books and papers. You slept there at that time," she said to Amparo. "He said that the room was acceptable, that he was going to use it; it worked out for him because it had its own door to the outside corridor, a bath, and a sort of dressing room that he could use, if necessary, as a waiting room. He would rearrange everything. Within a matter of days, he'd send a file cabinet, a bookcase, a desk, and a divan, in case he needed to take a nap. Ah, and it was essential that I tell the doorman, and if possible the neighbors, that he was going to rent the room. He decided that he'd always enter through my living room, that he'd keep the key to the door that connected his office with the rest of the apartment, and that he didn't want the servants to clean, except when he requested it, and always in his presence. I could keep a key, if the need should arise. If anyone came to see him, they'd do so through the outside door. He didn't talk to me like his sister, but like a doorwoman. He gave me orders. I repeated that we'd set up the room as Amparo's bedroom, as he could see from the furniture and toys, and he answered me calmly that, yes, he'd already heard, that I should move the girl immediately, as he wanted to use the room in a week at the latest. His work couldn't wait. I became angry with a vengeance. Martínez's revelations about my brother's escapades in Berlin blinded me. His escapades with the women in the zoo. It seemed as though the instructions he gave me with an authoritative tone were intended only to conceal the fact that he was preparing a room 'with access to a bathroom,' for his escapades. 'Do you intend to close your office on Avenida Juárez?' I asked. He looked at me sullenly, and said no, what was wrong with me, that he needed it more than ever. 'Then receive your honeys there and not in the room where my daughter sleeps,' I shouted. In my mind, he was showing the most unimaginable disrespect for me, for my husband and my children, that he would even consider installing a sex den in my home—forgive me!—and I told him so. I think I even cried, out of rage, nothing else. He glared at me in astonishment, then in disgust. He gave me one of those insufferable looks of revulsion that had earned him so many enemies. He didn't say a word; he turned his back on me, walked down the inner hallway to the dining room, where Dionisio was waiting for us to have coffee. Arnulfo told my husband that he wasn't willing to tolerate my insolence, and that he wanted the room vacated in a couple of days. That had been the arrangement. He'd paid regularly; now we had to comply with what we'd agreed. He needed to organize his work as quickly as possible. For the next few days, he hardly spoke to me. A man as cold as a stone! That's how he was! Then I saw that everything was indeed in order. He insisted that at four in the afternoon we turn on the lights in his office. He arrived every evening at about five, that is, an hour after the lights had been turned on, so that the neighbors wouldn't associate his arrival with the lights in his office being turned on. Silliness! He'd enter through the front door, into my living room, walk down an inner hallway to his office, and stay locked up in there for a while. Very few people visited him then, a few men and sometimes a chubby, middle-aged woman who looked like a retired nun, whom no one would ever mistake for a paramour. Shortly before finishing, his collaborator would come to pick him up.

"Martínez?"

"Yes. You mean, you remember him?"

"No."

"Then how do you know his name was Martínez?"

"Because you mentioned him several times tonight."

"I did? Oh, yes, of course! I told you the stories that brute told me about the loose life Arnulfo led in Germany. Well, he'd come for him. He always knocked at my door, not at the office. One morning, very early, Martínez arrived with a workman, and they put up a plaque next to the office door. 'Manuel J. Bernárdez. Permits,' it said. I asked my brother what that meant, and he said it was nothing. 'What does *permits* mean?' He answered, with a surly smile, 'Everything and at the same time nothing.' Possibly to throw off busybodies. We ignored the office, as if it had nothing to do with the house. No one would have imagined bothering him. No one applies for a permit in the abstract. Tenants were permitted to sublet one or more rooms. I paid the owners a little more; that was all. 'He's so clever!' I said to myself. 'He knows every trick in the book!' Little by little, we reestablished trust. In the evenings, after leaving his office, he would sit down and have a coffee with me. He talked about the gradual degeneration of the world. He said that if he'd known years ago, when he'd rented the apartment before traveling to Hamburg, what the building was going to become, he wouldn't have rented it. A Babel. The same was happening all over the city. People who had come from one didn't know exactly where. They were arriving from every corner of Europe, even from Turkey, like an Armenian Jew, the very wealthy Androgán, who came from Istanbul, to whom the whole city bowed, and who, it was said, had bought several of the best homes in the south of the city, especially in San Ángel. I was telling my brother that the same thing was happening in Colonia Roma, and in Colonia Juárez, and in Cuauhtémoc, not to mention in Hipódromo and Condesa, where Yiddish was heard more than Spanish, that it was happening all over the city, so we shouldn't worry too much. In the Minerva there were refugees from Germany, Spain, Hungary, Holland, and, what do I know, many other places. But there were also Mexicans, some of the finest, like the García Bañoses, who lived, poor things, in monastic austerity and supported themselves binding books— very expensive, opulent bindings, of the finest quality, but manual labor nonetheless. People who came out of the Revolution also lived there, such as Delfina Uribe, who wasted money with dreadful ostentation. Arnulfo listened to me very carefully. He was interested in knowing who was who, who was talking to whom. I kept him in the know. I tried to keep him on alert against that sinister Balmorán, a small-time hack reporter, a muckraker, who was about to publish a libelous article against our family, most certainly paid for by someone. Arnulfo listened to me; he said that all of that would soon be over, he was sure of it. If the world didn't correct itself, it would end in ruin, which couldn't happen. Order was necessary, and so order would come. We were on the threshold of a new history. No matter who opposed it. When he talked like that, a voice came out of him that was so tomblike that it gave me goose bumps. I just looked at him. His glazed eyes were full of tears. It was dreadful! He had aged so much during his stay in Germany! His skin had become wizened and mottled. His sight was growing increasingly worse. And the way he looked up, into the void, made him look even older. His way of walking, his faltering cane, his unsteady gait, all made him look more like my father than my brother. What an old dodderer! He was definitely ill. One afternoon, as we were leaving the Sagrada Familia, a mob of students surrounded us and began to dance and sing in unison: 'Crabs! Crabs! Crabs! Marching to the beat! Run! Run! Run! Crabs in retreat!' or something like that; they kept shouting, making faces, and wouldn't let us walk. Finally a traffic policeman came to our aid. I was very nervous, frightened. When the pack of hooligans scattered, a tall man came up to my brother and told him in very bad Spanish, I mean with a very thick foreign accent, that he deserved that and more. It wouldn't be long, he told him, before he'd hear from his firm, and he walked away. I all but had to drag Arnulfo off. He stumbled the entire time; he looked like an idiot. What a difficult man he was! He disapproved of my making friends, greeting the neighbors, speaking to Delfina. On one occasion I was going to take a trip with her to Guadalajara, and he made a scene that you wouldn't believe. Prohibitions, threats, hot air, that was Arnulfo."

"Wasn't he surprised that you went to Delfina's party?"

"Are you kidding! I'll say he thought it was wrong! But I hatched a plot to confuse him. Erich, his stepson, told me at Delfina's house that someone had called him in the morning, supposedly a boy he'd met at the sports club, to invite him to the party. When I asked the hostess, Delfina, about his friend, it turned out that she didn't know who he was. From what I found out, someone made those kinds of phantom invitations to people who, in some cases, didn't even know who Delfina was. The next day Arnulfo was frantic, a nervous wreck, and a finished man all at once. From then on, he lived in fear. He'd just made the arrangements for the funeral when I came to see him. He wanted to know what Erich and I were doing in that house. I repeated to him what his stepson had told me, and added, in front of Martínez (and some have the nerve to say that I have no courage!), that shortly before the party began I received a call and a voice identical to Martínez's asked me to meet Erich at Delfina's house. A good one, don't you think? He needed a taste of his own medicine, that nasty character, my brother's so-called 'adviser.' He waved his arms, grimaced, and without a doubt would've liked to strangle me, but I didn't flinch, and I cold-bloodedly repeated my tall tale and left the room. I would've liked to know how he explained his own presence in the room and his assault on Werfel."

"I never imagined you and Delfina were friends. 'Your aunt,' she said, 'is one of the few women in Mexico who has what can be called class.'"

"But how could I not have it! We grew up in very different

worlds. My grandparents still lived in the Palacio de Canalejos. It was wonderful! A house made of tezontle with stone mascarons, where there are now sugar warehouses, I think. I still remember being in that house as a child. By contrast, Delfina's grandparents were peasants. Barefoot Indians. She told me so herself. According to Arnulfo, her father was one of the pillars of Masonry in Mexico. Who knows! Arnulfo was forever seeing Moors with daggers everywhere he looked. He insisted so forcefully, pressured and threatened to such an extent that my relationship with Delfina was shattered. I was shocked that she invited me to her party, in fact. Perhaps we weren't as friendly, as you say, but we did get along well enough. Of course we did!" she said upon reflection, "We actually saw each other every day. Who would imagine! On one occasion she suggested that I work with her. Handling the public relations for her gallery or some such. They say she's made millions, do you think? That seems like an exaggeration. I stopped seeing her because of Arnulfo's fixation. He was suspicious of her and her relatives. Pure paranoia, Antonio would say. He thought everyone was watching him, persecuting him, and setting traps for him. Well, now that I think about it, he wasn't so wrong. But he could be such a pain! He was constantly interrogating me. Who is who? He was even afraid of the Bombón sisters, neighbors, harmless singers but a bit unsavory because they sometimes received politicians in their apartment. He'd say that one could never take too many precautions. Sometimes he made me see red. I've come to think that it was those precautions that brought him misfortune. 'You don't want me to talk to anyone. You insist that I have no friends, don't you? But instead, you have no problem if I replace the friends I lose with yours,' I told him one day when I was in a foul mood. Above all, I was annoyed by his refusal to allow Dionisio and me to have the relationship with his wife that we were entitled to. Were we or were we not brother and sister? We'd grown up under the same roof until the day I married. He invited us once, very ceremoniously, to have dinner when they finally moved into their home in Polanco. Until then I didn't even know where they lived. I was able to gather from Martínez's slips of the tongue that they were staying in hotels while the work on the house was being completed; every so often they'd change hotels. They lived in separate rooms. The German woman wasn't at all nice, but it didn't matter, she was my sister-in-law. Her French was bad, although it was good enough so that we could understand each other. Later, she claimed that she only spoke German, and communication became impossible. Who better than I to be her guide in Mexico? Introduce her to people, take her to those places worth knowing. Alert her to what could happen. In the end, she failed to give me the green light, and Arnulfo discouraged our friendship. Later I learned why. I was irritated by his obsession that everyone was against us. Sometimes I think so too, but in a different way. The whole world was our enemy, but he didn't lift a finger when I told him about a very dangerous one: Balmorán. I told him a thousand times that that man wanted to do us harm, that he'd brazenly told me about a relative of ours who'd gone mad from leading a licentious life. But there you have it, that didn't worry him. I told him, annoyed, that if anyone was interested in knowing whom he was receiving at his permit office they'd find out sooner or later. It was impossible for the maids not to find out, unless he thought I should do without them, which I wouldn't accept, because I was unable to manage the house alone. I didn't realize that that was exactly what he wanted, that people think that it was some sort of clandestine office, so that they wouldn't look for him anywhere else. He'd turned us into his laboratory rats. If anything happened to us, oh well, too bad! One day I told him that Martínez was snooping around the building too much, and that I had proof of his lack of discretion. He finally seemed to come out of his slumber. Why did I say that? Everything led to an interrogation. I told him very dryly that that busybody had shared with me certain aspects of his life in Berlin; he knew exactly what I meant. Something in my tone must have alarmed him. He jumped out of his chair, surprised, frightened. He shook me by the arm and demanded that I repeat what Martínez had said. Everything I knew. 'Everything?' I asked him, because in the end he didn't scare me anymore; on the contrary, his constant abuse only made me disloyal. 'Everything?' I repeated, my courage plucked. 'Can you take it? You know very well what I mean. Your first wife couldn't take it.' He let go of me, took a few steps backward and fell into a chair. He looked as if he were about to suffer a stroke. Then I let slip rather mischievously that Martínez had told me how successful he'd been with certain women who wandered the paths at the zoo. He was pensive; it was obvious that I'd taken a huge load off his shoulders; he finally burst out laughing. He labeled Martínez a joker. Then, in passing, he wanted to know if Martínez had told me about Hermelinda, which was the name of his honey, her illness, her treatment. Nothing, I said. And it was true. But, can you believe it, there was another mystery emerging, and no matter where you scratched it, it was the same. At last I knew why Arnulfo and his wife wanted nothing to do with us. They were hiding things that I learned about in a roundabout way. One day that monumental woman who'd filled the stairwell with her figure, Professor Werfel, stopped me. They say she was a prominent figure; I don't know about that. She was with Lala Carrasco, the wife of a well-known banker at the time. She and her husband made themselves out to be patrons, but they were nothing but a pathetic pair of showoffs whom everyone made fun of. I'd known Lala since she was a child; we studied at the French school together, so I stopped to say hello. I also said hello to Werfel, as was only proper. What means I had to endure to arrive at those revelations! She told me that she knew I was related by marriage to a famous opera singer from Dresden. 'A wonderful voice,' she said to Lala, whom she was trying to impress, but not to me, who was a mere pretext, 'particularly brilliant in the Mozartian repertoire. An extraordinary Doña Elvira.' It took me by surprise. 'No, señora, forgive me, but you're mistaken,' I answered with naivete. At the moment I didn't even remember that I had a sister-in-law or that she was German; that's how far Arnulfo and his wife had pushed me into the background. 'How strange!' replied the Jew, 'I must be confused. But by chance isn't one of your brothers married to Adele Waltzer?'

"'Yes, that's true.' At that moment I remembered Arnulfo's instructions. To run from those people, not to talk to them, not to open up, not to trust them. But it was impossible to deny something as public as my brother's marriage. Anyone who was of a mind could find out that Arnulfo was married to that German woman, whose last name I'd just learned for the first time, and that the couple and the wife's child were living in a house on Calle de Anatole France in Polanco. I was on tenterhooks. I didn't allow her to finish. 'Yes, that's right,' was all I could say. 'You see,' continued the professor, 'Adele is a biologist; Anette, a singer, a marvelous soprano. A specialist in Mozart, but also attentive to the most recent musical forms. The last thing I heard her sing was Strauss's *Die schweigsame Frau*, but that was in Amsterdam; she was a guest singer. A few days ago her sister-in-law's first husband, Hanno, the doctor, had visited her with his son. It was the young man who told me that his mother had in-laws in this building. I was pleased to hear that it was you. "I don't know her well,'" I said, "'but it's not difficult to detect a refined sensitivity in her."'"

"'Thank you,' I replied, because what else could I say? I was confused, or lost, rather, in that table of relationships that I didn't quite understand, and curious to know more about it since Arnulfo seemed to suspect even me, as he never trusted me with anything. 'So this is where the husband of a Mozartian singer lives,' said Lala. 'I'd like to meet him one day. Ida, see if you can convince him to give us a talk about Richard Strauss,' and then, playing the clever little girl, a talent she lacked, but always employed, she added: 'We've become cosmopolitan, Eduviges. Until recently we mingled only with our friends from Querétaro and Guadalajara. Today German singers, scholars, and artists from all over the world live among us, and this international monument to knowledge, our beloved citizen of the world, Ida Werfel.' Really! Lala was too pretentious, sickly sweet; a showoff, as I said. From a very young age she nurtured the ambition of one day hosting a literary salon. 'No, not Annette Waltzer's husband; I'm referring to Adele's former husband, the señora's current sister-in-law,' insisted the Jew, 'a man who discovered hell but managed to escape it and is here now.'

"'We're living in new time, Eduviges,' said the witless Lala, whom I could have killed, 'and divorce is no longer that Leviathan they taught us to fear for as long as I can remember, but a modern institution to which civilized people resort when necessary.' I was speechless, dumbfounded, as if lightning had struck me. I climbed the stairs as best I could, without realizing it, like an automaton. The apostle of tradition! The moralist to the end! Like a whitewashed tomb! I questioned Martínez, whom I found in my apartment. I detested going to him; he was becoming more and more presumptuous, to the extent that between Arnulfo and him one could no longer tell who was the boss and who was the subordinate. He pretended not to know anything. I bombarded him with questions as he had me. In his day, he said, reigned a beautiful woman from Tamaulipas, who couldn't stand the climate of Germany. He crossed paths with her in Hamburg, witnessed her illness and her death, 'absolutely natural,' he added, 'no matter what anyone says, I assure you, ab-so-lute-ly natural.' I don't know why, but I felt a shudder. 'I came to know Adele in Mexico,' he added, 'and that was, one might say, on sight.' Suddenly he began to lash out against my brother. He said he only gave him the dirty jobs, and he was getting fed up with the work. Some gentlemen were living the high life, but they were making the mistake of the century if they continued to treat him like a nobody. 'You tell your brother that I think it's time that we started respecting each other! Tell him I'm getting tired of having to take all the rough and none of the smooth! If I ever decided to open my mouth . . . !' With that, Arnulfo came out of his office. Martínez stood up like a lightning bolt. He was afraid, I think, of having been overheard. His voice changed. He rolled his eyes as he waved. 'Anything new, Martínez?'

" 'Nothing, señor.'

" 'Let's go then! I still want to go downtown and buy a book.' I couldn't say goodbye. I didn't want to talk to Arnulfo until I'd cleared up the situation. He'd deceived me again, like always. Just as he had done when he left me and Gloria without an inheritance. Today I hear talk of divorce, without giving it a second thought. I've gotten used to it. What's more, if someone told me that Antonio was thinking of divorcing Gilda, I'd be the first to applaud it. At the time it was unusual. That Delfina Uribe should divorce was nothing, logical, she came from nothing, a child of the Revolution. But the fact that a divorcée was brought into the Briones house, and that it was Arnulfo who caused the disarray, was another matter. I sent for Ida Werfel's daughter, a sort of trembling little mouse who was always frightened, and I said, 'Please call this number from my telephone and ask to speak to Erich Pistauer. Tell him to come here, that every year I knit something for the family, and I'd like to make him a sweater; I need his measurements. Tell him to come by this afternoon, any time.' The boy arrived. I had the Werfel girl come down again, to act as my interpreter, so that there'd be no doubt about our conversation. It was all true! That young man's father had recently arrived in Mexico. He was a surgeon. He had operated on the girl from Tamaulipas. He'd experienced many difficulties before leaving, but he was finally in Mexico. Didn't I tell you that story?"

"No!"

"Amparo knows it by heart. Oh well! I demanded an explanation from Arnulfo, and his answer wasn't entirely convincing, but he may have been correct as far as religion was concerned. I didn't surprise him, he wasn't alarmed, which is what I expected. I lost my courage. He was married in the Catholic Church. The ecclesiastical requirements had been met. Adele had been baptized. For me, all the effect was lost. I changed the subject; I repeated the threat that the documents Balmorán possessed posed to us. For the first time he seemed to listen to me. I repeated that he was linked to Licenciado Uribe's family. At that moment, Martínez arrived and winked at me, which I took as a bad omen."

"Balmorán's documents are altogether different," Del Solar tried to intervene. "They have nothing to do with your relative."

"Don't talk about what you don't know, please. Did I tell you he came to see me one day? Please, allow me to finish! I was testing the water. A few days later he returned to tell me that his house had been robbed and his papers stolen. He even called the police. Go tell that to someone else! I'm sure he wanted me to believe that if the papers were published he wouldn't be responsible. The only way to shut him up was to keep him permanently terrified. From time to time I let him know a few things. I have my sources. One day that clown Martínez showed up, whom I was beginning to loathe more and more, and after going around in circles he told me that Balmorán's papers had indeed been stolen but that he knew someone who could get me the documents I was interested in. He could show me a sample chapter, and I could get the rest at a very good price. I replied that it was his duty to share the news with Arnulfo, to tell him that the documents were for sale. He would decide whether it was worth buying them or not. Martínez didn't even flinch. He told me that his friend's acquaintance would be happy to involve the courts, that he liked publicity. I accepted his terms. He gave me photos of about fourteen handwritten pages where Spanish was mixed with something similar to a macaronic Italian, which according to the specialist I consulted was a mere Italianized Spanish. It was a vulgar and shameless tale about an Italian adventuress who knew a Mexican Indian woman and tried to pass her off in Europe as a eunuch. Everything was so vulgar that it was disgusting. I couldn't believe what they were translating. Martínez truly knew no limits! To what end had he given me that scandalous story? I still can't explain it. The next day, he came by to find out my decision. I told him that the pages were rubbish, that he shouldn't waste my time with such tasteless jokes. Somehow, I made him feel that there were fundamental differences between us, that I considered the incident the straw that broke the camel's back, and that I didn't want to have any more contact with him. That he would have to settle for my saying hello to him, and not to expect anything more. I mentioned the incident to Arnulfo. I insisted that he take care of that reptile. He was very worried. By then he was living in absolute anguish. There were days when he was in such a state of stress that I said, 'He's at a breaking point; when least expected he'll collapse.' And that's how it was. Well, they broke him, caused him to collapse. His last month was a continuous earthquake. He went from one catastrophe to another. What a frenzy! They killed his stepson; he tried to get his wife out of the country, deep down what he wanted was to flee with her, but they didn't allow them to cross the border. He stayed in a hotel in Ensenada for a few days. Then he went back to Adele; they arranged the documents, and before they finished, what we all know, happened."

"He'd also fallen out in those days with Goenaga, his cousin."

"Who told you that?" Eduviges asked apprehensively.

"Derny. But they reconciled shortly before the end. On the last day they were together. Strange that they should quarrel, don't you think?"

"Arnulfo was fighting with everyone. With me every day. There's nothing strange about that. He was very nervous. He was surrounded. To think that Haroldo Goenaga behaved badly with him is a mistake, an injustice you shouldn't commit. The foolishness that my brother was involved in concerned him very much. As it did everyone else. He'd reached a negotiated solution, he told me. They would let him leave Mexico provided he declare that he wouldn't get into trouble anymore. Poor Haroldo felt like a Judas; he wasn't able to hold his head up ever again. They'd made him a promise. He trusted them; he thought he was dealing with gentlemen; he wasn't. When Arnulfo arrived at Avenida Juárez he was struck on the back of the head and then a car ran over him. Remember that he was almost blind. It was very quick. Nobody saw. It was Sunday, the city center was almost empty."

"Who killed him?"

"What questions! How many times have I wished I didn't know! Dionisio said at the time that it would be unwise to investigate. Perhaps I wouldn't be talking to you if they had. After the funeral Haroldo didn't open his mouth again."

"And the wife? Adele? Did she stay here?"

"She collected the inheritance and left. With her first husband, I imagine. And we, contrary to everything that Arnulfo had promised us, didn't receive a cent."

They finished dinner.

"I'm going to try to locate Martínez. He must know something."

Eduviges looked at the clock. She became startled. She had to make a long-distance call. She got up from the table, said goodbye hurriedly, and disappeared.

Amparo changed the topic of conversation. She told him that discussing the subject made her very nervous. That night, unlike others, she'd been calm, because he wielded a calming influence on her. She thanked him again for the dedication in the book. She would start reading it that very night. She offered to take care of the many practical matters that he would probably have to deal with in the next few weeks. Looking at houses, schools for the children. She had nothing but free time, a car, and a driver. He said goodbye. As he headed for his mother's house, he told himself that it was a blessing to have a cousin like Amparo. He was interested in hearing her comments about *The Year 1914*.

CHAPTER 12

The End

DELFINA SAID GOODBYE TO A YOUNG girl with the look of a porcelain doll: a very pale face, extremely long black curly tresses, eyebrows, and eyelashes. She was a girl from the university, she told Del Solar, who arrived just then. She visited her once a week, and they recorded their conversations for an hour and a half or two hours.

"She has me recount anecdotes about the painters, galleries, the city's daily life and nightlife during this century. I like talking to her, but it tires me. I was born when the century was just beginning. I interacted with my parents' friends, my brothers' and sisters' friends, when I was very young. That is, I've known practically everyone who's figured prominently in one way or another in the country. Now in my seventies, I feel like a species that survived the flood. It's exhausting, Miguel; take my word for it. The girl turns on her tape recorder, I go about remembering, and at times I become terrified because it's like an army of shadows is marching through the room."

"The Love Parade?"

"Not always, alas," she suddenly smiled. "A movie, isn't it? And, if I'm not wrong, Lubitsch. Yes?"

"The Love Parade, and Delfina Uribe its golden majorette!" he said, unable to contain himself. She looked at him as if he were a madman. Her smile froze on her lips at the suspicion that Del Solar had disrespected her.

"Just imagine!" she said in a haughty tone, "Today I told this girl about the wedding of one of Carranza's daughters to General Aguilar, in Querétaro. A decadently lavish party! The high command with all the de rigueur accoutrements! What thunderous toasts! Thousands of those embraces that politicians give each other to know whether the other is armed or not. Infinite cheers to revolutionary unity. Months later, half of the attendees were fighting against the other half. Some rose and fell on the battlefield, others in villainous ambushes, or they ended up in jail. Some, like my father, chose exile. Yes, Miguel, after Carranza's death we set sail for Havana, and after a few months we continued on to Spain. Seventy years in Mexico, I assure you, are more than anywhere else! I've experienced many upheavals. Abrupt changes. And as a backdrop, uncertainty. I'm not sure that it wasn't all a big failure." She paused, noticing where she was and with whom. "You might ask, and rightfully so, what's the point of all this? Well, I read your book. It made me feel like an utter fossil. You know, I lived through and witnessed many of the events you describe. I must have been twelve or thirteen years old then. At that age one has very precise memories. As I said: I am old age." She laughed with her entire body. Her mouth suddenly became enormous. Somehow the fact that she survived, and did so with such personal success, must have given her satisfaction. "I wanted to tell you that although I generally agree with you, I find a certain intolerance in your treatment. You see, many of the caudillos, some of whom I met, so I'm not exaggerating, came from absolutely barbaric origins, and these men of gallows and knife, with astounding intuition and political sensitivity, you demand they behave and debate like full-time researchers at the Colegio de México. Just imagine the time! Good God, everything was new! Our parents emerged from swamps devoid of guarantees, rights, and civil traditions!

One thing I think you understand very well: in 1914 the possibilities of the Revolution were already in sight. The diversity of the ideological spectrum is surprising. Seemingly chaotic, it was the year of definitions," and without any transition she asked him: "Would you like to see my home? Come on! I have two or three little things that might interest you."

And she took him on a tour of the house. On the second floor was the library and the study. An immense space, broken up here and there by bookcases that seemed reluctant to outline a division of the space. Behind a door that Delfina didn't open must have been her bedroom and a bath. Everything on the floor was modern in design, geometrically functional, but the space was occasionally interrupted by a slender column, graceful, covered in a faded green antique velvet, which introduced an almost fairy-tale element into the ambience. Miguel praised the presence of those columns in such an excessively ascetic space, and she responded, pleased.

"As you may have seen, Miguel, I'm not what one might call an overly feminine woman, but I couldn't resist the idea of those felt columns. I always dreamed of having them in my home one day. When I was young, I saw a similar room in Genoa. Robles, the architect, refused to build them. He felt it was a violation of his poetics. Then, grudgingly, he became convinced that I was right. I've been told that in later works he repeated the use of columns of different colors."

The third floor, smaller, housed another studio and a large bedroom, with an excellent view of the garden. Throughout the house's three floors was a collection that spanned the last fifty or sixty years of Mexican painting, exceptional both for the quality of the works and for their placement: they established a relationship that emerged from within and permeated the house, as if each one were a moving piece in a set of signs. The entire house

reflected the face of its owner, a woman of meticulously cultivated taste: paintings, books, furniture, objects. But, at the same
time, as he contemplated the collection acquired over the years,
placed with intelligence, Miguel del Solar had the impression
that those vast spaces that circumscribed Delfina Uribe and her
world were an extension of sorts of her incommunicability, her
physical egotism, her reclusion.

A phone rang somewhere. A servant came in to say that Dr.
Gálvez wanted to talk to Delfina. She got up, took a huge book
from a side table, and placed it in her guest's lap. *Tiziano, l'opera ad affresco*. She asked that he excuse her for a minute and left
him alone.

Delfina was away for over a quarter of an hour. During
that time her guest leafed absentmindedly through the beautiful Italian edition. He thought about how little he knew about
Venetian painting. Fragments only, much like his ignorance of
Florentine and Flemish painting, Gothic art, the Baroque, Greek
sculpture, everything. It would have been wonderful to spend
a month in Venice before returning to Mexico. He got up and
walked to the farthest wall. Two paintings strongly caught his
eye: the famous portrait of Matilde Arenal in front of the mirror.
The diva! A desolate, aggressive, moving figure! Her expression
was one of coarseness, dejection, and, at the same time, per-
sistence, even defiance. A woman in stage makeup half-removed,
sitting in front of the mirror in her dressing room, contemplat-
ing her folly and helplessness in the mysterious glow of an indigo
blue spotlight. A kind of premature swan song. The famous
painting that had unleashed more than one storm. On another
wall, the portrait from Delfina's youth, painted by Escobedo
himself. No, there was no great difference between that young
woman, the restless student of literature, and the now aged,
powerful woman whose home and collections he was visiting at

that moment. From both faces, the current one and the one from half a century ago, emerge the same will to assert herself, the same defiant gaze. Ferocious on the young girl; cleverly devious on the aging woman. The same style of dress: blouse and skirt, a short jacket. No excess, and in substance (in substance and form, one could say) that inability to open up, that focused individuality, which neither demanded nor betrayed anything personal. Delfina, or the obstruction of communicating vessels. Delfina, or the dream of Onan. Impossible to imagine her next to one of the lovers or husbands she'd mentioned. One could only imagine her in bed with a book in her hand or reclined on large pillows, watching a newscast on television. Not vulgar; she was too civilized. Ferocious, yes, one of those ferocities that the person who possesses it can always keep under control. Since her youth she'd lacked curves. All her features could be shaped into straight lines. It seemed strange to him that she would like that portrait so much, the first painting of her collection as he heard her say once, as there was something about it that bordered on insulting, or at least reproving: Delfina and the management of her energies, Delfina and the frugality of her soul. In that sense the vilified "Diva" could be considered a tribute to generosity.

All of Delfina's invitations always left a memory of the unpredictable. She'd called him on the phone. She'd told him that they would be completely alone, that for the first time they'd be able to talk. It was true that for the first time they were alone, but they didn't talk. He seemed to sense in her a need to open up, but, as always, she waited for him to take the initiative, to question her, pressure her, place her between the sword and the wall. Perhaps in an extreme situation she'd decide to answer him, taking, of course, all the necessary precautions, knowing the lines she shouldn't cross in her response. The wise and reticent Delfina. Her request that he abandon the matter of the so-called crimes at the Minerva Building possessed perhaps the impetus that prompted him to continue the line of inquiry in which he was lost. He'd done so, no doubt, with the absolute conviction that she would act as she was.

But he'd had enough of her tricks. He would stop asking her questions. Allow her to direct the conversation! If she didn't broach the subject—patience!—he'd let the opportunity pass and would talk to her another time, and if not, some other time, until she finally decided to tell him what she knew.

Delfina returned. She became lost in a long and confusing conversation about a Dr. Gálvez Moreno who'd advised Margot Cruces to convince Governor Parra to buy a large canvas that someone would soon be putting on the market. And she became lost while explaining the reasons the doctor had given why Margot should convince the governor to buy the painting and donate it to a certain museum. Del Solar barely heard her, because the story was much more complicated than that and included a multitude of people he wasn't at all interested in. He had the conviction that she wasn't interested either, that she was merely using it in order to buy time. He made some comments about her paintings and she, elated, began to recount anecdotes about them: the circumstances in which they were painted and acquired, the relationship of the painters to her and her gallery; she related in almost exasperating detail her friendship with some of them. How she had to become a banker, a nurse, a confidant. How, at times, they demanded of her a degree of interest that should properly belong to their spouses, and later reproached her for the excessive intimacy that they themselves imposed, accusing her of wanting to subjugate them, of intervening too much in their lives, etc. At one point, it seemed to trouble her to talk about this topic, which she'd begun so energetically, as if she expected to have already moved on to other things. "But these things, Delfina," Del Solar thought, "aren't going to come out as spontaneously as they had until now; you'll have to be the one to look for them. Do you understand me?"

Del Solar got up and made a gesture that he was leaving. She, surprised, stopped him. She referred to Escobedo's painting once more with enthusiasm, adding that it required a great deal of effort to cope with the crises of his character, which over the years was becoming increasingly touchy, and since he didn't goad her on this topic either, the conversation again began to wane. Delfina seemed disconnected.

"The best Escobedo is one I have downstairs," she said. "*Angels and Japanese Plums*. I like to change the paintings from time to time. There are only two or three that have a permanent place here. My youthful portrait, for example. I don't like to part with it. I don't even lend it out. Without it I'd feel like an orphan. I also have a portrait of my son, one of the few things by Julio I don't like. For some reason I found it distasteful from the start. Malú and Bernardo have it in their home. One of these days I'm going to take it back and bring it to the office . . . Although this place is an office in name only. I never work here. I do, however, like to receive friends here. As well as to stay and read. I do all my gallery work at the office. And even there, in fact, I only do consulting work, a more or less vague form of public relations. I talk to the artists, attend to a special client or another. The administrative work, which is truly a bore, is done by Rosario, my niece. I try to concern myself as little as possible, and I've created a group of collaborators who work perfectly . . . One day I'll close the house and devote myself to traveling. I don't know if I'd be able to stand it, I think I could, but I'm not sure. I'm too accustomed to getting up first thing in the morning, taking a shower, getting dressed in a hurry, and heading downtown, arriving at the gallery, reading the mail, distributing it to the girls, checking the bank accounts. The first to arrive and the last to leave! Sad? No! Not at all!"

It was obvious that Delfina was prolonging the conversation. Del Solar looked at his watch and decided that as soon as he finished the cup of coffee she'd refilled, he would leave. He listened to her extend unnecessarily the subject of her obligations at the gallery, reluctantly saying that, of course, she now only performed a few formal duties, mere gestures to keep herself up-to-date, because she'd never liked living in the shadows. Clarity was necessary to her . . . Almost an obsession.

"I think it's getting to be that time . . ." and he explained that he had to pick up his children not far from there.

"I never thought," she said, without paying attention to his words, "that my life, in the end, would be so boxed in. When I built this house I imagined the future differently. I'm not complaining, don't misunderstand me. I was the one who decided that things should be as they are, and I believe I've been consistent. It's just that sometimes I get fed up." And she began to allow a tone of a whimsical ill humor to seep into her voice. "I've always found foolish people insufferable. And in a profession like mine one must deal with many decidedly impossible people. Absurd, silly people! You wouldn't believe what kind of clients I'm forced to speak with sometimes! It's not to be believed! And what kind of women! I've come to the conclusion that there's no world more bewildering than that of wives. I don't understand how their husbands tolerate them. What a pain they can be! I'm not antifeminist, let me be clear; on the contrary, sometimes I think I'm too radical. I was educated in another generation. Only a few women, a handful, had a voice of our own. We'd earned that right through hard work. The others, the majority, didn't exist. But they were better than those today; of that I'm convinced. You don't believe me? Just watch them! Listen to them!

They take for granted rights they didn't earn. I simply can't tolerate them!"

Miguel del Solar thought that if he stayed, he'd hear Delfina's views on the world of dreams, diathermy, the effects of the gold standard as a stimulus to international finance. He preferred to say goodbye. He asked her before leaving if she could give him a photo, if she had one, of one of the Lazos on the upper floor. He'd never seen them before, not even in reproductions.

"Let's go see, come with me." They went back upstairs. She went to an armoire and began to look; at one point she stopped, sat down, and began to tell him, as she looked at some photos: "When I built the house, this floor was going to be my son's. Some of these books were his. I couldn't accept, although all the doctors assured me, that his condition was so bad. I don't mean that I didn't do the right thing, that I neglected his treatment. Nothing of the sort. I took him several times to clinics in the United States, and there as well as here I explored every possibility. I was always sure that he would recover. When he died, my surprise knew no bounds. I was as unprepared as if he'd died in the street, shot. Ricardo was very happy in this house. He couldn't go out, but he enjoyed the garden and his study. I went upstairs every day to watch him do exercises. He did them twice a day. Breathing exercises. There were times when he couldn't come down to eat because he felt ill, so I'd come up and we'd eat here. I'd read to him aloud. He was, like me, a Dickens enthusiast. They were, in a somber way, the happiest months of my life. There wasn't a Sunday that my father didn't come to see him. One day he caught a cold . . . The slightest cold imaginable made him very sick; his pleura was filled up. They inserted a needle into his back and extracted staggering amounts of fluid from his lungs. The pain was so intense that he lost consciousness. One day he caught a cold, as I said. I don't even know how, because he hadn't been out in the garden that day. It seemed like any other cold. In the morning his nose was slightly purple, and when I came back from the gallery he was burning with fever. He barely recognized me. I began to speak to him almost in a delirium. I was screaming at him to try. I told him that what was happening wasn't fair, that he should do his part. He raised his head a bit. He looked at me with his eyes half-closed and said, 'Can't you see, Mamá? I'm doing everything I can. I don't want to die. You've got to believe me.' Those were his last coherent words. Hours later he died. If I were another woman, I would've closed this part of the house; but I didn't. It's a guest room, like any other. By the way, since I'm talking about my son . . ." she looked at him with a cruel, mocking smile. "Did you finally learn what happened at the Minerva Building?"

Del Solar had received his prize. The first step had been taken by Delfina. She should continue on that path. If the topic interested her, she should talk.

"What can I say? I've learned many things, but the meaning escapes me. I can't understand, for example, what Arnulfo Briones's activity was. You were right when you said that too many years have passed."

"Briones's activity? But I told you. Please sit down! He was an absolute and militant reactionary. He always was. He was up to his neck in the Cristero movement. There was a time when his cronies disavowed him, at least in part. He hid on a ranch in the North, then left for Germany."

"I know. But I can't figure out what he was doing in Mexico City in 1942. His export business to Germany must have been virtually finished. However, I've learned that he had offices in various parts of the city. To what end? He had one in particular, clandestine, in a building on Calle de Brasil. I also find the marriage to Pistauer's mother very dark."

"Why do you brood over these things, Miguel? What was Arnulfo Briones doing in 1942? The usual," she repeated mechanically, "conspiring against the government, allied to a bunch of shady sacristans. He never did anything else."

"Do you think his activities were dangerous for the government?"

She thought for a moment. Then she answered:

"I don't really know, but I don't think so. At another time, yes, at the beginning of the Cristero uprising. For the years you're researching, I imagine he was already a spent cartridge. It's possible that he used his name to disguise German property so it wouldn't be confiscated. Huge fortunes were made that way."

"Who could have benefited from his death?"

"Briones was a very unsavory character. To be honest, though, I really didn't follow the news about his death. After the operation, I stayed in the hospital all day. Ricardo was recovering. When he was discharged we went to spend some time in Tehuacán." She lit a cigarette. "Yes, I spent some time in Tehuacán with Ricardo. What a lovely place! It was there that I read the news of Arnulfo Briones's death. Hit by a car. An accident. The newspapers dedicated little space inside to it. I had someone go buy all the newspapers for me to see if there was anything else. But no, much of the information was irrelevant, and some of it wrong. I would've expected to see one or two glowing articles written by some of his coreligionists. Nothing! For an instant I thought about calling Eduviges to offer my condolences. Of course I didn't. Arnulfo was detestable, as was Eduviges, for that matter."

"Don't exaggerate, Delfina!"

"I'm not! I wanted to call her, out of curiosity. The news in the papers was very neutral, and I was eager for blood. The next day the press published a few lines that added nothing. I called my brother Bernardo. Of course he knew about it; it was that old fool, he said. Personally, the news didn't upset him. 'What I can assure you,' he added, 'whoever killed him was even worse than he was.' That's how I found out that what I'd suspected was true. It was no accident."

"Who killed him?" asked Del Solar.

"That's what I asked. Who? People in the same line of work, apparently. A settling of scores! My older brother, Andrés, for reasons that are irrelevant to what we're discussing, was one of the most informed men in the country. Bernardo promised to contact him and let me know. Not a week had passed when one of Briones's pals confessed to the crime and was arrested."

"Who?"

Delfina got up again. Without any sense of urgency, she placed one of her long cigarettes in a holder and lit it. She stood up. She crossed the room and stopped in front of a large painting by Tamayo. She began to move it, holding it by the frame. For a moment Del Solar thought she was going to take it down or at least put it aside, and that behind it, on the wall, would appear, like in the movies, a small safe, from which Delfina would pull out a few key documents that would clear everything up. He stood up and offered help, which she refused. She'd done all those maneuvers just to put the oil painting in the right position.

"I can't bear badly hung paintings. I can't. It must be an occupational hazard, but I feel ill when I see a badly hung painting."

Del Solar could have killed her.

"So the culprit turned himself in? Who was it?" he almost shouted.

"That's what they said, that he'd given himself up. I never thought he was the one. You get angry, Miguel; you accuse people of being negligent if they don't give you strict, precise answers. But as for Briones's death, two plus two was never four. As for the outcome, the press didn't say anything about it. I found out from my brothers. But, I'm telling you, I never believed that Martínez was the culprit."

"Martínez?!"

"Yes, I've told you about him before, haven't I? He attended my party uninvited. He assaulted Ida Werfel. Of course I told you!"

"But not this! So Martínez was the culprit! Or at least he agreed to be!" Del Solar was stunned. "Do you understand? I've been asking for information for months. I've spoken to half the world, and no one has ever mentioned this. It's impossible to go on like this, Delfina! I've just been with Pedro Balmorán; he almost finished me off with a cane. He threw me out of his house. He kept talking to me about his castrato, about astral planes that didn't coincide with the earthly ones, about the redemption that was yet to come . . ."

"A manifestation of madness that shouldn't be encouraged. He's come to believe that the character of that phony document that robbed him of his sanity, the apparent castrato, who was nothing but a hermaphrodite, was the mystical androgyne who will come to redeem and save the world."

"But he didn't tell me that Martínez was the culprit or that he'd confessed to the murder of Arnulfo Briones, which to me is more important than the fate of a castrato or hermaphrodite. I've been walking around completely in the dark."

"I always believed, and my brother confirmed my suspicions, that someone must have paid him a good sum of money to accept the blame. They must've also offered him a degree of impunity. Martínez was capable of anything for money. Although I only saw him a few times; that I'm sure of. Capable of anything for money. He thought he'd ruined my party by inviting a very famous duo from the time, the Bombón sisters, a pair of rather plump vulgarians who powdered themselves like pambazos. He failed; we were all happy that they were there, because when they sang they were truly divine. One of them died recently, Rosita."

"So Martínez pleaded guilty?" For a few moments, Del Solar wasn't sure if he understood correctly.

"Of having invited the Bombón sisters into my home?"

"Of Arnulfo Briones's death, Delfina. Why the hell should I care about the Bombón sisters?" Del Solar scolded her.

"Yes, that's what I think. They must have offered him money and, of course, protection. After two or three years, perhaps sooner, they probably got him out of jail. He'd be rich for the rest of his life. Perhaps he was thinking of going back to Hamburg at the end of the war and creating a harem with starving blondes whom he could fatten up. Who knows! Perhaps his dreams were more complex than one imagines!"

"When did he get out? Are his whereabouts known?"

"He never got out. He was killed a few weeks after entering prison. A brawl in his block. Apparently they were quite frequent at the time. And he had a sinister nature. He was one of those types who made enemies instantly. They lynched him. They made mincemeat out of him. They reduced him to a bloody pulp. It may be ugly to say, but I'm convinced he deserved it."

"Maybe it was someone else. Who identified him? Why didn't you ever mention this?"

"There wasn't the slightest possibility of confusion. Andrés would have found out. And you didn't ask me anything about it." She made a gesture of girlish innocence that Del Solar found very repugnant. "If it were up to me, I'd never talk about bloody deeds. Allow me to remind you that nothing you asked me has gone unanswered. I can't guarantee, of course, that my assessments are correct, but I warned you of that from the beginning."

They said goodbye. Del Solar didn't have a car that day. As he walked, he was certain that he now possessed all the information necessary to solve the enigma of the Minerva. The conversation with Delfina confirmed this conviction. But his gaze was unable to pierce the veil. As he passed by the San Ángel bookstore, he saw his book in the window. He pretended for a moment to be indifferent. Nothing was less true. The fact that his book was there implied changes, among others, a sense of freedom. He went in and walked around. On a table stood a stack of copies of *The Year 1914*. He could now devote himself fully to his new project. He was no longer convinced about 1942. After much, much love . . . ! The proximity could be risky, but the temptation even greater. He'd have to make up his mind in the next few days, and if he chose that year, he'd immediately begin to consult objective sources, to prepare his files, to interview the public officials at the time. He'd establish a rudimentary index. The international element alone could provide material for a huge volume: the declaration of war, its consequences, direct and indirect pressures, oil, foreign investments, Roosevelt and the New Deal. He'd have to forget about the diversion of the nota roja with which he'd been entertaining himself and the Minerva's confusing crimes, which, he had to confess, disturbed him more than he wished. To cancel the subplots for the moment. Everyone had spoken to him out of disgust, fear, derision for Martínez, the golden baton. Everyone also seemed to have conspired not to have mentioned his end. That period had ended. The presence of *1914* in the shop windows, on the tables and counters of the bookstore, was the best exorcism to vanquish all those perverse, almost shameful angles of his eventual project. In a few days he'd begin to work in earnest.

•

Miguel del Solar entered the long, narrow Calle de Galeana. He still might find Amparo and his children at the home of her friends the Ortíns. They were celebrating a child's birthday. The street was empty. He could hear their footsteps. A dark green car passed by, almost brushing him, slowed down, and stopped a few meters ahead of him. The car, with a broken license plate and an illegible number, began to back up slowly, carefully, until it was next to the historian. Suddenly Del Solar perceived he was alone. Only he and the green car were on the street. A blind, animal, instantaneous, and visceral hatred for Martínez flooded over him in those moments he believed to be his last. Inside, all he asked was that it be quick and painless. The car positioned itself next to him. The front window began to go down, and a brutish face, like that of a young boxer, asked him where he could find Calle de Santuario. Del Solar stood there, his mouth open, paralyzed. He wanted to say something, but he couldn't. He began to gesture with one hand, pointing to his throat and ears, and making guttural, strangled sounds.

". . . a fucking deaf-mute!" he heard the young guy say through the window.

The car drove forward, accelerated, reached the end of Galeana, and disappeared. Del Solar turned around, began to run, and didn't stop until he reached the San Ángel bookstore. Out of breath, sweat-soaked, and trembling with fear, he rested his body on the counter, not far from where the stacks of Zapata-style hats on *The Year 1914* caught the reader's eye. He looked as if he were about to break down and cry.

Prague, November 1983–Mojácar, June 1988

Sergio Pitol Deméneghi (1933–2018) was one of Mexico's most influential and well-respected writers. He studied law and philosophy in Mexico City and spent many years as a cultural attaché in Mexican embassies and consulates across the globe, including in Poland, Hungary, Italy, and China, with his final post being ambassador to Czechoslovakia. In recognition of the importance of his entire canon of work, Pitol was awarded the two most important prizes in the Spanish-language world: the Juan Rulfo Prize in 1999 (now known as the FIL Literary Award in Romance Languages) and the Cervantes Prize, the most prestigious Spanish-language literary prize, often called the "Spanish-language Nobel," in 2005. His Trilogy of Memory and *Mephisto's Waltz* are available from Deep Vellum in translation by G. B. Henson.

G. B. Henson is a literary translator and a 2021–2023 Tulsa Artist Fellow. His translations include Cervantes Prize laureate Sergio Pitol's Trilogy of Memory and *Mephisto's Waltz*, *The Heart of the Artichoke* by fellow Cervantes recipient Elena Poniatowska, and Luis Jorge Boone's *The Cannibal Night*. His translations have appeared variously in *The Paris Review*, *The Literary Review*, *BOMB*, *The Guardian*, *Asymptote*, and *Flash Fiction International*. In addition, he is a contributing editor for *World Literature Today* and the translation editor at large for its sister publication *Latin American Literature Today*.

Thank you all
for your support.
We do this for you,
and could not do
it without you.

DEEP
VELLUM

PARTNERS

pixel ||| texel

EMBREY FAMILY
FOUNDATION

ADDITIONAL DONORS, CONT'D

Mark Haber
Mary Cline
Maynard Thomson
Michael Reklis
Mike Soto
Mokhtar Ramadan
Nikki & Dennis Gibson
Patrick Kukucka
Patrick Kutcher
Rev. Elizabeth & Neil Moseley
Richard Meyer

Scott & Katy Nimmons
Sherry Perry
Sydneyann Binion
Stephen Harding
Stephen Williamson
Susan Carp
Susan Ernst
Theater Jones
Tim Perttula
Tony Thomson

SUBSCRIBERS

Ned Russin
Michael Binkley
Michael Schneiderman
Aviya Kushner
Kenneth McClain
Eugenie Cha
Stephen Fuller
Joseph Rebella
Brian Matthew Kim

Anthony Brown
Michael Lighty
Erin Kubatzky
Shelby Vincent
Margaret Terwey
Ben Fountain
Caroline West
Ryan Todd
Gina Rios

Caitlin Jans
Ian Robinson
Elena Rush
Courtney Sheedy
Elif Ağanoğlu
Laura Gee
Valerie Boyd
Brian Bell

AVAILABLE NOW FROM DEEP VELLUM

MICHÈLE AUDIN · *One Hundred Twenty-One Days* · translated by Christiana Hills · FRANCE

BAE SUAH · *Recitation* · translated by Deborah Smith · SOUTH KOREA

MARIO BELLATIN · *Mrs. Murakami's Garden* · translated by Heather Cleary · MEXICO

EDUARDO BERTI · *The Imagined Land* · translated by Charlotte Coombe · ARGENTINA

CARMEN BOULLOSA · *Texas: The Great Theft* · *Before* · *Heavens on Earth*
translated by Samantha Schnee · Peter Bush · Shelby Vincent · MEXICO

MAGDA CARNECI · *FEM* · translated by Sean Cotter · ROMANIA

LEILA S. CHUDORI · *Home* · translated by John H. McGlynn · INDONESIA

MATHILDE CLARK · *Lone Star* · translated by Martin Aitken · DENMARK

SARAH CLEAVE, ed. · *Banthology: Stories from Banned Nations* ·
IRAN, IRAQ, LIBYA, SOMALIA, SUDAN, SYRIA & YEMEN

LOGEN CURE · *Welcome to Midland: Poems* · USA

ANANDA DEVI · *Eve Out of Her Ruins* · translated by Jeffrey Zuckerman · MAURITIUS

PETER DIMOCK · *Daybook from Sheep Meadow* · USA

CLAUDIA ULLOA DONOSO · *Little Bird,* translated by Lily Meyer · PERU/NORWAY

ROSS FARRAR · *Ross Sings Cheree & the Animated Dark: Poems* · USA

ALISA GANIEVA · *Bride and Groom* · *The Mountain and the Wall*
translated by Carol Apollonio · RUSSIA

FERNANDA GARCIA LAU · *Out of the Cage* · translated by Will Vanderhyden · ARGENTINA

ANNE GARRÉTA · *Sphinx* · *Not One Day* · *In/concrete* · translated by Emma Ramadan · FRANCE

JÓN GNARR · *The Indian* · *The Pirate* · *The Outlaw* · translated by Lytton Smith · ICELAND

GOETHE · *The Golden Goblet: Selected Poems* · *Faust, Part One*
translated by Zsuzsanna Ozsváth and Frederick Turner · GERMANY

NOEMI JAFFE · *What are the Blind Men Dreaming?* · translated by Julia Sanches & Ellen Elias-Bursac · BRAZIL

CLAUDIA SALAZAR JIMÉNEZ · *Blood of the Dawn* · translated by Elizabeth Bryer · PERU

PERGENTINO JOSÉ · *Red Ants* · MEXICO

TAISIA KITAISKAIA · *The Nightgown & Other Poems* · USA

JUNG YOUNG MOON · *Seven Samurai Swept Away in a River* · *Vaseline Buddha*
translated by Yewon Jung · SOUTH KOREA

KIM YIDEUM · *Blood Sisters* · translated by Ji yoon Lee · SOUTH KOREA

JOSEFINE KLOUGART · *Of Darkness* · translated by Martin Aitken · DENMARK

YANICK LAHENS · *Moonbath* · translated by Emily Gogolak · HAITI

FORTHCOMING FROM DEEP VELLUM

SHANE ANDERSON · *After the Oracle* · USA

MARIO BELLATIN · *Beauty Salon* · translated by David Shook · MEXICO

MIRCEA CĂRTĂRESCU · *Solenoid*
translated by Sean Cotter · ROMANIA

LEYLÂ ERBIL · *A Strange Woman*
translated by Nermin Menemencioğlu & Amy Marie Spangler· TURKEY

RADNA FABIAS · *Habitus* · translated by David Colmer · CURAÇAO/NETHERLANDS

SARA GOUDARZI · *The Almond in the Apricot* · USA

GYULA JENEI · *Always Different* · translated by Diana Senechal · HUNGARY

UZMA ASLAM KHAN • *The Miraculous True History of Nomi Ali* • PAKISTAN

SONG LIN · *The Gleaner Song: Selected Poems* · translated by Dong Li · CHINA

TEDI LÓPEZ MILLS · *The Book of Explanations* · translated by Robin Myers · MEXICO

JUNG YOUNG MOON · *Arriving in a Thick Fog*
translated by Mah Eunji and Jeffrey Karvonen · SOUTH KOREA

FISTON MWANZA MUJILA · *The Villain's Dance,* translated by Roland Glasser · *The River in the Belly:
Selected Poems,* translated by Bret Maney · DEMOCRATIC REPUBLIC OF CONGO

LUDMILLA PETRUSHEVSKAYA · *Kidnapped: A Crime Story,* translated by Marian Schwartz · *The New
Adventures of Helen: Magical Tales,* translated by Jane Bugaeva · RUSSIA

SERGIO PITOL · *The Love Parade* · translated by G. B. Henson · MEXICO

MANON STEFAN ROS · *The Blue Book of Nebo* · WALES

JIM SCHUTZE · *The Accommodation* · USA

SOPHIA TERAZAWA · *Winter Phoenix: Testimonies in Verse* · POLAND

ROBERT TRAMMELL · *Jack Ruby & the Origins of the Avant-Garde in Dallas & Other Stories* · USA

BENJAMIN VILLEGAS · *ELPASO: A Punk Story* · translated by Jay Noden · MEXICO